MISS THING

Nora Chassler

TWO RAVENS
PRESS

Published by Two Ravens Press Ltd.
Green Willow Croft
Rhiroy, Lochbroom
Ullapool
Ross-shire IV23 2SF

www.tworavenspress.com

The right of Nora Chassler to be identified as author of this work has been asserted by her in accordance with the Copyright, Designs and Patent Act, 1988.
© Nora Chassler, 2010.

ISBN: 978-1-906120-46-7

British Library Cataloguing in Publication Data: a CIP record for this book can be obtained from the British Library.

Designed and typeset in Sabon by Two Ravens Press.
Cover design by Two Ravens Press.

Printed in Poland on Forest Stewardship
Council-accredited paper.

The publisher gratefully acknowledges subsidy from the Scottish Arts Council towards the publication of this volume.

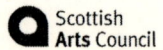

Scottish
Arts Council

About the Author

Nora Chassler grew up on the Upper West Side of Manhattan and attended state schools. She graduated from Hunter College where she earned a degree in English and Film Studies. She has worked as a fashion model, a Repatriation Case Worker and a housewife. She now lives in Dundee, Scotland, with her partner and her daughter, Frances.

She is working on her second novel.

For more information about the author, see
www.tworavenspress.com

For Richie

Author's Preface

We've become the Germans of our nightmares.
That we are also junkies, faggots, tax-
evaders, small time cheats & losers
is icing on the cake.
　　svz, 1981

I wrote the following when I was in rehab for the zillionth time. It is about two real people I knew. I wrote it from various points of view, but mostly his and hers. Initially I kept myself out of it; I suppose I had the idea that you don't put yourself in your own book, out of a kind of decorum. Or maybe it was more down to the fact that last year, when all this happened, I was fat and drunk.

But today I ran fifteen miles through Riverside Park and the whole time thought (to the tune of a pounding cha-cha) – Fuck it fuck it fu-ck it! Fuck it fuck it fu-ck it! I look better than Robert Downey Junior. I'll write the introduction as *myself*.

Andromeda appeared one day. She came and sat down on the bench next to the one I'd been monopolizing for years, took out a beat-up copy of *Being and Time*, lit an unfiltered Camel, and heaved a massive sigh – for such a skinny girl. I stared at her. I had no pride at that point. It was a point of pride. It was a very cold day. Andromeda was wearing this floor-length North Face puffy grey coat – it looked like a garbage bag – and shearling boots that went over her knees. Called Uggs, she told me later. I weighed 225 pounds, had a huge beard, huge donut head-phones my mother gave me when *she* upgraded, and my only

1

other worldly possession: a shopping cart filled with magazines.

Andromeda said, 'Stop looking at me. I'm nobody.'

I said, 'No way? Me too! ... Cutting school?'

'Yeah.'

'Where you go, Brandeis?'

'Used to go to public school, to Stuy, until last year, but my mother, who killed herself yesterday, made me switch so I'd get into a good college.'

'I'm really sorry. Was she crazy?'

'Yeah.'

'You know, I think you're in shock. Like someone after a car crash wandering around in the ruins.'

'Wreckage.'

Her breath was dove gray. 'Look – I feel nothing. This has been a problem for some time. I'm watching myself through a filter.'

She did say that. There were little ice floats in the river that day.

OK. Enough of that. I'll start with Andromeda's mother's obit, supposedly written by my boyfriend, Rob, who you'll meet. (He actually helped me write it, to make matters weirder. So I had to say, write this almost as yourself, as if you were someone imitating you. And on top of that he's hardly qualified to write an obit for *The Times*. *The Voice* maybe. Which makes you wonder, why didn't I use the real one?) Then I'll go to the parts in Sam's voice and Andromeda's voice, eighty-nine days after I met Andromeda on the bench, ninety days since Sophie died.

Ninety days, incidentally, and you get the AA gold star. Anyway. I tried. The wisdom to know the difference, and all that. Next week I'm taking the test for my NY real estate agent's license. I'm becoming a pragmatist.

The aphorisms are Sophie's. I found them in a shoebox in

the Meaningful Closet. I hang out in there a lot now that Andy's gone. I also found some other unpublished stuff, including a novel and a libretto for a rock opera.

Federico Escobar
Apthorp Apartments
August 2002

Sophie Van Zandt, Film Critic and NYU Professor, dies at 49
By Rob HARTMAN

Sophie Van Zandt, the film critic and feminist theorist, outspoken advocate of womens' and civil rights and holder of the Joel Lemming Chair in Film Studies at NYU, died yesterday morning after a fall from her eleventh-storey window. She was forty-nine.

An expert in silent film and Weimar cinema, an influential academic as well as popular mainstream critic, Ms Van Zandt (who always signed her name in print with the lower-case initials svz) will also be remembered for a number of controversial public appearances. Arguably the most notorious was the 1989 Bush White House Christmas dinner at which she scandalized guests, the President and First Lady by appearing in a dress constructed only of wire hangers. Ms. Van Zandt explained that the gesture was in protest against proposed legislation banning late-term abortion. She later conceded that her actions may have done her cause more harm than good.

Nonetheless Ms Van Zandt remained a popular figure. Part of her appeal to her many admirers was her ability – what at times seemed her desire – to side with her opponents. In interviews she often questioned her own motives and the efficacy of her actions; her essay on literary production, 'The Proof is in the Collapsed Pudding', a handwritten piece that is always reproduced as such, is a mainstay of many proprioceptive writing workshops.

While she embodied a recognizable type of intellectual self-doubt – referring to herself just last week in her column in New York as 'the worst thing to happen to feminism since feminism' – her humor softened what otherwise might have looked like sheer solipsism. If nothing else, Ms. Van Zandt's corpus always called into question the necessity of that certain, self-assured character she called the 'farting, assuaged reader'.

Though quieter in tone, svz's academic work constituted a formidable achievement in its own right, and included critically acclaimed translations of de Beauvoir's *Memoirs of a Dutiful Daughter*, and Roland Barthes. Her PhD dissertation at Yale, *Write of the First Night*, was effectively canonical upon publication in 1976, and is required reading in the majority of freshman Feminist Theory classes. At 1100 pages it drapes its thesis (which concerns the hidden nature and continuous presence of 'unspoken gender games (sic)' aka ugg(s), over most of Western history. Typically, she had recently distanced herself from the work, calling it 'a bloated spoof'.

While in some respects a very public figure who illustrated her theories with personal revelation and anecdotes, and who never shied away from a camera, Ms. Van Zandt was known by her colleagues at NYU as an extremely private person; her rejection of almost all social invitations was legendarily Garboesque.

She is survived by her mother, Polly Van Zandt, of Barrow Street, and a daughter, Andromeda.

In accord with her wishes, no memorial service will be held.

Every man is born as many men and dies as a single one.

    – Martin Heidegger

I'm very sorry and from now on I'm going to pay complete attention to everything.

    – Paris Hilton

A.

Narcissus in a Nutshell

This is not a prison
this is a trap
I am the bait.
     svz, 1972

On the first page of Andromeda Van Zandt's new Rembrandt artist's sketchpad.

5/15/01

Now that my mom's dead I have no one to talk to. So I bought this book. Twelve bucks. Rip-off. Today's her birthday. She would have been fifty. FIVE-OHHH. She would NOT stop saying it like that, imitating Bette Davis in *All About Eve*. It's ironic she turned out to be such a shitty mom, after all that waiting and planning, the hatching, the plotting, the BACKTRACKING: she wanted me for ten years; she wanted me to be so perfect she had two abortions when circumstances weren't exactly right. One – shit! bad genes. The other – she was 'too in love' and wouldn't have had the energy to spare for me.

FIVE-OHHHHHHHHH.

I'm cutting school. I'm down here on the Promenade, on what's become my usual sea-green, dirty-fingernail, rotting-wood bench. I chose it for a couple of reasons. Partly because this one and the one next to it are the only two that Guliani's fascist Park's Commission have yet to replace. But mostly because it faces away from the Promenade. In front of me there's a two-foot gap, a balustrade, and a straight drop down to the lower level of the park and the river. The whole thing is actually the roof of Amtrak tunnel. There are two drunks on the bench beside me. Actually, I know them – Federico Escobar and his new boyfriend, Jimmy, hanging out under their new Snoopy duvet. I'm this far from asking for a swig from their bottle of Nighttrain. Luckily, this far can be quite far enough.

Now the couple from across the courtyard are walking by. It's fucking *Mr. Roger's Neighborhood*.

'But what if it tastes divine?' she is saying to him. She has this ponytail that MIGHT be an extension. He is about a foot taller than her, with red hair.

He says, 'My love, I sincerely doubt anything is worth the price, or the risk.' Who the fuck does he think he is, F. Scott Fitzgerald? MY LOVE I SINCERELY DOUBT ... He's a writer, allegedly. Mom hated him because he once called her 'madam' in the elevator. Anyway. He's as tall as the lowest rung of leaves on the sycamores. His yuppess is small as a bowling pin. She keeps looking at him, talking, waving her arms. I can't hear them anymore. He's holding his eyes on the dog, an apricot Standard Poodle. The dog is pissing EVERYWHERE.

At night the guy stands in his kitchen. Their whole place faces the courtyard, poor dears. They could have bought a whole building in Brooklyn for what they paid for those two rooms, but no, they had to be here, in the grand old Apthorp Apts – anyway WHERE WAS I yes, he chop chop chops with a big Chinese cleaver; stares at his laptop on the counter; drinks little glasses of this and that; types with one extended finger, coming at the keyboard from, like, across the room. Meanwhile she paces around talking on the cell phone, flipping her extension to and fro, chugging water from a two-liter bottle. He and I have looked right at each other, me with the innocent urge to smile through the gloomy courtyard, to smile and wave with the sped-up flutter of a girl in a silent home movie – someone on Coney Island beach for the day, circa 1920. But no hellos allowed, it's against protocol. If you see someone see you and they see you see them or vice versa or whatever or any combination thereof etc... Look away. Under that kind of suppression I find myself with a different urge: I grab the hem of my shirt and have to hold it down with my other à la Dr. Strangelove to keep myself from flashing the bastard.

'You're the love of my life, Phaedrus,' Escobar just said.

'What's Phaedrus?' Jimmy replied.

'Andromeda, you tell him. Mommy was a philosopher.' Escobar waited, looked at me, sucked something out of his teeth, gave his mangy goatee a tug. We've known each other for a few months. We talk ideas. Still, sometimes I feel used. What am I, a party enhancer?

Last night I didn't sleep. I slept for about fifteen minutes. In the future everyone will ... sleep for fifteen minutes. Right after I nodded off I dreamed (again) that my headmaster, Lew Foresight, was trying to kill me. I jolted up and banged my head on the underside of my Non-Existent Sister's bunk bed. Anyway, seeking peace and at a loss, I decided to read the half-assed spirituality section of Mom's library. She compiled it while she was pregnant with me; felt she ought to give the idea of God a STAB.

All the books, even the *Tibetan Book of the Fucking Dead*, have those kind of fluffy lettered, early eighties covers, in shades of periwinkle and aqua. And the covers are nice and soft, felty, not like paper. 'Ah, the naive semiotics of lost years.' That's me practicing to take up her post. That's my heartless STAB. So I sat there, in her office, in that creaky old office chair, in front of the chill air of dark Broadway, no lights on in any of the apartments but those ghost columns of grey in back fire stairs ... I sat there last night, smoked a pack of Product Placement and read 'em all. I can read any book in forty-five minutes or under. I just skip the parts where the authors – or God, as the case may be – repeat themselves/Himself. The *Tao Te Ching*, *City of God*, *The Bhagavad Gita*, *The Yoga Sutras of Patanjali*, *The Poems of Rumi*, *Revelations of the Secrets of the Birds and Flowers*, and some others. A fancy edition of *The Book of Job*. They all get to the same point: Forget thyself.

svz never fucking managed it. Escobar and Jimmy (Jimmy can't be a day older than I am; he puts something on his tiny moustache, something reflective and greasy, so he'll look more MATURE) are suddenly very quiet. The shapes under the Snoopy duvet are puzzling.

No, I am not reading my *Being and Time*. According to her I should have finished it well before Christmas. No. I am trying. To forget. My fucking. Self. Writing this is just a preparation for that. So what do I see now? What is OUTSIDE of me?

The sky is red behind NJ. Filling in the spaces between the high-rises, like water displacement but with red light. I stand up and stare over the balustrade, what Escobar calls the verandah, down at the Hudson. It slithers. It moans, 'My pretty. My pretty.' No, a cross between a man choking and saying that in a low voice.

Jimmy whispers, 'Escobar, Escobar.' The pink leaves on the cherry trees that hang above my fingers, right above this book, about the size of my fingernails, go SHUSH. Or maybe SUSHI. From the West Side Highway a ... Doppler moan. Fuck! What would an even half-normal teenage girl write? In Botany, Ed Hanes gave me a look! Leaned in close when the teacher was talking about Venus Flytraps and said, 'The depravity' – which seemed almost ... at the time. But after class I ran into the bathroom and was in the middle of putting on my lipstick (it's rust-colored and called 'Toast of New York') when I just started to laugh uncontrollably. I mean, it struck me – there

I was, getting all gussied up, and what for? So Ed could say more, elaborate on his theme of depravity? Stand there in front of school and light my cigarette with the already-lit tip of his? (He's one of those guys who inhales so hard the cherry turns into an inch-long cone.)

Anyway, I washed the lipstick off – or tried to, it's sort of indelible – its middle name is '24-Hour Lipstick' – and snuck out the back door, past Headmaster Lew's office. The door was open a crack and all I could see were his feet and this ancient Guggenheim Calder poster he has up on the wall. He had his shoes off and his feet were retiring on the ottoman. That was the last time I was in school. About two weeks ago.

It's dark now. The lights of a thousand dental hygienists glint gold in the high rises. Time to go home. Granny will try to get me to eat. Ask me how I am doing. I'll tell her about all the fake activities I'm engaged in. Tonight: I've just finished presiding over my staff at the St Mary's c-literary magazine *Scion*. Escobar stands up, smiles at me, and pisses through a grate. I guess that's my cue.

LATER, FROM THE NON-EXISTENT MAID'S ROOM

Granny, who clearly resents having had to move back in here after forty years, shoves some raw meat she calls dinner in my face and bothers me about 'overextending' myself with extra-curriculars. I fantasize about taking a grenade out of my coat, doing a kind of pitcher's wind-up, and throwing it at her head, from a foot and a half away. It knocks her sideways, crashes through the closed window and lands in the fountain in the courtyard. Crack! Clank! BOOM! I'm a ticking bomb! The Upper West Side's own one-woman trenchcoat mafia! ...Please. I can hardly talk.

I blush and clam up. Another time in Botany, Ed said, 'Andromeda, that is SUCH a cool name.'

I said, 'Ya think?' when what I meant was, 'Really? I think it's the stupidest name on the fucking planet.'

While Granny and me were in the kitchen, I watched the yuppies. The girl one was getting ready to go out, her extension screwed into her brain just a little crooked. The guy was pretending not to look over here, as usual. Granny was saying, 'Maybe cut back, sweetheart, see FRIENDS?' Granny has a way of saying this like we are on a TV show, patting her hair, then blotting her lips on themselves. I've noticed a lot of people act like people on TV. I've been watching tons recently. Sort of a celebration after my mom's death. I took it out of the Meaningful Closet the day she kicked it, mostly cause I wanted to see if it was on the news. It was, in the human interest slot: 'Shocked students and professors, friends, and neighbors paid their last respects at a makeshift shrine erected…' Etcetera. There were about fifty bunches of shrink-wrapped Korean flowers in front of a wrought iron lion's head, part of the gate that encircles our building.

So I said to Granny, 'I haven't got any friends. No one likes me because I'm so pretty.' It was a joke. My ma would have got it. My ma would have made it. Granny was appalled.

'You should be out having fun.' Tears in her eyes.

'Today's her birthday, you know.'

The yuppie was frying something on high heat.

'For Christ's sake just let it out, sweetie.'

Fuck her. It is so obvious she would rather be back in her own apartment on Barrow Street.

* * *

Murray and Muckman letterhead ('Managers of Fine Apartment Houses. Where Tradition Lives') addressed to Ms. Lawson-Taylor, the female yuppie with what Andromeda thinks is an extension but isn't

5/15/01

Dear Ms. Lawson-Taylor,

In response to your recent query as to the status of the lease-holders for 11 E, I have been able to determine that after the passing of Sophie Van Zandt the tenancy has been automatically transferred to her daughter Andromeda. She is therefore entitled to continue her occupancy of the apartment, paying the Koch-era rate of $311.16 per month. If I can be of any further assistance please do not hesitate to contact me.

Yours,
Ted Gillian
Vice President

* * *

Handwritten on the convex backs of ten paper plates by Sam Taylor, the red-headed male yuppie

5/15/01

Tedious argument of insidious intent with Lar. Terrible. It started with an innocent discussion about fugu. I've been reading up on it all day. I'm thinking of working something up for *National Geographic*.

Lar'd come in from Reebok gym with no makeup and her hair in that high ponytail. Every since JFK Jr. and his wife drowned in their plane she's been affecting the wife's look – it's pretty disturbing. Still, she looked human (because she was flushed?) and it made me want to talk to her. It actually made me want to fuck her, but that was out of the question. Added up, we were 200% sober. I asked her if I could take her out. That was how I phrased it. 'You haven't got any money to take me out.' 'I do, my love. *Esquire*'s given me four hundred.' 'They were supposed to pay two and a half thousand.' 'It's a kill fee.'

They sent it for my 'Learn to Flirt' article. I'm punishing myself by writing on paper plates. I'm gonna sleep in the tub. I spent six months writing it. I went to flirting *seminars* at the Learning Annex, endured the most hideous suctioned morons… Let it go, Sam. Let – It – Go. Lara was in the closet in just her thong, changing into 'the little black dress'. No wonder I think in clichés.

'Anyway, you asshole … We can't. You forgot? My big sushi celebration with Mr. Yun? I'm selling him six old Woolworths?'

'I wanted to take you out to Haru. I wanted to get you to eat a piece of that poison fish, the one I'm researching?' (OK. I must've got the idea from the suppressed Mr Yun in the fucking first place.)

I leaned into the closet. She pulled the dress over her head and then hoisted a strapless bra up underneath. No doubt her putting the bra on afterwards is a sign of the horrendous state of the relationship. Midas was nuzzling her bare knees and running around her in circles.

'You didn't fucking walk the dog either?'

I told her I'd thought we both would, and that I'd envisaged we'd then come home, that she'd put on that dress she had on now – except without the bra – and we'd go out to Haru where she'd be poisoned as I held her clammy knee in my hand under the table …

She grabbed his rhinestone leash, stepped into her mules, said, 'So let's walk the fucking dog, then.' And on that note we set off.

How could I? How could I? All the way down 79th to the park, she wants to know. *How the fuck could I forget about tonight?* Tonight is the biggest night of her career 'thus far'. She needs my support. It's impossible that I care about her. I must never have. I tell her I'm sorry. We speak about the fish.

'Why do they eat it anyway? Is it the price? Is it that it's so

16

expensive?'

She's taking small bold steps in her impossible shoes down the bumpy path to the Promenade. She manages aorta roots of sycamores, tire-sized goiters of schist, thriving, piss-scented weeds with – great grace. The grace of ambition. The grace of real estate.

And it is precisely because she is where she is, at the end of the path, that she nails it. She doesn't care whether what she comes up with is true or not. She wants it done, solved, now, at this perfect moment, for she is about to step off the smelly path onto the clean, green and white Promenade: 'Men are attracted to danger. They want what they shouldn't have.'

'That's pretty deep.'

Ta da! We're off the hill. *My Wife with Picturesque Backdrop*. The red sun is sinking behind New Jersey like the giant tip of a banker's cigar. The windows in the high-rises glow like gold bars in a heist movie. The Hudson is sparkling, reflective, moving along. Lara stands akimbo in her perfect shape while Midas joyfully pisses on every clean lawn in the center of the monoblock walkway. We stroll beside the usual people-traffic: very rich straight families, very rich dog-walkers, very rich singles on their way to have drinks at the new café in the Rotunda, and the girl from over the courtyard, next to her fat, drunken pal, on their usual benches, their backs to the little Holocaust Memorial.

This is my last paper plate. Everything's my fault. She fell for the pained artist routine – in my defence, I was really *feeling it* – and now ... I am a foil for a real estate agent. I spend my days in imaginary conversations, defending myself to people I met at cocktail parties years ago. I'm lucky if I write a paragraph. I wander to MOMA, to the Ramble in the Park, to Gryphon Books. Last week I took the F train to Coney Island, and did ... nothing. Not a hot dog passed Midas' lips. Not a word issued from my gel pen. We stood on the boardwalk and watched: Russian gangsters in designer clothes, Hasidim in gangster hats, a magazine shoot where the models boiled in furs and hung around smoking cigarettes, having their sweaty noses powdered. I envied every one of them their place.

I'm looking down into the courtyard now. I watched Lara go, her ponytail wagging from side to side. She stopped halfway across and stared intently into the fish fountain. She was probably just thinking she'd complain to the Co-op board that it needed a polish, or maybe that she'd replace it when she is dubbed head next October. But her face, the tilt of her head, looked … thoughtful, looked OK. She can *look good*. Now it's almost dark. The sky above the courtyard must be lavender.

A blast of yellow light and the girl from the bench (who lives directly opposite me) sits down at her kitchen table and starts eating Cornflakes. She has that big kiddish box with the bright red rooster on it beside her. She eats like she has a gun to her head.

I'm slinking away like a mole to the only bottle we have left on top of the fridge, Calvados. I've propped it up next to this little machine that fans itself cool. Now I intend to write a *nice story*, with an old-fashioned omniscient narrator, one who's not afraid to tell it like it is.

* * *

Andromeda's Rembrandt sketch pad

5/16

Back on the bench. Supposedly at a volleyball game at Horace Mann, up in Riverdale. I'm the captain of the team… Please. Just the thought of it makes my forearm swell up.

Escobar waxes eloquent. Love is all there is to live for. L-O-V-E.

He's pining. Jimmy's off somewhere, working. So E's reading *A Lover's Discourse*, for the zillionth time. He wants to talk – about whether I've ever 'sucked a dick', about whether I'm gay. I tell him I don't know. He asks if my mom was. I tell him she said she wished, but men just 'did it for her'. He persists, says I should find out what I like, what quote turns me on end quote. He's drinking his third Product Placement forty, and thinks it's hilarious when he tells me it's gonna fall off if I don't use it soon and I say, WHAT?

Today I cut school, got all dolled up and went to Barnes and Noble. I went incognito in a big floppy hat and my famous purple sunglasses. Now that she's dead I've started going to chains. I have not been to church yet. Those were two big no-nos. Church is a joke, sure – but I do think in the future there will only be big business and that the thing to do is to work to improve it. I said that to my mom·once. She said, 'My own daughter, a bleeding-heart fucking liberal.' So I donned the Annie Hall getup out of respect for the dead.

It was worse than just a chain. It was the Self-Help section. But … I'm fucking desperate. I don't care how stupid a book is – if I pick it up and it tells me, EVERYTHING'S GONNA BE ALL RIGHT KID – I don't know, it helps a bit. I started to explain this to Escobar, who considers himself a clear-eyed cynic; I even played up the part about going dressed up, as an alter-ego, cause he digs that kinda thing – clothes and identity and gender or whatever but he immediately spread an old issue of a *New York Review of Books* over his face, said 'Oh, PULLEEZE!' and fell asleep. Fatso – always telling me he used to be prettier than I am.

Last night was awful, worse than my usual. I'm in the habit of traipsing from room to room of an evening, a book under one arm, The Old Moth-Eaten Cashmere Throw under the other. I sit down here or there until I pass out somewhere. I fell asleep in the bathroom the other day. I am afraid to sleep. I have bad dreams. Cheap horror-movie affairs, body parts, monsters, gleaming blades. My ma was actually into slasher movies; we had to keep that under wraps. Anyway, I tried 'dream journaling' for two weeks, as recommended in the S-H aisle. Painstakingly recorded every gory detail of my gory-ass nightmares in a *Hello Kitty* notebook and what happened? My nightmares got about a thousand times worse.

Other suggestions from the aisle: practical measures. It's sometimes a good idea TO MOVE. I fastened a necktie to a cardboard box and dragged all my stuff out of my room and across the hall into the Nonexistent Maid's Room. I've always spent a lot of time in there anyway. I hang back and spy on the neighbors, or lean way out and look down into the green shallows of the broken fountain and at the tops of bald men's heads.

Last night I lay in there reading, on some cushions I stole off the couch. The yuppie milled around in his apartment. Mrs. Kasbaum watched the Home Shopping Network. Hugo On Nine (whom Mom hated; she called him a 'Seventies Feminist' because they had a bad date once) did his ironing. By midnight they were all asleep, their lights off. The courtyard purple-gray, the fountain black and gray. At about two, I was finally sort of liking some of this Heidegger. I got up to this part about what H thinks is the right attitude towards death for the dying person – she appears to have had it ALL wrong – when the tacky chandelier blared on in the yuppies' place. Their maroon curtains, that I'd seen him pull shut at eleven, were flung wide.

It was such an odd pose. He has this wild red hair and must be six foot five – he stood at the window in only those karate or whatever pants he always wears, talking to her over his shoulder. She had her back to him too, in a little black cocktail dress, and was fiddling with the locks on their door. They looked like they'd been posed by a photographer making some obvious point about human relationships. Long untraceable shadows and beams of light, very *Dr. Caligari*. Except for her fiddling and his mouth moving, they were completely still.

Then, when she got the door open a crack, he came up behind her and slammed it shut again. She took her mule off and started to hit him in the face. He was running around the room while she went leaping from the couch to the coffee table to the chaise longue – newspapers were flying off the Pottery Barn table, a lamp off the Pottery Barn desk, cushions from their courtyard-view window seat.

Until he stopped, suddenly, in the middle of room, froze for a moment and then took a flying leap across the room onto the couch. He pulled the heavy reproduction Chat Noir that everyone has straight off the wall and threw it on the floor. A very loud crash. Other neighbors' lights came on, changed the shadows in their room. He had her mule in his hand now. She was leaning back on the couch. He held it over her head. He was pulling her head back. By the attachment.

I'd been on my knees hiding behind this batik thing I nailed up over the window, but civic duty compelled me, or something, and I ripped it down and opened the window and said 'Hey!'

He came up to his window, his hands crossed over his naked chest. A look of ... supplication? I think that's what I mean.

I ran away, to the other side of the apartment, to the living room, where the window was open like a door into the sky. I haven't closed it since she opened it. I looked down at Broadway, at the four dark corners of 79th Street, the twin traffic islands facing each other. The traffic lights above them, swinging slightly.

You used to see people there, selling shoes and paperbacks on blankets, getting out of cabs, making out, buying cigarettes, getting into fights. Now there's just an endless stream of tightdoored new taxis, flying uptown. There was not a single light on in anyone's apartment, just those grey columns of back staircases.

I started thinking about how she readied herself, while I was standing there, freezing my ass off in her flimsy old slip. What did she think of, looking down at the thick white lines on 79th, across at the asymmetrical cornices of the Baptist church? Then … exactly how she fell, what angles her body formed, whether she flopped, was sort of suck-plummeted, or what. There's this famous photograph, a postcard now, of a guy diving out of a window. I think he's in Paris. His back's arched, chin up, legs clamped together, toes pointed like an acrobat. I sometimes think it was like that. Except with her, there's her long pink hair too, rising above her head.

* * *

Andromeda's Headmaster Lew's letter to Polly, on St. Mary's stationery. On the header: 'An Independent School for Highly Gifted Children.' On the footer, the school motto: 'Question Authority'.

5/16

Dear Polly (Van Zandt),

First: great to see you at the Met. Second: please tell Andromeda to come back to school. She's been here six times in the past eight weeks. I thought I'd let you know what's going on; I imagine she hasn't had a chance to mention it.

Good thing I haven't believed in synchronicity since the sixties: right now, as I was writing you, a woman from Child Protective Services called. She said there had been complaints from people in the Apthorp – about Andromeda being left alone, and fraternizing with 'undesirables' in Riverside Park. Ugh … these fascist co-op boards. Anyway, after I stopped laughing I assured 'Mrs. Bream' that

Andromeda had cleared her absences with us. I told her she was taking some sanctioned time off.

My advice? be brave, Polly: talk to her, tell to come back to school.

Also, you looked radiant when I saw you yesterday. Can I take you to dinner sometime?

All best
Lew

* * *

Polly's Counter Receipt from Vidal Sassoon

5/16

Cut and Color, *Volumizing* Tonic, Manicure and *Youthifying* Facial: $429.43

* * *

Sam's new 'Marble Mead' composition notebook, the kind elementary school kids use.

5/16

Lara would like to get pregnant. I would not like Lara to get pregnant. Lara would like to beat me about the face with her fucking mule, the one with the squat little heel with the *nail* in it. Jose the doorman would like to know – this morning, as I went out for coffee – if I got into a fight with my razor.

She must have had ten saki martinis. She came in looking like Joel Grey in *Cabaret* – showed a definite lack of judgment in the amount of pancake she'd reapplied in the cab home.

No. Fuck this. I'm *not* gonna detail the fight. I'll write about what's much more important. Maybe I can work this into the Unsellable Memoirs. Something I saw today. The end of the world, actually:

A cherry-patterned curtain in the window of the maisonette

on 83rd Street has been removed. It's been there for fifteen years. I've always imagined it hid a little apartment untouched by time, a place from between the wars, where a husband smoked a pipe and a wife in an apron (cherry-patterned too, lazy imagination) prepared his one-pot supper.

The sky is yolk-yellow, bruise-yellow. It feels like thunder. I remember walking these streets as a boy, getting drenched to the bone, along with the buildings, the stinky ailanthus trees poking through asphalt playgrounds, the fishnet hookers. Another misty fucking watercolor memory of the Upper West Side.

People still got mugged. I look back on it fondly. Janet had dressed me in my too-short suit. It was bright, not quite the navy blue it was supposed to be, and 100% polyester. She used to say, 'I wonder how many poor little polyesters they killed to make this', as she pulled it over my underwear. I was still wet and cold from the tub, and her long fingernails, always painted the same shade of rust, dragged gently down my back. She'd turn to stand at the open kitchen window, where she put on her makeup in a little round mirror and smoked a joint 'for her nerves'. That was when we lived on 100th Street, in the place she had with my dad. It was that kitchen window he threw the leg of lamb out of.

I've watched this movie a thousand times: the glass is opaque with steam; it's Thanksgiving; he hates turkey, and my poor mom is trying to cook lamb the way his mother did. My mom slips up, is feeling too at ease from the vermouth she's sneaking herself as she cooks; and she makes some funny remark, says something true, but slightly mean, about his mom, his family, him.

I see him open the oven and grab the roast with his bare hands, then hurl the haunch like the football star he was in high school. *Thwap!* It makes a comic-book hole, a jagged lamb-leg shape … I don't *remember* this at all. I see it this way because that's how she told it: short, brave, haughty, with her trademark theatricality. 'That, Sammy dear, is the window *your father* threw the leg of lamb out of.'

My father. It's no wonder I couldn't live in reality, had to keep to my own little world. What a prick. I'd never ask her what she saw in him, though, because she would certainly tell me.

The only semblance of peace I knew was on these very streets, out of that damn house. I walked down to school under the filtered light of Riverside's trees, past the Normandy Apartments on 86th, where Nick Charles knocked Nora Charles out in *The Thin Man* with the butt of his gun so she wouldn't be witness to a fight. I headed down West End, under wide flat awnings, above me masonry intricate with gargoyles.

Other kids would have taken the bus – it was a mile and a half – but it was the happiest part of my day. I waved hello to the doormen who loafed in front of buildings, betting on baseball and talking politics. They smoked mini-cigars, Café Cremes, and wore steel-gray three-piece suits. Zaftig livery cabs moseyed up in front of buildings to gather businessmen with wide lapels who climbed in, looking hung over. There was a softness of smog, of drugs and graft that hung over New York in the 70s. It's odd, the way cynicism and softness are so closely related, brother and sister.

The only drawback – the only snag in my prepubescent love affair with the streets of the Upper West Side – was that I got mugged about once a week, usually by this Puerto Rican kid, Escobar. We got to know each other. At first I was scared. I convinced Janet we needed to bleach my hair, to throw him. She thought it was fun. Said she was deprived of this kind of thing because she didn't have a daughter. We stood over the bathroom sink, working two bottles through this ketchup-colored aberration, till the fumes made us cry.

The next time Escobar and I crossed paths he just said, 'Your hair still looks like shit. Give me your money.'

So I tried taking a different route, down Broadway, past the hardware stores, the stationers, the just-opening coffee shops. What mountains of garbage you saw on the street in those days, steaming like puddings.

Now the phone's ringing. It's Lara's voice on the answering machine. 'Pick up, Sammy. It's important.' No. But Escobar always found me. He always wore the same Crazy Eddie freebee T-shirt that every fucker was wearing that summer. Just when I'd gotten used to him, when I started keeping my pinball money in my front pocket for easy access, just when *I almost liked him*, he stole my fucking forty-dollar Bass loafers. He couldn't have known it'd ruin my life.

What does Lara want? For me to look through her pockets for a phone number she wrote on the back of a receipt. She couldn't remember if it was Barney's or Bergdorf's. 'I know you're there, Sam. I know you think my business isn't as important.' I turned the volume down.

And yesterday, The Old Man Himself called from some convention in Miami drunk as shit, and drawled in his best Ernest Hemingway, 'Come on, son, if you brighten up I might leave you something when I'm gone. I'm getting old, you know, and this blood pressure thing isn't going down. Why don't you call me?' That such a man exists.

Oh, and my stupid agent's now trying to sell the 'Flirting' article to *Sassy* – some man's-perspective angle. Dear God. Now to walk Midas. To get out, into the sun, under the patterns it makes through the leaves over the little Holocaust Memorial.

* * *

Andromeda, in her Rembrandt

5/16

Tonight Granny lit into me in the way only she can. Very Claus von Bülow. Most people probably wouldn't even have noticed. First, she made what she persists in thinking is my favorite meal, capellini with pesto, because when I was five and precocious I said I thought it was the best food known to man. KNOWN TO MAN. Ha. Then – she served it in the dining room, a place I avoid at all costs. It's the portrait of Granny as a little girl, nailed over the sideboard. She must be about seven in it. The eyes. Such happy-happy eyes. Then the mouth, which looks like a sunken boat. In the background someone's big Newport Mansion (i.e. Bates Hotel) rises up. Such hopeful eyes; such a shitty, gloomy mouth. Pollyanna-tie-me-to-the-train tracks. She still looks EXACTLY THE SAME.

Fine. Fine. Fine. Give her a break. She is an OLD LADY. She really did try. Even with her drunk first-cousin parents it was still a big deal for her to give up her rich-girldom in the Apthorp and move down to the Village on her trust fund. She knew Elizabeth Bishop. That's her big claim to fame. And it's not like she didn't really WANT to hock all the stuff we have in here now: the Tiffany lamps, the ancient dishes with bleeding blue pastoral settings, the silver etched with dead people's initials, the claw-footed tables and chairs. She would have in an instant, but my INSANE mom guilt-tripped her into keeping them. She said that I might want this shit someday.

Whenever we met Granny for lunch downtown (she never came here) it was always a variation on the same convo. She'd tell my mom she wanted to sell stuff, and that she needed the money (never trust a trust fund not to run dry) but my mom would tilt her head, suck in her checks, nibble the tip of her Waterman and fucking intone: 'Money comes and goes,

Mother.' She could say the STUPIDEST things, but manage to make them sound really, really profound. This is from a woman who collected foreign and rare editions of *Das Kapital*.

Anyway, in my experience money goes ... and goes ... and goes until you're sixteen, stuffed up in this sprawling rent-controlled shithole with hardly enough money for cigarettes but thousands of dollars-worth of antique furniture and china that's falling to shit.

Granny had set the places at opposite ends of the table (*Citizen Kane*). We sat for a long time not saying anything, chewing daintily, listening to the capellini twisting around each other's forks. I looked out the window and down three floors into Mrs. Kasbaum's apartment: she stood in her kitchen preparing a tray, brought it into the living room, put it down on a fold-out card table that is not usually there, fluffed up the pillows on her gold couch and turned to the mirror to pat her dome of hair. Then she saw me (*Rear Window*) and – I had to look at Granny. I haven't looked directly at anyone in a really long time.

It was the time of day when everyone has their lights on, but no one has closed the curtains yet. The lit windows made a chunky tiara around Granny's purple hair, one made of those plastic cubes, the kind that usually have tiny sea-horses, or real dried flowers suspended in them; except in hers there were people, tables, the big green leaves of houseplants, and Nora Kasbaum. Granny had a lot of make-up on, and looked somewhat plastic herself. And like a woman who'd outlived her daughter. The first and last thing she said during that joyous meal was 'I was afraid to ask the cheese woman at Citarella if the pesto was fresh. She's so intimidating. I remembered you said sometimes it's green on top and grey underneath. But I got up my nerve.' She paused. 'You must go back to St. Mary's. Tomorrow.' That was, literally, it. I didn't even say anything in

28

reply, just smiled at her. I can make my smile very reassuring. Very down to earth. Very sane.

What's funny is while she said it, the Yuppie appeared at Kasbaum's door with like a hundred bags of groceries. He gave her a big hug then sat down right in the center of the cushion she'd fluffed up and – RUBBED HIS HANDS TOGETHER? Do people even do that anymore? It's like out of a silent movie, *Mother Krausen's Trip to Happiness* or something. For a second I felt like we were all innocents: me, Granny, him, even my mom.

* * *

A printed-out Mellel document. Sam has inserted a ^ between 'or' and 'a' on the first line, and 'the morbid carnival of' is handwritten above. 'Flesh-colored' on the second line has been bracketed, and has a question mark above it

5/17

I face the river. Sometimes, if I'm lucky, as I watch a seagull, or a garbage barge, or the sun sink between the flesh-colored high rises of New Jersey, I forget myself. Then the air is luminous. I am luminous. Like stained glass. That beautiful. When my mother dropped, flew, cascaded out the window to her death, she passed the stained glass window in the high arch of the Baptist church. I wonder, was it upside down, with the blood-blue stained-glass sky on top? Did she see the pearly tips of His intricate thorns?

OR

The girl sat before the river, looking down into her book and then up at the sun, which was slipping down between the high rises across the river in Ft. Lee. She liked her book, and that was why she kept looking up. It made her think.

29

A man who lived in her apartment building walked by with his dog. He saw her there every day. Until today, he had never

* * *

Handwritten on the back of the above

5/17

Had the asinine idea to write about the girl across the courtyard. She's called Meadow or something. I thought, 'It's the thinking man's *Bridges of Madison County*!' They'll laugh. They'll cry. I mean, it is an awful story. Lara says the doorman came up and knocked on the door to tell her. Meadow's mom landed, thud, in front of him. She was some sort of famous academic. And Christ, what an apartment they live in. Lara said it would sell for at least three mill, even in the shape it's in. All the details are there. The girl is really beautiful. She reads. I see her in the park, Heidegger on her lap. She walks around half-naked too. But I avert my eyes.

* * *

Note to Sam from his literary agent Lynne Gerlitz on a miniscule Post-it ...

5/17

Sam I Am. This came for you. Whatever you want – to do! Nothing on the memoir yet! Lynne xx

... which is stuck to a handwritten letter from Sam's ex-girlfriend Hillary Schwinn, a fashion editor at the teen fashion magazine SASSY

Dear Sammy,

I hope this note finds you and Lara well. Funny to be writing through your agent – you could have called me yourself, silly boy. Oh well –

great to see you at Ashby's after so long. Your article. Lynne is right about the tone. We aren't *Esquire* and can't really do cynical. As it is, I think 'Learn to Flirt' is hilarious, but just not – as Lynne put it – '*Sassy* reading.' At *Sassy* we use exclamation points. Not sarcastically!

The only possibility that comes to mind is we do a monthly column, 'From His Angle.' Maybe we could morph it into that? It's only a thousand words, but we always feature a big photo of the author. Considering Lynne's (joke?) request for it to be published anonymously, I can't see how this would suit you. But your call, if you want to follow up. The fee is a princely $250.

Look, honey – I want you to know that I think it's really great that you finally putting yourself out here again. Just drop your airs. C'mon, we'd all be so happy for you. We'll Photoshop the hair.

Let's have a drink sometime, soonish?

Hill xx

* * *

Andromeda in her Rembrandt

5/18

Basically, you JUST KNOW to look in the sky for the moon and not under the park bench you're sitting on – that's Heidegger's Comportment. He says it's an inherent logic, an ingrained connection between me and the world. Well, sorry guy, but on a subtler level I don't know where the hell to look. Today (back in school after being subjected to a lecture / saki-soaked lunch special with a sleazier-than-ever Lew) I embarrassed myself in 'Kafka in Context' because I hadn't noticed that the protagonist in *The Judgment*, uh, KILLS HIMSELF at the end. Plus, I like, REALLY LIKED IT. I read it like THREE FUCKING TIMES.

'Andromeda, he throws himself in the Vltava,' said Anorexic Trish with an unsightly shake of her skeletal skull. Everyone else joined in the general concern, including 'He's my gay teacher'

Rob. They, the whole class, all eight of them, gave me the look I'm getting a bit bored of: it's the 'your mom killed herself' look. Whatever. You know what I DID notice in the story? The big gesture. The big gesture of his dad standing over him while he lies in bed. His face like a totem pole. I waited a few minutes so it wouldn't seem too obvious I was running away, slowly packed up my bag, smiling at it, then slipped out the door and down the back stairs, past Lew's office and out the back. He called after me, 'Hot date?'

Now the yuppie's dog's at my knees. Escobar is nowhere to be seen. His shopping cart's here. But it's always here. He keeps a tarp on it.

Anyway, after that catastrophe I went across Montague Street and then across Pierrepont and into (another forbidden chain) Duane Reade, where I found myself staring into a locked case of expensive hair products. The labelled manageress, Cherise, came over and asked me if I would like to see something. Even though I only had five bucks I said yes, thank you. She opened the case, took out a metal jar, which was pale blue and cost twenty-one dollars, then went to show an old man where the Cheesenips were. I wanted this goo. I took another one off the shelf. When Cherise came back I handed one jar back and kept the other in my hand. Then I perambulated. Browsed the make-up. Flip-flops. Fondled a loofah. If someone said anything, I would explain, 'I'm sorry I was preoccupied as my mother has just killed herself.' I held the line in my head like a mantra. The repetition cleared my mind.

I went to the back wall. Feet stuff, Dr. Scholl's, bunion pads. I made sure no one was around, that there were no convex mirrors in the corners of the ceiling, then peeled the quilted sticker off, the one that sets the alarm off – and just dropped the goo in my bag before buying a pack of American Spirits at the counter. (I've switched. Lew said, 'If you must smoke at least get the ones without chemicals.' OK OK OK.) Cherise called after me on the way out: 'You have a good one, sweetheart.' I felt like she was giving me the stuff. Like she knew about my mom. I ALMOST CRIED.

I was still technically on my lunch break but since I never eat lunch I had half hour to kill before Botany. We continue to dissect oranges. Anyway I just went back to school, took the stairs up to my favourite bathroom – the handicapped one on the eighth floor, the one with the private lock and good view – and locked myself in. I stood in front of the mirror: matting, sculpting, teasing. All the things they told you you could do with it on the back of the jar. It looked really awful. Try as I might, I couldn't wash it out with hand soap.

I gave up and leaned out the window and smoked, being very careful of my coiffure, which might have exploded like Debbie Harry (*Hairspray*) with the slightest heat. It was such a clear day. The Brooklyn Bridge was sparkling. The sky was blue as an enamel egg. The Twin Towers (monstrous spokes) were gleaming. Down below Ed Hanes and Anorexic Trish, who I guess is his girlfriend, were arguing. She was playing with the buckle on her very expensive 'hobo' bag. He was pacing around her in circles, smoking one of those dumb miniature cigars he sometimes has. Then he looked up and saw me.

No matter what comes of it; no matter what he thinks, or decides to call it, I can truthfully say that Ed Hanes, ex-jock, Ritalin snorter and sometimes club-promoter, loved me. He put his hand out and squeezed Trish's shoulder, still looking up, then turned her away and they went towards Boro Hall.

Now the Yuppie is standing right behind my bench, on top of the Holocaust memorial. It is just a bit of marble, three feet square and flush with the ground (guarded, though, by this pathetic knee-high fence). There's something wrong with the memorial even without him on top of it. Why the Lilliputian monument for six million? Even the dog ('Midas', no less) looks embarrassed. He's hiding behind a tree.

You know what my Comportment is? How I can see him? Because I'm pretending I'm looking over my shoulder up the slope to Riverside Drive, smoking and squinting hard. Like I'm looking for someone in a window. I'm fiddling with my bag, searching for cigarettes, for water, for matches, for my phone (which I only use as a clock, which never rings its Work-of-Art-in-the-Age-of-Mechanical-Reproduction Bach ring). He won't acknowledge me for all my show of busy-busy-busy. He's fucking standing there in the Holocaust Memorial staring at his sneakers.

LATER:

Escobar came back to the bench after that with a bag of groceries containing: five Hostess cherry pies and three forty-ounce bottles of Ballantine. He gave one to me. I've never drank before, just a sip here and there. The fighting yuppies must have been drunk the other night. My mom may have been drunk when she offed herself. She was half the time. They actually asked me if I wanted an autopsy 'to determine the cause of death'. I mean: she jumped out the window.

Escobar keeps insisting we talk about it. (Right now I'm waiting for him to come back; he said he was going 'to the loo', but it's been a while.) The truth is he's a bit ... touchy-feely. Probably from being in rehab so often. He said he'd been reading my mom's first book, and he's come up with some theory to ''splain my psychology.' Even though I loaned it to him on the condition that we never talk about it.

'She's got this thing about when you are a girl, you're both the seeker and the sought. She says you're rent, splintered, tortured. I think the stealing thing is symptomatic of this –'

He was eating a pie. I wanted to change the subject.

34

'Where's Jiminez?'

'Working.'

'Aren't there child labor laws?'

'He's a hooker. He sees himself as both seeker and …'

Escobar thinks it's all very funny. But it is not funny. And there is some truth to what she said. I think. I don't know. As he was inhaling the disgusting bright red cherry glop, coated with a layer of icing not unlike putrefying, deeply cracked flesh, I drank the rest of my (first) Ballantine.

The row of shiny black bars on the fence that separates us from the little hill sort of swayed. I took off my shoes and put my feet up. My chipping purple toenails swayed pleasantly, too. I arranged everything in a line, the toenails, the pin-thin windows in the high rises, the bars of the fence.

* * *

From Lara, to Murray and Muckman Managing Agents on Douglas Ellimen Realtors' letterhead

5/19

Dear Mr. Gilliam,

Thank you for your prompt reply. Andromeda Van Zandt will not be eighteen for another thirteen months, and is therefore illegal in her occupancy of 11 E. I mention this not because the legality of her tenancy concerns me, but out of neighborly concern for her welfare after the tragic death of her mother. The child is disheveled, she smokes constantly, and she comes home late. Last night I saw her drunk in the lobby, asking Jose Hernandez, one of our doormen, if he had a cigarette. She might set her apartment on fire, or intentionally harm herself.

I understand that her grandmother has moved in to look after her, but I never see her: they keep their blinds open, and our place looks right into theirs. It is clear that the elder Van Zandt is rarely there. (Since she still maintains a rent-stabilized lease on Barrow Street – please see the enclosed xerox – she is not herself legally entitled to live in the apartment anyway.)

This morning I put in a call to Social Services to ask that a home visit be made. It seemed like the right thing to do. I will keep you informed.

Yours Sincerely,
Lara Lawson-Taylor

* * *

Sam, in his Mead notebook

5/19

'xx.'

Two *x*s.

… Should I schmooze Hillary? At that asshole reunion she drank too many Cosmos and kept running her hand along her belly under her sweater, *exactly* the kind of thing *Sassy* suggests you do, the kind of signal you send to let a guy know… Anyway I had the receiver in my hand before I realized that sleeping with her would make me … *a bit* of a bastard. And I have to admit, I kind of set this up the last time I saw her. Looked at her a few times from across the room, wearing Sam Taylor Serious Face Number 5, the I-might-be-talking-to-this-guy-but-my-attention-cannot-be-long-diverted-from-your-beautiful-face face. But still. Oh, how I've sunk! For chrissake she's an assistant editor at *Sassy*, not Helen Gurley Brown.

I can't go near Lara now, and Meadow – or whatever that girl from across the courtyard is called – is wherever I turn. I really do see her everywhere. Yesterday she was down on her bench without her friend, that fat Puerto Rican guy who's been there for years. He is very well-read, this guy – bodily attached to a shopping cart full of periodicals, and not *Playboy*. He reads *The Nation*. It was quite funny, actually; she was fidgeting around like crazy, trying to get me to look at her, and ended by giving this big theatrical wave up Riverside Drive. To a spot in the sky. I know the views of the park well.

Then this morning on the subway, en route to have coffee with my agent, she was on her way to school, sitting there with her nose in *Being and Time*, as usual. I stood almost right on top of her with my hand on the roof. She didn't look up for the whole ride.

At Twenty-eighth I stood back to let the hordes off. Meadow was among them. Several businesswomen pushed in front of her. She waited patiently, with an almost singular composure and ... patience. I put my hand on the door to keep it open for her. Still no recognition. On the stairs, she stopped to take out a cigarette. I hung back. Her hair was up, but hundreds of single strands had broken loose, making a kind of messy aura around her skull. She was wearing a long straight slip, a milky color, like a moonstone – the same one she had on the night I almost killed Lara – and this weird black shawl she always seems to have draped over her. It might be a real Spanish mourning shawl. She lit up in a shaft of light that led up the dirty steps to the Hickory House coffee shop.

We climbed into the sun, walked east. I was going to Park, I reasoned with myself; I wasn't following her, which was both true and not true. I did wait while she stopped on the stairs, but only because it would have been awkward to run into her, so late in the game.

It was ten-thirty and the flower markets were open. The flower district has not changed since I was fifteen, like her. If anything, its simple business has grown more robust, has flourished, in our bubble economy of appearances. There is not one shop now on Twenty-eighth that sells anything but flowers, and they spill their wares out onto the sidewalks, leaving only a two-foot wide path for pedophiles. I mean pedestrians.

For she moved through the big spotty lilies, and slack-jawed irises, shot-in-the-face daisies and glossy rubber plants, past spongy defensive cacti and topiary trimmed so tightly it made you suck in your stomach, between walls of trellis that crept with kumquats, she moved like ... the spirit above this muck of flesh, more air than earth, more sky than flower...

Lara *must* be fucking drugging me. Part of the get-pregnant plan. But – in my defense – the flower-guys agreed, paid their respects, called her 'pretty lady', old-fashioned things like that. One very fat man in a tank top even offered her a sunflower. No one said anything sleazy. She, for her part, ignored us all. Seemed, in fact, to be only interested in that gigantic Samsung billboard, the one over the parking lot on Seventh, where a naked girl looks out from behind a huge cellphone.

Moving east, the flower district gives way to wholesale. Persian rugs in cavernous musty shops, luggage in all makes of pleather, notebooks, photoframes and bracelets stuck with bits of cut glass and plastic pressed in by nine-year-old fingers three thousand miles away. Everyone rushing in cheap business clothes. Women in smoky pantyhose. Men in ties. Hot kiosks and piles of frying onions, preparation for a day of shwarmas.

I erased the present. I made the famous-artist lofts above the street back into old garment factories. I set ten thousand Sister Carries to stitch and pedal at ten thousand metal machines that roared like crickets. Meadow walked through the gun-grey streets, beside women in long dresses the color of rats, under swinging black gas lamps.

Scratch that. Back then half of everyone was coughing up a lung. I razed the horse-shit-impacted roads, lifted the fire-trap factories. I unzipped her boots and set her bare feet down on cool dirt and moss. We walked under the domes of five-hundred-year-old oaks. It was quiet.

On Park Avenue South I almost got hit by a cab. I had to head south anyway, down to 23rd, for Stupid Lynne and the Venal Pastry at the Globe Café. I watched Meadow walk on, further east. She'd finished her cigarette. I stepped on it for her.

Lynne Gerlitz is the type of woman whose boulder-like reality makes you afraid you'll never be able to buy into a movie or a novel again. (Ten years ago I liked that about her.) She gets sight of me and raises her arms in exasperation. Over her head there is a giant Earth suspended from the ceiling, too large for the room; for a moment, from the door, it looks like she is holding it up. Sally Jessie Raphael as Atlas. I kiss her hello. Please let it be good news. Please let someone want my piece-of-shit memoir. She tousles my hair.

'What are we going to do with you?'

'Sorry I'm late. So! What's the latest?'

'Well I'm still getting some good noises, but the consensus seems to be that it's a bit light on … event. I've got a plan in the meantime. Look. Take the staff position at *Sassy*. Develop a following of teenage girls. Memoir sells like crazy. Dave Eggers, only backwards.'

'Ass-backwards. Anyway *he* can go fuck himself. You admit there are sinister parallels. '

'No, Sam. I don't. You met him at party once. He'd finished his by then.'

'I know the truth. Anyway, you know it wouldn't work at *Sassy*. They'd hate me.'

'You *can* and it *would* and they *wouldn't*.' She gives me a once-over. 'Imagine yourself, walking into the office every day. A *writer*. With a haircut. And a suit on.'

Half of me wants nothing more than to please Lynne and all those like her. The other wants to throw her iced latte at her blouse.

'I don't know, Lynne. I might wanna just cut my losses. Just leave it. I've started – I'm starting something new. Sort of a sly omniscient narrator. An inverted one –'

'Wait, what, *sweetie*?' She only calls me sweetie when she wants to kill me.

'Inside out.'

'I know what fucking inverted means, OK? I thought we were working on selling *A Freak Show of Candor*, if that's what it's called today. What's it called today, sweetie?'

'*Leg of Lamb*.'

'___'

The tables at the Globe are arranged in concentric circles. All around clean men and women are making deals, shaking each other's hands, smiling. Their white teeth glimmering. There is a bowl of cold strawberry soup in front of me. A blade of something floats forlornly in the center, like a stick insect. Lynne stirs the long spoon in her latte, prods the half-eaten Napoleon on her plate. Her voice, which has lowered incrementally throughout our conversation, is now a husky whisper. I have to lean in to hear this:

'What am I doing here? Can you please tell me? Because *I* have no idea what I'm fucking *fucking* doing here.' She's balancing the long spoon between her thumb and her fuck-finger like a see-saw. 'Seriously. This *is serious*. Don't you smirk at me.'

'OK. Hold on –'

She throws the spoon. She means to chuck it on the table, but it bounces off, flies a foot in the air and lands on the pale gold carpet. I nod, lean down, and am struck – by the interstices in the weave of the canvas of my Converse. I slow. The carpet is so clean. Lynn's wearing mules too. I need to see my dad. When I come up for air, I put the spoon gently back on the white tablecloth. Like a gauntlet. I forfeit. Lynne won't look at me.

She takes two calls about Susan Summers' memoirs. The check comes, and I pick it up. Thirty bucks of my dwindling kill fee to sit there and be the world's biggest asshole.

Outside the Globe it starts to pour, the afternoon rain of late May. It gets hot, and then it rains. Some things are so clear. Office workers are huddled under dripping awnings, smoking. I run west in the darkened road. To my dad in Naples. Florida! Two skinny girls in the Hickory House coffee shop smile at me, as I leap down the steps and onto a waiting number 9 train. The doors close. The air conditioning's on and it's freezing. My clothes are soaked. The car is empty. Me and the Reaction ad: a drugged model posing with her shoes. *Hi, I'm the Reaction model, and these … these are my shoes. Wanna buy some?* Empty orange plastic ass-shaped seats. The sound of my own deep breath. My heart hurting my ribs. Please stand clear of the closing doors.

* * *

Andromeda in her Rembrandt

5/19

Got soaked coming home from the shrink Lew made me go to. Ever since I'm back at school, Lew's following me in and out of every class, offering advice on books, movies, my HAIR … I will remain in denial about the fact that he might be coming on to me. My mom slept with him once or twice. Said he had certain talents that it would be in poor taste to disclose. Anyway, he recommended this shrink when I told him about the self-help aisle. 'No. Just say no to Deepak Cho, Andromeda.' The shrink's a REICHIAN, for God's sake, a German no less. Dr. Gorling. He was floored when I told him I don't masturbate, and made me promise him I'd keep an eye out for a guy or girl I'd like to quote have end quote. Gosh golly darn. He had a swastika on his wall that he claimed he was re-appropriating.

I'm kind of reeling, because the instant I got in, soaked through – not only was Granny here (haven't seen her much in the last two weeks, I think she's given up), but she was sitting IN THE LIVING ROOM WITH A SOCIAL WORKER. I literally can't remember the last time there was someone new in the house. Granny and 'Brenda Bream', a Jamaican lady from central casting, sat straight-backed on two different couches, about twenty feet apart. Something called a homestudy was apparently in progress. I joined them in my wet slip, and tried to act as dignified as I could, under the circumstances. I partook of tea from tiny gold-edged cups I've never seen before.

Brenda seemed almost as nervous as I was. Granny was laying it on thick, i.e. the blueblood thing. She thought it would make us look more respectable. She's been known to throw the weight she claims to hate around – big time, when it serves her purpose. Poor Brenda shifted around on her ass and futzed with her clipboard. She asked if that was our church out the window. She had on a cheap pink skirt suit and bright blue plastic earrings. Granny said, 'No, we go to Collegiate'. What a fucking lie!

Brenda said there had been an oversight when I met with the social worker after my mom died. (They made me go into St. Luke's Roosevelt hospital and talk to some dude. He was very lax. He said, 'You have friends? They'll help. Friends are the best,' and kept looking up my skirt.) At that time, it should have been registered that Granny was moving in to look after me. That fact that it wasn't wouldn't have come to light, had it not been for the intervention of a 'concerned neighbor'. Apparently someone put in a call saying that Granny was never around and I was drunk all the time.

Granny raised her teacup and her over-tweezed eyebrows. 'I can assure you there's not a shred of truth there. They're trying to get us evicted. We have a very desirable rent-stabilized lease.'

'I wouldn't put it past them,' said Brenda, and looked at me. I was chain-smoking. I tried to imitate Granny. I crossed my legs tightly and held my eyebrows up. 'You doing OK, Andy?'

No one ever calls me Andy. Even though I tell them all to. I must have put it down on the form at St Luke's.

We walked her to the door, as well brought-up ladies do, then all stood in the cramped front hall, the tiled hall, the one with the hideous mosaic. Granny pointed out this charming 'period feature' – a shit-faced little man with a wreath on his head and a jug in his hand. Mom and I always kept him covered with the coat rack, but Granny likes him. We are having an unspoken argument about it, actually. I move the coat rack in front of him, and she moves it away. It's handy, though: I can always tell when she's been in.

After Brenda left – assuring us that it'd all be fine, she could see there was 'no problem here' – me and Granny stood there not speaking for five minutes. Then Granny said she thought she'd go to a movie. *Barry Lyndon* – the longest movie Stanley Kubrick ever made, and that's saying something – was playing at Film Forum. She didn't invite me. I would have accepted.

I came back in here, into my new room, and sat down on one of the two couch pillows I'm using as a bed. I felt awful. I decided I'd watch the Yuppie take a shower. Again, my comportment was a bit off: this was not the place to look. He had the window open wide, his hair was a foot high with white foam, and he was soaping himself with a pink sponge the size of my ass. I've never really looked at his face before; I guess I've been so overwhelmed by his hair. It's nice, his face; hard to describe. He has wide lips, high cheekbones, and his eyes are quite far apart. That sounds like a cow. Maybe I liked it because of what he was thinking about. His eyes looked inside, the eyes of one remembering. I actually ran in and put on another coat of 'Toast of New York' in case he should look over and see me. I didn't want to think any more about fucking comportment. I had it all planned out. I would stand back from the window in my dark new room, and watch him for the rest of the night. For the rest of my life.

When he'd rinsed the bubbles off and left the shower, I waited, staring like a hypnotist into the warm smoke-colored courtyard. His dinky chandelier did not come on. I waited. I WILLED it to come on. The windows got darker. He'd have to turn something on soon to see in a drawer, to get dressed... I stood there for ten minutes, twenty minutes. No sign. Finally, I looked down at the floor. And there – there I saw her fucking eyes looking out from inside the pillow case. This photograph of my mom that Robert Mapplethorpe took in the eighties. I swear it always appears when I like, seriously, least need to see it. In the pages of a book, under a blanket in the closet, in a fucking Cracker Jack box. She must have had five hundred prints made. I started crying.

I did not cry when she died. I felt like a tear would've been in order when José came up to tell me, but I couldn't.

She's naked in the photo except for the necklace she always wore, an heirloom, a cameo. She wore it on a leather choker. Granny wanted to bury her in it, but I kept it. I dumped her laptop in the eco-coffin instead.

What the FUCK does that face she's making mean? One second it seems murderous; the next, just neurotic. Or is it supposed to be sultry? She's kneeling, on a swivel chair, with her choker on and a face like a ... what? Why couldn't she just have taken SSRIs like everyone else? I used to ask her when she went to bed and cried for WEEKS. And she would sob, 'I don't want to kill my soul!' 'But you don't believe in the soul!' 'Don't simplify. Don't literalize. Don't undermine me. Don't fucking NITPICK, Andromeda.'

I just kept crying, kissing my own knees that I had pulled up under me. I was convinced that if I looked at her face long enough I would understand everything. But I almost didn't notice when I stopped. I stopped because it got so dark I didn't have to look at it anymore. Nothing had changed. The only thing that was different was that my makeup had run and my face was all sticky.

Now I've got a bottle of Chateau Lafite. It was a hobby of my ma's. She made a fair amount of money off her bullshit treatises but blew it all on extravagances. Anyway, I've moved to the living room, where I haven't hung out for a while. I used to sit here with her and eat dinner. We sat here, at the coffee table, and had Chinese. She got Revolution Diet number 9, which is tofu and vegetables with sesame sauce. On the phone to the guy she always said, NUMBER 9, NUMBER 9, like in that Beatles song. I'm sure he thought it was hilarious.

We'd sit here, by the wide open windows, with the sun in the windows of the apartments across the street. We'd eat and she'd ask me what I thought about everything, and I'd tell her, but as I was telling her I was always thinking about what she wanted to hear. I might have been leaning out the window looking at the church smoking one of my, or one of her, cigarettes. She smoked Virginia Slims. YOU'VE COME A LONG WAY BABY!

* * *

On the back of a Zabar's receipt of Lara's for a quarter pound of Nova, half an applestrudel and a small Greek salad

5/19

AvZ 2,5000,000 x .20 =
NK 675,000 x .20=
Hugo 345,000x .20 =

45

Sam in the Mead

5/20

Pablo Picasso Was Never Called an Asshole
1st draft

Lara has left papers strewn all over the floor. She's been promoted to exclusive agent for the Apthorp. I read her contract. Whenever an apartment sells, she gets 20%, which is … an enormous sum. If a place sells for 1.5 she gets … 300K? Fuck.

There were many complicated calculations, on satanic Post-Its: how much will she make if Mrs. Kasbaum's remission goes out of remission? Or if Hugo Greenberg spends one day over six months in his electricity-less artist's shack on a dune in Provincetown? One day over six months (I read, on a highlighted Xerox) and the Apthorp is not his 'primary residence'.

There were also some notes and a letter about Meadow – whose name isn't Meadow, it's Andromeda.Van Zandt.

In a last-ditch attempt to know what the fuck drives Lar, and maybe even to cultivate a little compassion, I used all her fancy products in the shower. I lathered up with her big pink sponge and something called Lux de Mer. It smelled of coconut and felt like sperm. I lit her aromatherapy candle. The price tag was still on the bottom. Fifty dollars. *Fifty dollars!* But the effect was … kind of nice. It was called Clarity.

When I got out I sat on the floor, Indian style, in the dark. Midas came to me and rested his jaw on my thigh. And Lo, I *got* some clarity: my flirting article was a lie. I was putting on this voice, the *Esquire* guy. The point is, some real fucking guy writes those articles, *and he is not being ironic.*

Lara came in. She was just passing through. She had to pick up a Tiffany's flask and get it monogrammed for some clients.

She set in on Van Zandt. 'That girl has twelve rooms all to herself. There are families who *need* these apartments.'

I gave her the Jimmy Stewart good-guy routine. 'Come on, Lar. The only family that could afford to buy her place is Tom Cruise and Nicole Kidman's.' The room is still dark; she can put on lipstick in the dark.

'They're in Trump Plaza. Tacky bastards.'

I grabbed her foot and held it fast. I said, 'Be nice.' When I let go she didn't move right away.

'I *am* nice.'

And that minor, debatably non-existent victory – that's what really set the ball rolling. A drink was in order. Because. Not only had I uncovered one of my most crippling misconceptions – it was now a inflamed axiom, it was now: No One Is Ever Being Ironic Even If They Think They Are – but I had also convinced Lara to let up a little on Andromeda.

I started out on Burgundy but soon hit the harder stuff.

Her lights came on across the courtyard. I left mine off. She had a plastic Fairway bag tied to her head like a kerchief, was wearing a salmon-colored kimono, smoking a cigarette and drinking red wine out of the bottle. She looked about thirty-five, with all her hair off her face. She leaned too far out for a while, peered down. Then she settled back on her radiator.

I opened my window and sat on the window seat. We saw each other. She raised her bottle. I lifted my glass. Then … we did not look at each other; we looked up at the sky and down at the fish. I pretended there was something between us. A thin silver wire. We were attached by our wrists, connected in some great Calder mobile. If I moved I'd jerk her into the courtyard. I even stopped drinking my wine, stayed perfectly still. She held her kimono closed high at the neck, right under her chin. Then she went in. I tried to see into her room but it was too dark.

I'd finished the bottle and was feeling not drunk, but *fan-*

fuckingtastic, when I picked up the phone and called Hill. Hell, she *did* put two *X*s. She was free! Her dinner party had been cancelled! The hostess, Fatuous Ashby, was suffering with morning sickness but was thrilled to be *blah blah blah*. I cut her off. Did she want to meet at the Dublin House? This was foresight: I knew a Guinness would round me out. No, but she would meet me at Isabella's. She was in the mood for one of their Manhattans.

A *Manhattan?* I regretted calling the moment I hung up. But I'm a *good sport*, I told myself. I can be *a good sport*. I have this thing, I ... jolly myself along. I put on my dad's voice, give myself his chummy pressure. It's fine when you're drunk.

I decided it would be responsible to stop at Plimpton's. The sky was glorious, almost dark, that ultimate, twilight blue. In spite of myself, I felt a surge when I stepped out of the Apthorp's grand wrought-iron gate. The king of his castle, after all.

Plimpton's was closing, and the saleslady, Genie – who Lara confides in and who therefore hates me – was spraying the glass cases with Windex. I picked up a three-pack of Trojans, kind of slammed them down on the counter and gave her a shit-eating grin. Then the bell on the door dinged, and we both turned and watched Andromeda stumble in. She had her old book-bag across her chest, but everything else was black, purple and gauzy, even more risqué than her usual. She'd even donned purple-tinted glasses. She looked ... almost *awful*, like a darker Stevie Nicks in the cokehead era. When she saw me she opened her mouth a little in surprise, then turned away toward the makeup displays.

Genie called after her, 'Hi, Andromeda.' Then to me, holding her hand flat with my coins in it: 'Two-*sixty*. I got forty here.'

I fumbled. There are seven pockets in my wheat-colored corduroy jacket. Breast. Two sides. Internal left and right. That secret one in the back. Who the fuck was I pretending to be, anyway? And why oh why did I choose *this guy?*

Then Genie darted out from behind the counter with her arms over her head. I thought a display case was teetering.

'Stop!'

Andromeda had frozen in the doorway. Genie tugged on a bit of pink that stuck out the corner of her bag.

Lara's Pink Sea Sponge.

Andromeda said nothing, just looked confusedly at me.

And miraculously, I got it. I got it or I invented it. Sometimes, booze is *good* for the reflexes, right before it's catastrophic. 'So, how much do we owe you? For the rubbers and the sponge?' says I.

Andromeda and I were smiling at Genie as if our lives depended on it.

'She was trying to steal it.' It came out with an astonished guffaw.

The offending item had been placed on the checkout counter. I balled it up. It disappeared in my fist. I let it spring open.

'I'm closing. You want it? Fine.'

I paid fifteen dollars and seventy-five cents.

Outside it was a *bit* awkward. We stopped by a parking meter. We were not really standing together, exactly. The subway had just let out and there were people everywhere. Finally she said 'I can't believe you paid sixteen bucks for that,' and blew a stream of smoke sideways so it wouldn't go in my face.

'I'm going for a drink, to meet someone. We're old enough to be your parents, wanna come?'

'I'm sixteen.'

'So what?' We headed into the crosswalk.

'I'll get carded.'

'Drink mine.'

'How old are you anyway?'

'Thirty-three.'

'You'd have to have had me when you were seventeen, which seems demographically unlikely.'

We crossed Broadway, passed Mrs. Ellie's Homesick Bar and Grill, a sentimental restaurant with a stencil of a cowgirl lassoing a martini on the door. I've never wanted to go in. Andromeda walked close to my arm, then swung way out, walked on her tiptoes in the gutter and swung back again. She did this a few times. It slowed the pace. At the top of the hill on Columbus the high flat wall that forms part of the extension to the Museum of Natural History came into view. It used to be a mural of the earth looking like a beanbag of the earth. I liked it. They redid it recently. Now it just says 'The Museum of Natural History' in black courier on an orange background, like the old NY license plate.

'*Pablo Picasso Was Never Called an Asshole*. Do you know that song?' I have no idea what made me think of it. She'd have been about one year old, if that, when it came out. I went on. 'It's about how artists, male artists, tend to suck all women's energies up to fuel their own art. But the funny part is, the women don't hate them for it. They feel honored.'

'How do you know?'

'I dunno. I've read biographies.'

She stopped in front of the liquor store on Amsterdam. Her head was framed by deep-colored bottles of booze, flashing Christmas lights and cut-out pictures of half-naked girls.

'Of the women?'

'What?'

'Have you read books *by the women*? The muses?'

'I didn't say *muse*.'

'That's what you meant.'

'No, that's not what I meant. Your hair's purple.'

'It's temporary.'

50

'Why don't you just come in for one drink?' The idea of showing up with her filled me with monstrous glee. Across the street from Isabella's, a crowd of about fifty MBAs were talking on their cell phones. Nobody wants to be alone anymore. Nobody wants to be alone with anyone else anymore.

'Who's gonna be there?'

I handed her the bag with the pink sponge in it. 'A woman I'm hoping to sleep with.'

'Let's just walk around the block once and then you can go in? By the new Planetarium?'

She started crossing the road before I agreed. I followed her. Then we were on the quiet street beside the dark museum. I watched the pointed toes of her boots landing in the small octagons that make up the dented sidewalk.

'May I ask why you were trying to steal the sponge?'

'You made it look so appealing.'

We headed up from Columbus Avenue on 81st. I had hoped the sight of the new Planetarium, dumb as a space station in a Disney movie, would offset the somber mood that seemed to be creeping in. But no. There it was, glowering, at edge of the Park, in all its fucked-up nightmare snow-globe glory.

'Do you remember the old one?'

'They only tore it down about a year ago. I guess that's a long time for the likes of you.'

'It was nicer.'

'It was definitely more to scale.'

'Can you describe it? I can't remember it. I can't… I can't see it.'

She gave a quiet, nervous laugh. It got to me.

Ye Olde Planetarium was a giant gobstopper that had fallen in the dirt of the Museum's grounds. It was patinated copper like our fish fountain. Inside it always smelled like it was raining out. I didn't say any of that. I turned around and craned my

51

head to look up at the Beresford Apartments. Impossibly warm yellow windows, tiered terraces like tarnished silver. When it was built, there was this idea that we might be perfected, that we had perfection in us. I didn't say that either. I turned back and looked at her, at her old face. She jaywalked across Central Park West and leant on the stone wall that separates the sidewalk from the trees in the park. There was no one around. I watched her there a long time, deciding whether to cross over or not. The reason to go was the same as the reason to stay: I wanted to.

I went. I said, 'I'm sorry. I'm sorry about your mother, Andromeda.'

She pulled herself up, and yelled. 'Fuck you! You think – I hate – I hate my stupid name. It's a joke! And your wife? The real estate agent? She's trying to get me fucking evicted!' She laughed. Her teeth and lips were stained purple with red wine. Her hair stuck to the lenses of her sunglasses, and black make-up had run down her face to her neck. She took off. She ran fast, even in her ridiculous high-heeled boots. She'd only gone about thirty feet when her sunglasses flew off, clack, into the gutter. She didn't slow. Her hair flew, her mourning shawl flew, everything flew behind her. I almost went after her – I did, for about ten yards – but then I stopped. She wasn't faking it. And anyway, what the fuck was I going to do once I'd caught up with her?

N.

A Lover's Discourse

*I'd rather be run over by
a milk truck.*
    svz, 1977

To a Poet Dying Young

Can I have your apartment?
    svz, 1979

* * *

Sam in the Mead (continued)

5/20

Strange how that story lends itself to The Story. Maybe I'm just hopeful because of the hangover. I'll turn Andromeda Van Zandt into an anemic queen, high at her Broadway window. (Never has there been such a case of window envy. To know that every time she disappears from my view she goes off to her east-facing windows and sees things I can only dream of: the uneven roof of the church, the little traffic islands, the corner of 79th where the West Side Democrats' Club used to be ...)

I could feel it contorting itself into The Story, grasping towards the confirmation of some Big Picture. The Great Account. The Marriage of Cause and Effect. The dialogue is recorded, shoes and bones carefully noted, so that ... so *what*? Just to enthrone our icky human feelings? Just so they can reign between the lines, underneath the words? Fuck this. I've spent years documenting, obsessing over, this problem. You see: I believe in the myth of the Narrative Myth. And I'm not about to slip back into it like some drunk with a bottle. My lack of faith in people – or rather people and their motherfucking monocausal explanations of who they are and why they are and why they do what they do – was hard-won! So I'll usurp my queen. I'll stage a romance, and then, when they least expect it…

Why do I suck? Why can't I just concoct a nice story? Self-consciousness is an auto-immune disease. So I wrote that thing, the Picasso thing, and it was going OK, but I can't hold off, I feel like if I don't dismantle it all on the next page I will be encouraging people in their delusion. Like, who the fuck am I? Jonathan Edwards? Cotton Mather?

The *likely cause*, though, for my artistic failings, would have to be Janet's remarriage to my stepfather, 'Uncle Sam'. But I'll get to that. At least it was the catalyst, the thing that got me spinning this self-referential web of bad faith that culminated in my marriage and what is shaping up to be its weak dénouement: the rejected flirting article.

I'm hardly wiser for the passage of the years, but Janet's much stupider. She looks younger than I am, thanks to Loni Anderson's plastic surgeon (true). Her tits point straight up. My mom, who I remember without a bra, drooping under a tee-shirt, half-hidden behind the leaves of the ficus, smoking a joint and watching New Jersey wake up in the winter dark, saying things like, 'What if you put a musical note to each light, and then videotaped them. You'd have a nice little movie and tune, after a year, if you sped it up.' A born speculator, aside-comment-maker, lover of men. When I was twelve and we lived alone together she was beautiful. Now she's the kind of woman that makes me turn away on the street. A piece of litter, a candy wrapper.

OK.

The End of the End of the Story, one assumes.

After Andromeda ran away I just stayed where I was for a while. Not much was going on. A Chinese delivery boy rode by on an old bike, hands on his hips, cigarette hanging out of his mouth, his empty basket jangling. Some drunk white kids hooted their way into the Diana Ross playground at the 81st entrance to the park. Seinfeld came out of the Beresford in a tux and got into a waiting SUV. An ancient station wagon with an old brown couch strapped to the roof moved slowly up Central Park West.

I went to the curb, picked up her purple sunglasses and put them on. They were cracked. The new Planetarium glowed even more cheesily. And then the street went dead still. I felt something on my shoulders, something I used to feel when I had feelings. A gargoyle, shifting his uneven weight, finding his balance. The dirty consciousness of the city itself. Unearthly. Andromeda.

But I pulled myself together and started walking. I remembered that, like my father, and his father before him, and all the way back to those who lost their lives in the Negro Insurrection of 1810 (hint: they were white) I am disgusting. Obviously, as Lar put it when we fought the other night, I just want to fuck a sixteen-year-old girl.

I headed down to Isabella's to fuck Hill. Its garish front grew large in my cracked Purplevision, the flat white awning, the polished gold railings, the little wicker tables that line the sidewalk. Then I stopped about fifty feet from the entrance. I saw something. I *imagined* something. The trees at the edge of the museum were shifting their thick trunks over the stone wall. Dragging their joints, their soft leaves, their *costumes*. I heard a low murmur from their spacious leaves.

Reign it in, son. Can't. My blood's too thin with alcohol. You know why I wrote that asshole memoir in the first place? I was convinced that I was personally heralding in the End. I would be the rallying cry for those of us ready to stand up to all the bitter disappointments of our fictions, all those neat little Beginnings, Middles and Ends, ready to yell *fuck you*! and not fear the silence that ensues.

Please, it's not silence, there's an *echo* ...

The mob of MBAs in front of Isabella's had thinned out. I saw Hill *and Paul* the moment I opened the glass door, the kind of door that you only touch and it flies open and hits someone in the face. I would have left. I would have fallen to my hands and knees and scuttled out through the panty-hosed legs, the chinoed ankles. But one of Paul's qualities is his quickness. He is very fast and very large. He boomed 'Sammy! Sassy-glasses!'

(A note about these two, as it is a Story: we all went to Oberlin together years ago. Lara too. Back in those days we did not know that what we felt for each other was simply competitive curiosity. Now it's too inconvenient to undo, and we are 'friends'. We see each other much more than any of us would like.)

Back at Isa's. I took off the shades and had to put my thumbs in my eye sockets to stop the objects glittering screaming to be touched, absorbed: the jewel-colored booze-bottles, the tree branches painted shiny white and twirled with tiny Christmas lights, Hill's iridescent, sleeveless satinate dress. (With a thick purple scarf to 'dress it down', as Lar'd say.) I'd reached that no-man's-land of belligerence and self-pity. I was the Undrunk. There are endless variations. Tonight: one who drinks alone and too early, then is shocked into sobriety.

'Hello Red, what'll it be?' Hill's kiss smelled like my mother, like department store make-up.

'Straight double Jameson.' After a bottle of wine, on an empty stomach.

Hill and Paul were in the middle of the usual conversation.

The one about what everyone that any one of us has ever met is doing. A frantic who's-seen-who. I asked Paul what he was up to. He's a Corporate Motivator.

'Is that kind of like a fluffer?'

'No, it's not *kind of like a fluffer*, asshole.'

Hill said, 'It's about understanding boundaries, basically,' and put her hand on mine under the table. Then Paul very much wanted to share with me the fact that he'd got a huge advance to write a self-help book, something about applying 'effective management principles to your emotional life'.

'Much?' One Jameson down.

'A lot,' Hill told me. 'But Sam's back on the ball. He wrote a *really* funny, a *real* tongue-in-cheek thing about flirting. Too sophisticated for us, though!'

I put my hand on her thigh. 'Oh *you*. But seriously, Paul, how much really?'

'The idea is that there is such a thing as emotional literacy.'

His eyebrows move as much, if not more, than his mouth. 'It's a subject English majors like us are a little afraid of: We're afraid of losing The Mystery. Afraid to be practical about our feelings.' During this he was staring at a pretty waitress across the room. I can't be sure, but I think she was laughing really hard at something Ben Affleck had just said. Isabella's is a place celebs go to be seen by out-of-towners. Under the table Hill was moving her hand around too much. I held it still. 'For example, I take the model of hot-desking. And I re-apply it...' I inched my hand up Hill's dress, half-listening, half-thinking about the distance from one side of the courtyard to the other, half (yes: another half) wondering how to make a definite move towards Hill's place.

After a few minutes she got up to go to the bathroom. We watched her take the stairs. She looks nothing like she used to. She must spend half her life at the gym. In college she was soft;

she's naturally kind of soft. She disappeared into a door with that painting of a smear-faced can-can girl, another Toulouse.

Paul said, 'Hill looks great. How's Lara?'

'She looks pretty good.'

Bitterly – he's so in touch with himself – 'Remember all your bullshit about the death of narrative, about facing life on its own random or whatever terms? Well – where would marriage fit into it? I've *wondered* about this.'

'I'm flattered.'

'I mean, why marry her? Why marry Lar when you might have just cohabitated?'

'For her money.' I finished my second double in two swills.

'She doesn't have that much!'

'I'm lazy!'

He was disgusted. He's a fucking Boy Scout, a fucking homicidal African-American Boy Scout. I mean: he's still pissed off I stole Lar off him. It was fucking ten years ago! He can have her! Luckily, the waitress showed up with another round. If she hadn't he might have punched me. I could see him gearing up for it, but luckily for me hunky guys like Paul are easily distracted by small-talk, lipstick, a nice ass. He smiled at it as she walked away, then tipped his Bass Ale back in his throat. There's something about looking at the ass of someone waiting on you that offends my delicate sensibilities. My dad does it.

'What about looking at the waitress's ass? Is that "playing by the unspoken rules"? Is that "emotional teamwork"?' His terminology's nothing if not catchy.

He kept his eye on her. A change came over him. I wasn't worth the trouble. He decided to practice for Larry King.

'Sex and caring about someone are not necessarily on the same page. They can be, and that's beautiful.' That's the *miracle*, Larry. 'That's when you propose the merger. See. I believe in fairy tales.' On *fairy tales* he raised his fingers above his head like he was clacking little castanets. I didn't realize how far gone he was. I was kind of in shock. 'But, sometimes they're not, ya understand? Sometimes they're *not* on the same page.' He found the waitress's ass again, smiled at it, finished his ale and gave me a guy-to-guy look. I hate him.

Hill was back with more lipstick on, and what I'm pretty sure was a crumb of coke under her nose.

'We've been talking about the difference between sex and love. Sam thinks there's a *gray area*.' He stood up. 'I'm gonna bleed the weasel.'

There was a howl of laughter from the vicinity of Ben Affleck. A romaine leaf sailed into the air. I tried to give Hill a dirty look. An old one from my repertoire. Somewhere between condescension and seduction. My face was too sleepy.

'What?'

'Paul is here.'

'You both called. I thought it would be fun. No. OK. Truthfully? You've both been MIA for months, and then you go and call on the same night, so I figured – fuck 'em both. Or, rather, I won't fuck either of 'em.'

'It's kind of funny. Good one.'

She spun her Rolex around.

'So you hate me cause I haven't called?' I held her hand again. *I suck.* Then she looked me in the eye and *fucking fell for it.* 'I'm sorry I haven't called, Hillary.' I kissed her. She didn't taste good; her mouth was parched. She pulled back coyly, and at that pregnant moment –

The cute waitress walked by carrying a platter of fried calamari. The last thing I'd eaten was a spinach and feta croissant when I took Midas to the dog run at ten in the morning. I was starving. I could think of nothing but sex. I put my hand back under her skirt, and pushed it up so far so fast she squeaked. I felt her eyes on my face, on my mouth in particular. Then – I

59

shouldn't have let myself do it. I don't know what possessed me to do it. I *met her gaze*. Andromeda Van Zandt. I had to look hard at her and I still couldn't see her. Hill's the opposite: if I look at her for one second, I see everything. Hill smiled a – what is it? Sad? It's a smile, it's shaped like one. She'd like you to kill her, please. I slid my hand out from Hill's underpants and put it next to the other, flat on the slab of marble. I slammed out a tune. Shave-and-a-haircut, two bits!

Paul appeared beside us. I said, 'I feel like the third wheel here. I'll leave you guys to it.' Then I pulled Paul down with one arm and Hill up with the other and gave them both a little cuddle. I used to act like this all the time, so they weren't that surprised. That old I-don't-give-a fuck thing I had when I was gonna be somebody. Well, I still don't give a fuck, even if I'm no one. Fuck you! Etc

I swallowed the rest of my drink, and half of it fell out of my mouth. Then I tried to walk a straight line to the door. I was staring down at the maroon tops of my Converse. I had forgotten Paul and Hill and was *deeply* involved in considering my pizza options. Anchovy? Mushroom? Sicilian! When Hill called out, 'Sam. You are the weakest link.' In this bad English accent. I turned around to give her the finger, blow her a kiss, something – but just as I did the door hit me in the face with such force it opened the cuts from Lara's shoe.

Now.

Then.

I'd like to believe there was some coherent explanation for my appalling behaviour: alcoholism, testosterone, *thanatos*, a change in the means of production. I wish I could buy one of those, and then buy its antidote. But I don't *believe* anything. My brain is quivering in aspic. I feel like a little mouse curled up and died in my mouth. It can be like hell in our apartment. A fucking dungeon. Out the window, walls of blank decent-people-at-work navy blue windows. I need to see Broadway, the river, the trees. Midas wants to go out and I can hardly move. Lara didn't come home last night. Or call. She's not picking up her cell phone.

Across the courtyard, that basket-case has closed her bathroom window on the sponge, a splash of garish pink amidst our gray and silver limestone. It's a bright clear morning. The phone's ringing. I let the machine pick up. It's the plasticated woman who brought me into the world.

Oh. Epilogue:

On the way home, staggering along the gutter, dabbing the blood from my face with my jacket sleeve and eating two slices of Big Nick's poisonous mushroom-and-anchovy pizza on top of each other, I passed Andromeda's grandmother getting out of a cab. She was with this very dignified-looking gentleman in an orange cravat. White-haired, well-read type. They locked in an embrace. They're old and they stood there making out like kids. It was very sweet, actually.

* * *

Page torn from Lara's Filofax

5/20

Sweetie, You only need a thimbleful of Lux de Mer. Also, should I book you an appointment with Shoshanna? She does an awesome French manicure. But seriously, are you gay? Not that there's anything wrong with that.

xxoo Lara

* * *

61

Andromeda in her Rembrandt

5/23

Escobar knows Sam the Yuppie. I told him about the other night, the parts I could remember, and he said, 'El PELIRROJO? The one with the POODLE? I know HIM.' We were sharing a Ballantine, for my hangover. Escobar called it the 'hair of the dog that bit me'. Apparently, when I was nothing more than a twisted fantasy of my mom's, they were sort of enemies. Escobar used to steal Sam's pinball money.

'He just let you get away with it? You didn't have to beat him up or anything? He's big. He could defend himself.' He's taller than me. I'm very tall too.

'Oh please, Andromeda. Don't get like this on me. Not you. I can't handle it.' As far as E's concerned there's nothing more passé than heterosexuality. Anyway it was practically an appointment they kept in the mornings. They were sort of friendly. Escobar called it an affinity. He said: 'This kind of affinity only exists between men. Women are exempt.' He was getting on my nerves.

'So what happened, if it was so beautifully Platonic? Why doesn't he even remember you?'

'Don't be naive. He liked me. He liked me so much, and he didn't want to be a fag.'

Subtext: Jimmy has decided he's not gay, and has run off with some older woman he met online at the Korean's. At least that's what he told Escobar, who thinks bisexuality 'is bullshit'.

'Maybe Sam's bi too. Maybe everybody is.' I took a swig from the Forty. He grabbed it out of my hand and some spilled on my dress.

'What you gotta get with, Andromeda, is that everybody wants the dick. That's why your mama was so mad.' Then he lurched towards me and grabbed his crotch to accentuate his

62

point.

I hate when he gets like this. I stood up and started to pack my books back into my bag: *Being and Time, Being and Nothingness* (which Lew just gave me), *Listen Little Man* (that Dr. Gorling lent me), *The Castle* and *The Concise OED*. I can hardly walk.

'Come on. Don't go. Have a heart. I'm lonely today.'

'Fuck off,' I said, and I sounded just like my mom.

LATER:

Now hungover after my mid-morning beer. On the floor in the Meaningful Closet. I'm under a pile of clothes that smell like svz (Paloma Picasso and cigarette smoke). I think I'll spend the rest of my life here. I'll order in from Big Stav's. Eggplant parmigiana. Anchovy pizza.

This closet, her closet, has got to be about the size of the living room of that fucker across the courtyard. What they call a 'walk-in'. Maybe having grown up in this falling-apart dump, using this closet for so long, actually accounts for some of her more far-fetched theories. The Closeting of the Text, for one, whatever the hell that means. She was always talking about layers, shading. And here they are: fur coats, stiff kilts, sweaters in every conceivable shade of green, lace-up and high-heeled boots, and that shoebox of sex toys I opened once when I was twelve. It's a NIKE box. JUST DO IT!

It seems like a normal closet at first, though very disorganized. The wire dry-cleaner hangers face both directions, each buckling under too many items, which have been thrown, not hung on them. Their function, just to keep clothes off the floor. Because a path must be kept clear to the back. You have to know it's there. The closet starts off narrow and you expect to find a wall a few feet farther in. But push on and it opens out, into something almost as big as a room. Shelves line the walls, the smell of old papers is almost unbearable. (A library smell, the smell of the shiny pages of old illustrated books.) There are boxes and books and yellow loose papers jammed in everywhere. In the middle of the ceiling there's a funny old light fixture, a grapefruit-sized ball of amber glass. On the wall a brass plate with buttons, the kind you'd use to call the help. ANTOINETTE! I CAN'T FIND MY FUCKING GOWN. What's in the boxes? Endless academic 'correspondences', rows of defunct academic journals (*Feminism Today, Sister's Keeper*), jaundiced family photographs with crimped edges and three generations of female juvenilia (me, her and Granny) stuffed into plastic Fairway bags. Then, at the very back, on the wall facing the door you can no longer see – there, we find the low dresser with a hazy, copper-tinted mirror screwed to the top. When I behold me, moving towards my dim reflection (and the Hammacher Schlemmer mini-wine cellar), backlit, emerging from the chaotic fabrics and old newpapers, when I see my huge belladonna pupils, these expectant, curious, wide-set eyes, moving forward with a lover's relief towards my own image, I sometimes think there is something to all her Lacanian crap. I look almost not human, a chimera, a ghost, half girl, half book. ALL TEXT. Duh! Of course I fucking don't. But if I become the new her, the next 'Van Zandt', maybe then I'll believe it. Or I'll have to pretend I do to get enough money to buy my wine, because maybe it really is all genetic. There I was again, kneeling under the mirror to unlock the cellar she bought with her Merrill Lynch Visa points.

'Look at this sweetheart! My wine cellar came! Check it out! It has a padlock!'

That was about two years ago. I open the bottle exactly as I've seen you do it: Bottle between the knees, and a stern pull with one hand: THOP! My bottle is now half-empty. HALF-FULL, DEARIE! I'm holding my feet in my hands. Observe the chipping purple toenails, the purple tips of my hair dangling over them.

I used Granny's old lady hair dye. What a mistake. And – I'm not doing well in school, got an 80 on a trigonometry test and neglected to hand in my paper on Leni the web-fingered love interest in *The Castle*. Just now while I was not writing my Bach rang out. It's the first time it's ever rung since my mom and I tested it out in the shop. She insisted I have one 'just in case' someone tried to kidnap me. Maniac.

'Uh, Andromeda?'

'Hi Ed Hanes from Botany.'

'Yeah (guffaw). I'm writing this thing ... I'm working on this thing and I was wondering if you'd be interested in auditioning for it. It's just some shit to get into Tisch.'

He's an aspiring screenwriter.

'God. I don't know.'

'We could just, ya know, hook up, anyway.'

We're going to meet at the museum.

I can't find my very important purple sunglasses. Whatever shall I wear?

ANTOINETTE!

***

Handwritten letter from Lynne to Sam on Gerlitz Management stationery.

5/25

Dear Sam,

Meeting you eight years ago, my excitement at the prospect of being a part of your future was great. I'm not sure where we went wrong. I like to think that I have done my best by you. I've just reread the three stories you had in the New Yorker, 'At the Old Loews', 'Spigot' and, of course, 'The Unstrung Harp'. You know how disappointed I was that we couldn't place 'Some Unpleasantness'. I remember when I first met you, you played them down, saying that if it hadn't been for your mother's connections you would never have got them published. I told you this was not the case. You were young, and faith in yourself is such an important thing to instill in any young artist. Not that I'm qualified to know anything - as you've so often pointed out, I'm nothing but a huckster. Maybe it would have been better if I had agreed with you that those initial breaks were all down to Uncle Sam's gig at the NYer. You'd have struggled with the realization, overcome it, found a way to deal with the reality of it, made the conundrum of privilege your own, whatever you needed to do in order to move on artistically, if not personally.

Instead, there we were again, at the Globe last week, you kvetching about the same woes you did when you were twenty. And of course, if you were Brett Easton Ellis it would be different, but you are not Brett Easton Ellis, you are Sam Gordon Taylor and at this point in time that means very little.

I don't know how to say this.

As for the Freak Show of Lamb or whatever it's called this week, it's true what you said about Dave Eggers' success doing you harm, though your reasoning that it was intentional on his part still strikes me as extremely paranoid. At this time your memoir is a hard, if not impossible, book to sell. I was willing to stick my neck out for you. I think it could be an important book. The truth: I've been laughed off the phone on your account.

Sam: you will never get it out there unless you are willing to play the game by the rules. They aren't mine. I just wanted to help you win. But after our meeting last week I think it's

66

clear that this isn't working out. I think it's time we end our professional relationship. I wish you the best of luck for the future. Please find enclosed a termination-of-contract agreement to be signed and returned.

Lynne

Sam / Mead

5/27

I am going to quit drinking for a while. I should thank her. Thank you, Lara. You fucking fuckhead. This morning she went out early, bought me *The Post* (she usually won't: too 'of the people') and a coffee and brought them to bed. She sat there at my feet staring off into the courtyard, complaining ... lamenting, almost. She asked me if I'd noticed her grey hairs. I said 'Heavens, no.' The slant of the sun as it rose above the twelfth floor showed everything she's trying to hide. Her small bluish teeth (the whitening backfired), the little hairs growing back into her plucked eyebrows, some blue goo left in the corners of her eyes from yesterday's liner. She wouldn't believe me if I told her that I *seek out* flaws in pretty things. That I *love* them. She told me she was going away for the weekend, to schmooze some new clients. She actually met them through Paul. He'd be there too. She didn't suppose I wanted to come.

I said, 'No. I don't want to come.' After I said it, I just looked at her for a while, in her little Barney's slip. I suppose I've been getting a bit horny. It's been a while. But it feels spiritual. That's another problem I need to consider when I remake myself (starting right after I finish this cup of coffee). Something Lara once called *aggrandizement*. Not that she doesn't have her own issues. The moment we ... make love, fuck, sleep together, have sex? ... I never know what term to use; each one's wrong in its own way. Now, if I was the type of fella who could write the

67

Esquire article, I'd know – I'd have the categorization down, and there might not be all these ... shades of gray. Anyfucking-way ... the moment we do whatever it is we do, she starts acting – switching from one persona to another as if in the throes of a one-woman show that, when I'm done, leaves her less herself, but happier. Previously, I thought she was protecting herself. Women are vulnerable. But screw that. I'm now convinced she does it to amuse herself.

So, between the first-reel teen slasher victim and Carmen Miranda there was this very loud crash in the courtyard. She gasped 'What was *that*?' and knotted my tee-shirt in her fist, like we were alone in yonder log cabin on the frontier. I propped myself up and, lo! Andromeda Van Zandt was half out her bathroom window, her purple hair hanging down, with ... *knotted brow*, her expression exaggerated like someone in a silent movie. A *boy* came up next to her and leaned out too, his hand on her shoulder.

'Come inside me,' said Lara, whom I'd forgotten about. And I did.

No, it wasn't exactly spiritual, but I felt better than I had in weeks, like an undone knot. We lay in bed. She complained about her boss, about her clothes, about me, but in the funny way she used to. Then almost as if she'd just noticed the time, she cut to the chase. Told me I needed a 'reality check'. Why didn't I just take the job at *Sassy*? I didn't remember telling her about it. As she was leaving, with her packed bag and her hand on the doorknob, she said that she didn't feel like she could keep living with me and that I should get out before she got back. It was so politic, so empty, so clearly premeditated. Life is so often like this: inevitable yet ... inevitable, *not* surprising. Yet the question sprung to mind: *Then why the fuck did you tell me to come inside you, you fucking lunatic?* But I didn't ask. I resented its obviousness. As for the future, I'm fucked.

68

I have no money. There are a few guys who would take me in, and two girls, but I can't face them. My mother and Uncle Sam would lend me some. I could get a real job. But now it's Monday, 5:30, time to pick up Mrs. Kasbaum's rations. If I'm lucky she'll serve me canned fruit on pancakes. They're very good. Made with love.

* * *

5/27

Triplicate receipt (the hard-to-forge kind, used only for 'drugs of abuse') for Edward Bruce Hanes: 60x5mg Ritalin, 30 Halcyon. Forged by Andromeda, filled at Plimpton's pharmacy

* * *

Andromeda, on Crane's 'Florence' stationery shoved into a matching lined envelope and left with José the doorman. All caps in thick purple marker:

5/27

DEAR MR. TAYLOR,

I AM WRITING TO APOLOGIZE FOR MY APPALLING BEHAVIOR THE OTHER NIGHT. I AM REALLY EMBARRASSED TO HAVE INVOLVED YOU. STILL I DEEPLY APPRECIATE YOUR COMING TO MY (THIEF'S) AID. I HAVE THE URGE TO EXPLAIN IT ALL TO YOU, BUT I'M AFRAID YOU WOULD PROBABLY FIND IT QUITE BORING, QUITE KITCHEN-SINKISH. AS IF OUR COURTYARD RELATIONSHIP WEREN'T UNCIVILIZED ENOUGH. SO I WON'T. AT ANY RATE, I'LL SEE YOU AROUND.

ANDY

ENCLOSED PLEASE FIND A CHECK FOR SIXTEEN DOLLARS.

* * *

On another piece of Crane's stationery, thick purple marker

5/27

NOTES FOR ROB'S PAPER

LENI ISN'T HUMAN. SHE HAS WEBBED FINGERS. UNLIKE SANDERS (CITE QUOTE) WHO SEES THIS AS A REFERENCE TO OUR MIASMIC DARWINIAN PAST, I THINK THIS IS A CASE IN WHICH KAFKA IS MAKING YET ANOTHER ELABORATION ON THE (TIRED OLD) FEMALE-AS-ANIMAL PARADIGM. THEREFORE I POSIT THAT HER DEPICTION NOW WHY WOULD KAFKA (K), WHO CERTAINLY UNDERSTOOD ALIENATION

BUT THAT HAS NOTHING TO DO WITH IT

Andromeda Van Zandt Andromeda Hanes
Andromeda Van Zandt Andromeda Hanes

Andromeda Taylor Andromeda Taylor *Andromeda Taylor* ANDROMEDA TAYLOR Andromeda Taylor Andromeda Taylor Andromeda Taylor ANDROMEDA TAYLOR

* * *

Receipt for Mr SG Taylor, one week's rent at the Bellclaire Hotel, Broadway and 77th Street, Room 831

5/28

$490.00 Paid in cash

* * *

Andromeda's Rembrandt, purple marker, beginning to run out towards the end

THE STORY OF MY FIRST DATE WITH ED HANES, WRITTEN ON TWO OF THE RITALIN I STOLE OFF ED, 2:45 AM MONDAY, END OF MAY, ALMOST JUNE, NOT SURE

5/28

Started out a perfect spring day. Cherry blossoms in the park in the morning, where I went to watch old ladies feed ducks. Then came home, drank three cups of coffee, smoked half a pack of American Spirits and got dressed to meet Ed. I should have had some zippy soundtrack, like the guy in *Saturday Night Fever,* like the beginning of a movie with the credits rolling, establishing my routine, my decent yet funky life. Cause it was Sunny Spring Saturday on Broadway and everyone was HAPPY. Happy to be spending money, spinning in and out of the revolving doors of chain shops. Usually, the men whose attention I attract on the street are drawn to a certain *Les Mis* waifishness. It's depressing. But today the comments came from the more respectable tier of sleazeballs, i.e. those with jobs: construction workers, doormen, one hot-dog man. I assert: I was ecstatic on the way to meet Ed Hanes.

I never use the Central Park West entrance to the museum, climb the grand staircase and marvel at the bronze balls of Teddy Roosevelt's horse. It's too crowded. Tourists littering up the steps. Riffraff. I went in through the cavernous Seventy-seventh Street one. The service entrance. The scientists who work upstairs poking pins into moths, public school kids anxious to get to the astronomical gift shop, the infirm who can't make the steps, me – we all slither in this way.

Ed was late. I detest lateness. It's some recessive WASP gene. (Then again Granny's always two hours late, but reeks of Jardin

71

de Bagatelle.) I stood there tapping my toe and twisting my hair, getting more and more pissed off, losing air, trying to deflect the glances of middle-aged dads, the glare of a certain totem pole in the corner. I rummaged in my portable library and found Lorca's *Poet in New York*. Escobar recommended it.

I'd settled into that familiar state of forced absorption when I felt a hand on my elbow. I jumped. Ed looked perfect. He was smiling from ear to ear, his dark hair matted just so. He's got a big nose and dresses like a junkie rock star. He gives himself away, though, with that Downy-Fresh scent. His Dad's Guiliani's shrink and his maid does his fucking laundry. I've been doing my own, downstairs, in the Apthorp's creepy basement, since I was eight.

He kissed my cheek and went 'Mmmm... You know, you said to meet you in the boat. I thought I'd see you sitting up there with your Heidie.'

We were standing there, as planned, under the long boat with the 'Indian' wax people in it, each one doing something different: rowing, skinning, eating corn on the cob; at the end, one dude – I've never been able to figure out WHAT he's doing – in a mask, a bird mask, looking out. Ed studied the cover of the Lorca, a Miro-inspired doodle, opened it and read something in a Puerto Rican accent. I wanted to reply in German but the only thing I could think of was Homo Homini Lupus. In a loop. Homo Homini Lupus. Homo Homini Lupus. I have no idea why. He gave me the old 'your-mom's-dead' look as he took my hand, flipped the palm up in his, and stared into it. I don't like my hands. The nails are chewed to bits.

I said, 'I once dreamed I woke up, or that I couldn't wake up, and I was in that boat.'

Which was a total lie. I once dreamed, when I was about nine, that I was trapped in the museum with Freddie Krueger and he kept jumping out and stabbing me and I had to hold slices of Wonderbread (which was verboten at home) on myself to sop up the blood. When I told my mother she muttered 'Fear of menstruation.' I felt ashamed for having such an 'easy' dream.

Ed wanted to go to the IMax movie about elephants. I was hoping to stroll around the museum, through the big dark galleries, past dusty taxidermied animals in glass boxes. I like to think about how they would have been dead long ago anyway, even if one of Teddy Roosevelt's thugs hadn't shot and killed them.

The film was sort of a kids' movie. There were lots of toddlers crying. The whole plush auditorium smelled of tuna sandwiches freed from Tupperware. It was sad. Elephants died. You couldn't help but be affected. The screen's six storeys high.

Predictably enough, about halfway through, Ed put his hand on my knee. My wraparound skirt dropped off the leg nearer him with the ease of a sail gone slack in no wind. He kept making these little noises (I can hardly bring myself to write it, it's so embarrassing), mms and ahs. The sort of noises WOMEN make in the movies. I thought he wanted ME to make them. I would HAVE LIKED to make them, I could feel myself try – the moans rising from my throat, then getting stuck between my tongue and the roof of my mouth. Anyway, it was almost faked. I did feel something. A very slight something. But his moaning, the expiring elephants, the sandwiches…

When the film let out he said, 'So what would Heidegger say about that, about the elephants? Would he think they had souls like a human soul? He was a Nazi, you know.'

I didn't.

The sky was blue and Ed wanted to smoke a joint, so we wandered into the park, which was packed with Europeans in little quilted jackets and rollerbladers showing off. Ed wanted to go into the Ramble. I've always been afraid there, of how you don't know what's coming around the corner; I like open spaces, but I didn't tell him that. I managed to lead us to the point with the widest view, though, to the tip of a bit of schist that juts into the lake. He took a joint out of the cellophane wrapper of his pack of Marlboros, and with a VERY cursory look around, lit up.

I watched three couples in boats. Two sets of gay guys rowing, wearing wife-beaters, showing off their huge Popeye arms; and one straight date, the passenger a girl in a shift dress, with miniature Popeye arms. They were all headed to the boathouse. It was starting to rain. Ed handed me the joint, and I took a long inhale, and held it in; impersonating what I'd seen my ma do. The smoke was heavier than a cigarette's, and pulled around my lungs like rope. The boats were in a tidy little chain, stern to bow, stern to bow, everyone rushing (in slow rowboat motion) to get out of the rain. The boathouse guy got flustered and kicked the straight couple back in line. I felt like I was looking through a magnifying glass. Shapes bulged, wide surfaces caught the pale yellow light.

Ed said 'You all right?'

I wanted to smile my best reassuring smile but my eye got stuck across the lake, on a little wood gazebo. It was empty, and the rain was darkening it. Everyone in the park had disappeared, as easily as if they had turned into trees. The boats were suddenly moored, their dull colors rocking. I looked up and Ed was looming over me, the dark sky behind him. He really does look like Bob Dylan.

'About a year ago a thirteen-year-old girl and her fifteen-year-old boyfriend killed a guy there,' I told him.

He had a chest full of pot which he exhaled very slowly. 'No shit,' he squeaked.

'Yeah. And then they cut him open.' I made a gesture in the air like Zorro, like a conductor at the Met. 'And took his guts out.'

Ed held the joint in his hand. A drop of rain hit it and put it out.

'Then they filled him full of rocks and dropped him in the lake.'

When it happened I obsessed about it for a long time. I bought *The Post*, *The Times* and *Newsday* everyday. Of course Mom thought it was to do with the Phallus, the stuffing up, whatever. My interpretation was less abstract. It was a local story. I have a taste for melodrama.

Ed put the roach back in the cellophane. It made a huge din of crackling. 'You're freaking out.' It was pouring now. He took off his fuzzy sweatshirt and held it in his hands and looked at it. Then he came over, knelt on the rock in front of me, draped it over my shoulders and tied the arms in a knot. It was just like being in a teen movie. 'Let's go.' He was trying to pull me up. I shrugged him off and started to laugh. He started up the rock, calling over his shoulder, 'Come on, An – drom – e – da,' the way someone does who knows you dislike your name.

There was a flash and crash of lightening near the boathouse. A thin rope of smoke actually rose behind it. The theatrics added to my hysteria.

'He didn't sink!' I yelled after him. I laughed until my face hurt. Rain got in my mouth. I laughed because I was thinking, they tell you all these things, how humans are above animals because they bury their dead, think about thinking, think about themselves. But it's all just a terrible, hilarious vortex and all it does is fill their tummies full of rocks!

It doesn't seem funny at all now.

I caught up with him and he clipped his arm around my waist and sort of laughed. The 'your mother just killed herself' look can be a laugh, too. He told me he thought I was ACTUALLY crazy, and I told him I didn't ACTUALLY care and that all I wanted in the world was my sunglasses even though it was raining.

We passed the Planetarium, next to where Sam the Yuppie and I stood a week ago tonight, and Ed said 'It must be hard for you, man. I'd be pissed off if I were you.'

I kept looking back at it over my shoulder. The dome inside seemed stiller for the thunder outside it, the way a room is stiller when there's classical music playing. I stared, fixed my attention on its bald face. I wanted it squashed flat, collapsible, a pancake. Ed turned around to see what I was looking at.

'I'm not pissed off.'

I wasn't. I took out a cigarette and tried to light it. I cupped it in my hands. I ran ahead and leaned against a wet black lamppost and unzipped Ed's sweatshirt and tucked my head inside. I used up every puny match in the book; they fizzled and popped in the wet wind. Then I gave up and just let it hang out of my mouth. That's all I wanted it for anyway. It started to fall apart.

I guess I should be pissed off. The worst part, I think, was after José came up to tell me about it, this cop came to the door. He had a cup of coffee from the Galaxy coffee shop in one hand, and a blown-up Polaroid in the other. They needed next-of-kin ID. Apparently like right away. Her face was dented in like a side-impact car wreck. Her eyes were open wide, like she was very surprised. All I could think as I looked at it was that she looked just like Cindy Sherman, imitating a suicide. Ugh.

Granny just called and said she thought she'd 'not be home tonight', having been to the Met with 'a friend' (i.e. Lew). God, imagine her at intermezzo, fingering the strands of three-storey-length glass beads in front of the three-storey windows – politely chided by the man whose sole occupation (I'm pretty sure: Mom and I watched him for a long time one night) is to tell theatregoers to PLEASE NOT TOUCH THE BEADS – Granny's baby eyes sparkling with coy wonder, discussing Lew's new kitchen and holding an empty plastic flute, all the while that huge, flouncy fucking Chagall mural floating above their heads.

* * *

In a MOMA Rodchenko greeting card, showing cutouts of flappers, kangaroos, spoons, an old-fashioned telephone and a man with a pince-nez in a driving cap. The card has been ripped in half and is fluttering in a wrought-iron garbage can on Broadway

5/31 Memorial Day

Dear Andromeda, I started writing a story about you. Sorry. Maybe if I talked to you again

* * *

Ed Hane's third and final screenwriting assignment, handed in two weeks late. Rob Hartman's class. Grade: F

5/31

YOU COULD HAVE KILLED SOMEBODY

SCENE I

INTERIOR: GRAND DECKED OUT LIVING ROOM IN THE APTHORP APARTMENTS. ASHTRAYS FULL OF BUTTS. HOLES IN THE CURTAINS AND CARPET. CRUSTY, DUSTY OIL PAINTINGS ON THE WARM ORANGE WALLS.

JOSH, A NINETEEN YEAR OLD WITH SCRAGGLY BLACK HAIR AND A BIG NOSE PACES AROUND THE ROOM WITHOUT HIS SHIRT ON EATING A BOWL OF CORNFLAKES, HE INTERMITTENTLY LOOKS OVER HIS SHOULDER THEN PICKS UP AN OBJECT, A LETTER OPENER A BOOK A CHOTCKE, THEN PUTS IT DOWN AGAIN.

JONI MICHELL CROONS CAYOTE IN THE BACKGROUND

77

GALAXY ENTERS IN A FLOOR LENGTH PINK KAFTA HER HAIR WRAPPED IN A PINK TOWEL. SHE CARRIES A BOTTLE OF RED WINE UNDER HER ARM. SHE LOOKS LIKE THE GIRL IN THE SAMSUNG AD.

GALAXY (PICKING UP THE NEEDLE): I CAN'T LISTEN TO THIS SHIT.

JOSH: YOUR MOM DIDN'T HAVE MUCH OF A SELECTION.

GALAXY (SITTING DOWN ON THE RUG SHE PULLS UP THE KAFTAN TO REVEAL SLENDER LEGS): IT'S MINE NOW. ALL YOU SEE IS MINE! (BEAT, SADLY) MINE!

GAL STRUGGLES TO PULL THE CORK OUT OF THE BOTTLE. JOSH TAKES IT FROM HER, PULLS IT OUT AND HANDS IT BACK. SHE TAKES A FEW LONG SWIGS.

JOSH: WHY DID YOU SWITCH TO ST HILDA'S? WHY DIDN'T YOU JUST STAY AT STUY?

GAL – MY MOM THOUGHT I WAS DEPRESSED. SHE THOUGHT I WAS SUICIDAL.

JOSH: WERE YOU?

GAL: NO. (SWIGS) NO, NO. NO. THOUGH I THINK I WOULD HAVE BECOME A DIFFERENT PERSON IF I STAYED. I LITERALLY SPOKE TO NO ONE THERE. NO ONE. I GOT UP IN THE MORNING. IRONED MY CLOTHES LIKE SOME HAUS FRAU, SMOKED CIGARETTES AND GOT ON THE TRAIN. I ATE COUGH DROPS FOR LUNCH IN THE LIBRARY. IT WAS LIKE PRISON.
JOSH: SOME BOYS MUST HAVE TRIED TO TALK TO YOU

GAL: NO THEY DIDN'T. YOU'RE THE FIRST.

JOSH (STOPS PACING AROUND THE ROOM SITS AT GAL'S FEET): LIES

GAL: I NEVER LIE

JOSH: I LIE ALL THE TIME. LIFE WOULD BE BORING WITHOUT LIES.

GAL: NO ONE HAS ANY IDEA HOW IT WOULD BE TO LIVE WITHOUT LIES. I MEAN, LOOK AT THIS SHIT.

HE TOUCHES HER BARE FOOT AND SHE SHAKES HIM OFF. SHE WALKS TO THE WIDE EXPANSIVE VIEW AT DUSK. A GLIMMERING CHURCH, A FULL MOON, VOICES.

GAL (CONTD): WHO NEEDS LIES?

JOSH: ITS BLATANT. LIKE ME. I'M TRYING TO COME ONTO YOU.

JOSH: (ROLLING ONTO HIS BACK, P.O.V SHOT OF A HUGE BROKEN CHANDELIER FROM DIRECTLY UNDERNEATH)

GAL: WHY?

JOSH: CAUSE I LIKE YOU.

GAL: YOU LIKE ME BECAUSE I LOOK LIKE THE GIRL IN THE SAMSUNG AD.

JOSH: IF I LIKED HER I'D LIKE HER.

GAL; IF YOU KNEW HER YOU'D LIKE HER. ANYWAY, LISTEN TO THIS. I'M BORING. I'M CRAZY. ALL I EAT ARE CORN FLAKES AND COUGH DROPS. OH, I KNOW WHAT IT IS. IT'S THAT MY MOM IS FAMOUS.

JOSH: WAS FAMOUS.

GAL: IT'S THAT SHE'S DEAD, THERE'S REAL DEPTH IN THAT.

JOSH: YOU WERE OK STONED, YOU NOT GOOD DRUNK.

GAL: AND LIZ. YOU HAVE A FUCKING ANOREXIC GIRL-

FRIEND TO THINK ABOUT.

JOSH: WE'RE JUST FRIENDS.

GAL: (HOLLERING OUT THE WINDOW) THEY'RE JUST FRIENDS. JOSH AND LIZ AND JUST FUCKING FRIENDS! (TURNING INTO THE ROOM) OH, I'VE FORGOTTEN THAT'S INTERESTING BECAUSE IT'S A LIE.

JOSH: (LIKE A SHRINK): EXPRESS YOU'RE ANGER. YOUVE A RIGHT TO IT. LIVE IT. ONLY THEN WILL YOU BESET FREE.

THEY SIT DOWN ON THE COUCH

JOSH: WHAT WOULD YOU HAVE BEEN LIKE IF YOUD STAYED AT STY?

GAL: VERY ORDERLY. SOMEONE WHO ATE THE SAME THING EVERYDAY, WORE TURTLENCKS AND BIG NECKLACES AND THEN (SHE PAUSES AND SMILES AT HIM, PUTS HER HEAD ON HIS SHOULDER) THEN I WOULD HAVE BEEN SOME KIND OF ACADEMIC BUT NOT THEORY, LIKE A MIDEVILIST OR SOMETHING. A SPECIALIST IN ELOISE AND CHECK NAME

JOSH: (LOOKING IN HER EYES, TOUCHING HER FACE) I THINK YOU WOULD HAVE BEEN EXACTLY THE SAME.

HIS PHONE RINGS, ITS ON LOUDEST. HE HAS IT ON CARMEN. THEY SIT AND LISTEN TO IT, THEN HE GETS UP AND LOOKS AT IT. HE PICKS UP.

JOSH: I THOUGHT YOU WERE IN GROUP?

GAL SITS ON THE CHASE AND FINISHES THE ENTIRE BOTTLE OF WINE. SHE'S BEEN DRINKING IT LIKE WATER. SHE STAGGERS OVER AND KISSES HIS NECK MAKING EXAGGERATED NOISES.

FAINT SCREAMING IS HEARD THROUGH THE PHONE, THEN

THE SOUND GETS LOUDER AND LOUDER UNTIL IT SOUNDS AS IF IT IS IN THE ROOM

LIZ'S VOICE (OFFSCREEN) YOU FUCKING CHUMP DICKHEAD!

GAL (TAKING THE PHONE): LIZ? HI. YOU KNOW I'VE NEVER KISSED A BOY BEFORE. AND I'M GONNA TRY AND CONVINCE HIM THAT IT'S THE RIGHT MOMENT TO DEFLOWER ME! ISN'T THAT HISTORIC!

(JOSH GRABS IT BACK. GAL GETS IT AGAIN. THEY STRUGGLE, THERE IS A LOUD DIALTONE. ED IS ON TOP OF MEADOW ON THE FLOOR, HOLDING HER DOWN)

JOSH; WERE YOU IN ANYWAY RESPONSIBLE FOR YOUR MOTHER'S SUICIDE. CAUSE THIS'LL BE TWO. HE KISSES HER. SHE RESPONDS PASSIONATELY FOR A FEW SECONDS THEN SHOVES HIM OFF, ROLLS ONTO HER BACK AND P.O.V SHOT OFF THE CHANDELIER.

MEADOW: THAT WASN'T A VERY NICE THING TO SAY. DOESN'T IT LOOK LIKE YOU'RE LOOKING UP SOME VICTORIAN LADIES SKIRT. P.O.V SHOT OFF THE CHANDELIER AGAIN (ED PUTS HIS HAND UNDER HER SKIRT) I WANTED TO SHOW YOU SOMETHING. (SHE STANDS UP, UNSTEADYING HIM. HE FOLLOWS HER, BUT SHE STOPS HIM, PICKS HIS SHIRT UP AND PUSHES IT TOWARDS HIM.)

GAL: PUT THIS ON, THE WINDOWS HAVE EYES. SEVERAL SHOTS OF THEM FROM ACROSS THE COURTYARD, THROUGH THE WINDOW

DOLLY SHOT THROUGH HE DIM HALL, LINED WITH BOOKS (CLOSE UP OF TITLES, MARX, HEGEL, CIXOUS, DERRIDA, FOUCAUX ETC)

THEY ENTER THE BATHROOM, IT'S DARK THEN SHE

SWITCHES THE LIGHT ON. THERE'S A FULL ASHTRAY ON THE CLOSED TOILET SEAT. SHE PICKS IT UP WITH ON HAND AND WITH THE OTHER TAKES A FLIMSY NIGHTGOWN FROM A HOOK ON THE WALL.

GAL: DO YOU LIKE THIS? WELL. I STOLE IT. I STEAL THINGS.

JOSH KISSES HER GENTLY THEN PULLS BACK. SHE TURNS, CLEARLY UNSETTLED, AND THROWS THE FULL ASHTRAY OUT THE WINDOW. A LOUD CRASH FOLLOWS.

GAL: GOD. SHIT. FUCK. I MEANT TO THROW THE NIGHT-GOWN. SHE LEANS OUT.

SHOT OF THE DOORMAN AND A LITTLE OLD LADY NEXT TO THE SHATTERED ASHTRAY

DOORMAN CALLS UP, HIS DEEP VOICE ECHOING THROW THE COURTYARD: DAMN ANDROMEDA, YOU COULD HAVE KILLED SOMEONE!!

DISSOLVE OVER CLOSE-UP OF SHATTERED ASHTRAY

ROLL CREDITS ECT

* * *

Rob Hartman's comments in red Le Pen, written on the last page of the above.

31/5

Ed, yikes!

What happened to the retelling of *The Picture of Dorian Gray* in a Soho setting? I thought we'd agreed on that for this assignment. This made me cringe. Were you going for that?

Incidentally dolly shots are prohibitively expensive. Ditto 'across the courtyard into the window'.

Please keep the DP consistent. You should fix this before we do a class reading. I don't think Andromeda would appreciate the cameo.

And, it's way too short. In order to give you credit you'll need to get me something of the same length again by June 11. Look at a real screenplay. Copy the format. Turn on your spellcheck. Then I won't fail you.

I liked the chandelier. That's doable.

Any questions, call or email me.

Rob x

D.

The English Novel Pre-1912

*A fool and his money are soon
Married.*
  svz, 1984

* * *

Sam /Mead

5/28

The problem with this avz thing is I can't get her voice right.
Or maybe I can't get mine right. My mother is on the phone

* * *

Douglas Ellimen Realtors' letterhead

6/4

Dear Mrs. Bream,

  The other night, May 27th, Andromeda threw a lead-crystal
ashtray out her window into the pedestrian courtyard. I have left a
message on your voicemail to this effect, but wanted to put this in
writing so that it goes on her permanent record.

  All Best,

  Lara Lawson-Taylor

* * *

Sam, on yellowed Hotel Bellclaire stationery

6/11

I set it up so I could watch my mother from above, from my eighth-floor window. I wanted to watch her walking into Big Stavros's new upscale venture, Stav's. I chose the venue maliciously, because I knew she'd have trouble finding something to eat on the menu. The last time I saw her, at Uncle Sam's retirement party five years ago, she was 'off wheat and dairy' (but on wine and coke). She got out of a cab on the other side of 77th street, in front of the old Broadway Bay, and slammed the cab door, hard. She was in tight, all-black clothes and high heels. She'd dyed her hair red, the color it used to be. You could see her a mile away, still, and she likes it that way. She's never considered the option, the possible joys, of blending in to the woodwork.

I made myself wait exactly ten minutes before I ran downstairs (it's faster in the Bellclaire to run down eight flights of stairs than take the elevator, which automatically stops at every fucking floor).

She was sitting at a booth in the back, looking put out. The first thing she said was 'I can't believe you can't smoke in here.'

I leaned down and kissed her – I was out of breath – she's my mother, after all – while she continued to pack her skinny brown Moore by tapping its tip on the table. Then she gave me the once-over. I was in the new suit I've bought to wear to work. I've been hired by Barnes and Noble. And I think the suit will help me get promoted faster. I need to make more than six-fifty an hour, soon.

'For Chrissake I wish they'd turn off that damn polka music. You're looking good, Sam.'

'It's Greek. Greek music. Lara left me.'

'Is that good? Cause you *look good*.'

'How's Uncle Sam?'

'Don't call him Uncle Sam. Anyway, darling, wonderful.'

She didn't look at me. She opened the wine list and snorted,

85

'*Greek* wine!'

The specials were written in neon blue pen on a black plastic board behind her head: Mahi Mahi with cherry tomatoes and feta, clam pizza, scallop burrito, ceviche. Big Stav is pretty undiscriminating. He'd sauce a cat. This fancy Greek place is his big step up. His dream. To my mother's left, there was a glass refrigerator-case filled with very fresh dead fish. You can tell by the clearness of their eyes; Stav told me that once. He'd been pretending not to look at us since we came in, standing over in the corner watching the same Greek Tourist Board video that he's always got playing on three monitors mounted near the ceiling.

He ambled over and propped his drooping belly on the edge of our table. That degree of shamelessness is refreshing.

'Your sister?'

'Oh come on.' Janet wasn't having it. 'There's no one else back here. Can't we smoke?'

'I may have to pay a five hundred dollar fine.' He shrugged his shoulders and smiled. She lit up with a gold Cartier lighter.

Stavros insisted we have cocktails before the wine. I didn't take much convincing. I didn't take any, to tell you the truth, though I haven't had a drink since that night with Hill. I had planned to not drink indefinitely. I ordered a martini. My dad drinks them thusly: straight, Tanqueray, one empty olive, in a frozen highball glass. Nick brought it out in a red wine glass with an umbrella in it which sheltered three pimento-stuffed olives speared on a miniature blue pirate sword. I swallowed it in two gulps.

Janet sipped her *Greek* white wine. 'I suppose you'll be needing money. The suit tipped me off. You're trying to look grown-up.'

Two sips of wine and it's the old badgering Janet.

'Actually I've got a job. Barnes & Noble.'

'No one wears a suit at Barnes & Noble.'

'I've been reading up on this career shit. The suit makes the man.' I adjusted my tie.

'Nice you're still reading.'

'Nice you're still smoking.'

When I saw myself in the pockmarked mirror back in the Bellclaire, I thought I looked alright. Now, through her eyes, I was incredibly fucking pathetic. Lara has about half of one percent of the money Uncle Sam, or my dad, for that matter, has. My low-level gold-digging is a blight on the family name.

Janet refilled her glass, played with the tip of her cigarette, rolling it around in the ashtray. Then she said, and sort-of giggled, 'I'm nervous.'

'So am I.'

'Sam is really sorry about what happened. He blames himself.'

He blames himself for my punching him at his retirement do? Big of him. Big Stav of him.

'As long as you're happy. I just think people should be happy.'

'Do you have someone else?'

'Have? No.'

'Jesus, Sam.'

'What?'

'I always feel judged by you. You're judgmental. Lara probably couldn't stand it. The little creep.'

'Whatever. Oh: Lynne dropped me.'

'I'll get Sam on the case.'

'Don't. Please. She dropped me because I'm a ne'er-do-well and a dick.' I finished the rest of her wine. It warmed me. Stav's got a thing for Christmas decorations. The ceiling is layered in gold, silver, and turquoise tinsel garlands. Accordioned cut-out paper fish dangle between plastic crabs and strings of glass

87

beads. It's a beautiful, gaudy nightmare.

I had avoided looking at my mother until now. I was overwhelmed, being so near her. She's impenetrable, but see-through. I don't know. I don't know about women, but when I drink they seep into me. The dead fish glistened behind her, their skin like mercury, their open mouths pink as ... My mom's surgeon, he's really not bad: she doesn't look pulled or tucked. She looks ... well, there is something strange about her face. She doesn't exactly look *younger* than she is ... I don't know what she looks like. Probably just like a rich fifty-five-year-old who goes to the best and wasn't so badly off to begin with. I found myself staring at her décolletage, which – strangely – she's neglected to have fixed or bleached or whatever the fuck they'd do to it. If you pulled on the skin it would stand up for a couple of minutes.

She hacked and put out her cigarette. 'So you hate Sam? You hate me.'

'I don't hate him. I *resent* him.'

'So you do hate me.'

'Mom, I love you.'

We laughed. Nick brought me another tepid martini without my asking. I started telling Janet about this new thing I'm working on – the avz thing, which so far is ... disappointing, Sammy boy, you loser, but stick with it ... Anyway, Janet feigned interest: being married to an editor, she's really good at it, *ohh*s and *ahh*s at all the right moments. It isn't that she's not interested. She's just beyond it. She *is* a good story.

She got a call on her cell phone and took it outside. I watched her through the plastic fish, the stenciled sign and nets in the window. People turned back to look after they passed her. She was very involved in the conversation, and spoke quickly and earnestly. Then she was wiping tears from her eyes.

I caught myself in a convex security mirror on the ceiling:

amidst the clutter in my clean shirt and tie I looked like an animal in a man suit, on the prowl. I looked sort of big. Inflated. She is still soft. I am not. I will be kind to *this woman*. My mother.

I stood up when she came back in. She was now smiling. Cheery. 'He's jealous.'

'Why were you crying?' I looked at her rings. She has many gold rings, one of them a Tiffany's yellow diamond from Sam, in the shape of a fucking heart.

'He doesn't want me to bail you out. Basically he doesn't want me to love you more than him.'

'Do you?'

She looked at me and smiled. Then she reached out and touched the top of my big hair. 'He really likes you, that's the sad thing. He's just a kid too. But he thinks you're great. He wants to see what you're writing.' A long look, and then this Italian mama accent she does, with her mouth full of tiramisu: 'How much ya need?'

* * *

Andromeda / Rembrandt

6/10

Ran out of Ed's Ritalin and have to wait a week to fill another scrip. Felt the most crappy I've felt in my whole life. I must have stolen five hundred dollars' worth of cosmetics to console myself. I've come back to my bench, hoping for Escobar. He might have some insight. He was just in a bad mood the last time I saw him. When was that? It seems like ages ago. Maybe he's dead.

God, here comes Sam looking like a used car salesman.

I couldn't keep writing, after he sat down. He just plopped down on Escobar's bench, and didn't look at me, or say anything for about five minutes. As if he was just some normal yuppie sitting down for a rest. As if we'd never met. Fuck him. I figured I'd leave. I packed up my stuff, stood up and was lifting my bag when he finally mumbled, 'Your check bounced.'

I took out this old chainmail purse of my mom's, what they call a CLUTCH. In it were two fives, two ones, and about a million stolen lipsticks. They all spilled out onto the ground in front of the bench. I crouched down, held the bills towards him with on hand and threw the lipsticks into the bottom of my bookbag with the other.

'Forget it.' He didn't move.

I said, 'We all have our little foibles and mine is the prompt settling of accounts.' Which is what Charlotte Bartlett says in *A Room with a View*. I did it in an upper-class English accent. I'm good at accents. He didn't laugh.

'You shouldn't sit here alone. It's dangerous.' His beard was growing in the color of saffron, and his eyes were bloodshot.

I gave his suit a dirty look. 'What are you going as?'

He jerked his head at my dress and laughed – I guess it's a bit weird too. It's a floor-length cream cotton thing that buttons up to the chin. The sleeves used to cover my hands but I cut them off this morning. It may be a hundred years old. I found it on the floor of the Meaningful Closet.

And just then, as we were actually looking at each other – me crouching, him hunched over – his weird laugh reminded me of the first time I spoke to him, in the elevator. She wasn't even dead yet. I mean, we each knew who the other was by then – we'd watched each other across the courtyard for months. Anyway he asked me if the other elevator was broken, because

I was riding in the one on his side of the building. I said 'It's on the fritz.' I can tell two weeks before that the elevator is going to break. I can feel the little changes. My mom used to call me the Mystic Mechanic. He said 'No, it's not. I just saw Mrs. Kasbaum going up.' But I didn't feel like getting into my paranormal talents, so I didn't say anything. We rode in silence. When we alighted, and he was going into his stupid apartment, getting out all the keys to open all his stupid expensive locks on his stupid door (we have one lock; renters all just have one, practically state-issued) and I was making my way through the big heavy fire door and into the great gray greasy garbage hall on our side of the building, I heard him say, 'No it's not. Asshole.' And he laughed at himself, the same laugh.

And IT'S NOT DANGEROUS. Maybe it was in the seventies. It was nearly dark, but there were still tons of people around. Two yuppie girls in short skirts, their waxed legs crossed, conspired on a bench on the other side of the Promenade. A woman jogger, in gear so hi-tech she must have been sponsored. Another woman walking several tiny dogs on complicated connected leashes.

'That seat is taken, by the way. That's Escobar's place.'

'I used to know a guy called Escobar.'

I pulled on my bag. I can hardly lift it. I bent forward and it swung into the cavity of my stomach. It occurred to me that I hadn't eaten anything but three blueberry muffins in the past two days. He stood up, much too close to me. He invaded my space. He reeked of gin. I took a step back. He took a step forward, kind of smiled, then pulled something out of his breast pocket and stuck his arm straight out over the balustrade. My purple sunglasses. I reached for them. He flicked his wrist and they flew down to the path thirty feet below us.

'What the fuck?'

'I didn't know what to do with them.' Which is also from

A Room With a View.

I leaned on the VERAN-DUH. It was dark. You wait and wait and wait, and you pay attention to the fact that you're waiting, and then the second you stop waiting for it, it's just dark.

He lifted my bag by the top handle. 'I'm gonna carry this for you.' The strap was still across my chest; he picked it off me very carefully, so he wouldn't have to touch me, like I was covered in cat piss or radioactive waste or something. Then he turned around and walked away. Clack Clack Clack – he had on cheap new Fayvas – over the metal grate in the middle of the Promenade. The park lamps lit just then, while I was looking at the back of his head, trying to decide if I was offended or not. They made this bobbing chain of amber beads to 94th street, where the Promenade ends in a curve, and there's that tunnel that goes under the offramp from the Henry Hudson Parkway, and that playground with different concrete levels and concrete fountains. Suddenly there was no one around. The thin reflective strips of one jogger; that was it. Sam was disappearing up the dirt path to Riverside Drive. The way he had my bag, by the top handle like that, reminded me of a father putting his daughter on a train (I can't remember what movie that would be from). I ran to catch up and ended up about three feet behind him, tripping over the roots of the trees, the bits of schist, the empties.

Halfway up some crackhead appeared. He said, 'Hey man?' As if he was about to try and con us, or something. Sam stopped. I stopped. It was really dark.

'Hey man,' he said back. In a monotone. He was scary. In his cheap suit. Like some yuppie who's been pushed too far. They're the worst. The guy zipped down the hill, passed me without even looking. Sam rubbed his eyeball with his thumb and didn't move on.

'What if you were alone?'

'I'm always alone.' I wanted to get out of there.

'What ARE YOU afraid of?'

'Drunk yuppies.' I went to walk past him, but he held my bag out and blocked me. Then I tried to go over a rock, off the side of the path, but my stupid high-heeled flip-flips wobbled. He got in front me again. It wasn't clear if wanted to obstruct me or to keep me from falling.

'Listen.'

I tried to get around him one last time. He put his hands on my arms.

'Listen!'

'OK!'

Then he said, 'Some people die because people kill them. And some people kill themselves, that takes the uncertainty out of it. But you – you have to look after yourself now.'

'Fine. Thanks. I will. ' I know about drunks. Don't engage them.

He moved aside, dropped his arm and gestured up the hill with the bag, like an usher.

I ran up to Riverside, to the thick sidewalk, the predictable traffic of cabs. A dog-walker hung limply over a Learning Annex Pamphlet dispenser. The light was red. I pressed the button on the green iron box. The light did not change. The dog walker crossed. Sam came out of the park and stood behind me. He put my bag on the right way, over his shoulder. I watched him open and close his hand to loosen it up. He doesn't wear a wedding ring.

'What have you got in there?'

'Some guy's head.'

The laugh again, it's nice.

'I am drunk, Andromeda. I'm not a yuppie though. I fucking wish.'

I pressed the button again. Across the street a doorman was unloading Fairway bags out of the trunk of a green Mercedes.

Martha Stewart got out of the driver's seat. She ignored the doorman and walked into the lobby. Sam and I looked at each other. 'Thank you!' he yelled across the street. Martha turned and gave us the finger. We were still waiting obediently for the light.

Then we crossed. The light still hadn't changed. As we walked up to West End he told me that when he's alone on the street he does two things. One, he imagines the gargoyles or faces or figures on the buildings coming to life, circling around him and landing on top of his head, holding on with their claws, pulling his hair. Other times, in a worse mood, he imagines the city stripping itself away, layer by layer: toilets, kitchen sinks and radiators flying out windows, like the black and white tornado at the start of *The Wizard of Oz*. I thought it was cool. Maybe I shouldn't have told him. Because then he took the opportunity to tell me he was writing a story about me. And was that OK? I told him definitely not.

The Apthorp gate was in view. I said, 'So, you just came to tell me my check bounced?' José and Mrs Kasbaum were just inside the courtyard, shooting the shit. Kasbaum took two cans of kidney beans out of her plaid shopping cart. She was in a huff about something, as usual. She got more and more exasperated, holding one can up and then the other. Sam took my elbow and turned me away from the gate.

'No. I came to tell you Lara's gonna get you evicted.'

'You know what? Let her.' I started to walk into the building. He pulled me back. Kasbaum and José noticed us. Sam said, quietly, his thumb back in his eye: 'You hungry? I really wanna sit at a table with YOU, with things between us, salt and pepper shakers and hot sauce and a metal napkin holder.' As he said it he moved his hands, pretended to shake salt and pepper, outlined a metal napkin holder. I said OK.

La Caridad or Big Stav's? The only two options for the non-rich. They've both been around FOR-FUCKING-EVER, as my mom would have said. I told Sam that she and my dad, The Other Leonard Cohen, were good patrons of Big Stav's during their six-month fling. Back when they went, people drank rosé out of those teardrop-shaped bottles in plastic nets, and generally had a better time. Then they'd go back upstairs to the Apthorp and fuck their brains out. That's how she put it. Sam said why didn't we go to La Caridad.

It was filled with driven, single men eating alone at orange tables. These guys all migrated here last week from Staten Island to get nouveau riche on the stock market. So they can BUY a wife a Lexus a boxer. An eight ball. But the 00s or whatever they're gonna be called are still just like *The Man in The Grey Flannel Suit*, except he takes Viagra instead of martinis. Still, the chiccarones are pretty good. I said all this. I couldn't stop talking.

Everyone stared when we went in. There was one table of girls my age, all very made-up. He ordered a Presidente and rice and beans from the waiter, who said, 'Hello my friend. For the lady?' I thought it would be cool to get a beer too, or at least a café con leche, but I got a can of guava juice and fried pork chops. If I was with Ed I wouldn't have. The other day I tried to eat a poppy bagel in front of him and was worrying the whole time I had seeds in my teeth.

The girls at the table were still ogling me. It reminded me: 'Some nut left a note in my lobby asking me if I wanted to be a model in *Sassy* magazine. They do this "real people" thing.'

'What was her name?'

'Hillary something.'

I didn't think it was THAT funny.

'I'm not gonna call. I mean I don't want to encourage anorexia in nine-year-old girls. Make 'em buy things they don't need…'

'Especially when they can steal 'em.'

I sat there and tried not to say anything. But the longer I said nothing, the more pissed off I got. Partly because I wouldn't shut up. Why was I even there? With him? His face just ... bothers me. One at time, I picked up the napkin holder, the empty plastic bread basket, the jar of hot sauce. 'Are you happy now that these stupid things are on the fucking table?'

I NEVER act like this. My mother did. Maybe it's coming off Ritalin.

I stared out the window at 78th, feeling like I was going to cry. I concentrated on the iron fence between the Apthorp and the sidewalk, the shiny black rail as big as my neck. The way he was looking at me made me feel like one of those Hirschfeld cartoons in the Arts and Leisure section on Sundays, the caricatures. He always hid his daughter's name, Nina, between two strands of hair, the folds of a dress, a crease in the hand. I was always better at finding them than my mom. I could find them in a second; I could find the names in a second. He was just STARING at me.

He said, 'You might be too pretty to be a model. I used to know a guy called Escobar. Don't cry.'

'I'm not. It's the same guy.'

'No. Uh uh. My Escobar was... He's not that guy.'

'Believe it.'

'He looks like shit.'

The food came. I was fucking starving. I'd eaten all the bread and butter. I started in on the plantains. Sam shook hot sauce all over his mountain of rice and beans then didn't touch it. He sat there watching me eat. But watching someone eat can get a bit boring, even when they're as gorgeous as me. He started looking over my shoulder, past the traffic island to Kandila Pizza.

'Do you mind if I disabuse you of your pristine image of Escobar?'

'I don't have a pristine image of fucking Escobar.'

'Can I tell you a story?'

The story was about this time – around when I was born – when Sam and Escobar were teenagers, and Escobar stole Sam's penny loafers. He told it pretty well; he'd obviously been thinking about it for a while, how to tell it. Or maybe not. I thought it'd be impolite to ask. He kept interrupting it with lots of asides, asking me what I thought, etc. He had this way of elevating (or is it lowering?) the story to the level of the metaphysical, and I go in for that. Honestly, though: I didn't really get the point of the story, if there was one. But I don't think a story needs a point. A story is its own point. I mean, what's the POINT of *The Judgement*?

'You think that Escobar stealing your shoes ruined you life?'

I guess it's hard not to look for one.

'Without a shadow of a doubt.' He took a triumphant, final swig of Presidente, muttered 'shithill' and jumped off his chair and got under the table. I crossed my legs. His hand was on my foot.

The waiter came over 'There a problem?'

Sam hiss-whispered, 'Do you see two guys in black suits, with sunglasses? On the corner?'

'Friend, you got problem?' The waiter was getting angry.

'Are they gone?'

There were no guys. There were very few people out. Across the street, in front of Mueller's cheese, there was one yuppess in a thick purple scarf. She was on her phone and kept turning back to look at us, at me. She was making me really self-conscious, actually. I put down the pork chop bone I was chewing on. There was nothing left on it anyway.

I said, 'Sam, there's no one there.'

When he came up his tie was loose and his hair was even more messed up than usual. 'Sorry,' he said to me. 'Sorry,' he

97

said to the waiter, who looked from him, to me, and back again.

'Somebody looking for you?'

I took one of my fives out my clutch. Sam waved it away. 'Take that out of Granny's drawer?' He picked up my bag and walked to the register.

'Where do *you* get money?' I followed him.

'Well, tonight I borrowed a thou from my mom. Basically I scrub off whoever's closest to hand.' He paid twelve bucks at the register and gave the guy an eight-dollar tip.

There was a low, full orange moon over 79th Street, rising over boarded-up Woolworths, which will be gone in a few weeks. They're going to build a new condo there. I know cause Granny's got a friend on the Landmarks Commission. We stood near the Apthorp gate, not saying anything. He gave me my bag back, put it over my shoulder. Then he straightened my shawl, which was caught underneath it.

It was a weird night. The first hot night. The air gets qualities, personality, a disposition. Someone was pissing against the window of Mueller's Cheese. Very off: we have order in Guiliani's New York. The pisser zipped up and headed to the crosswalk. When he stopped on the traffic island I saw it was Escobar and he'd lost about a thousand pounds. I was about to point him out to Sam, who'd been somewhere else, his eyes stuck where his hand had been on my shawl. Then José boomeranged out of his booth – they make him stand in this little copper booth – like a comedian running onstage for a second bow. He whispered, 'Heads up!' skipped sideways to the edge to the gate, and adjusted his cap, doorman-style. I've never seen him move so fast. Sam took two big steps back.

Lara was with Midas, who stood up on his hind legs, threw his paws on Sam's chest and licked his suit. Sam said, 'Hello, boy. Hello. All right. All right. Jesus FUCK.'

Lara looked Sam up and down, and said, 'Hill just called me.

98

You. Are. Vile.' Then she turned her attention to me and added 'Bring him up. You're grandma's not home yet.' She dropped Midas' leash and a squeaky toy newspaper with the word EXTRA written on it at my feet, and headed uptown, hanging back for a second on the corner to give Escobar – who thank God didn't see me – a wide berth.

José came over and stood with us, a nickel poised over one of those scratch-off Lotto tickets he always has. We stood in a line: Sam, José, me, Midas, the squeaky paper. Click click click, and around the corner she went, in those little pink mules. She kept reaching up to adjust the pink scarf she had tied over her hair like fucking Doris Day. The last thing she did was reach into her Hermès bag, pull out her cell phone, and stick it on her ear.

Sam eyed José's scratch-off. 'Do you really think you're gonna win that? You know your chances never increase. Even if you play the same numbers every day, your chances never get any better.' He tried to smile as he said it but he looked more like he might cry.

My mom used to make fun of José too. She called him Hey Ya Never Know. He called back You Gotta Be In It To Win It.

Cynics.

* * *

In the Case Notes field of the New York State Child Protection Database file for Andromeda Van Zandt
6/12

Received another call from Ms. Lara Lawson-Taylor who said the minor is living alone and was caught shoplifting, though no charges were pressed. She also claimed that she was involved with a married forty-three-year-old who lives in her apartment building.

* * *

6/12

A Good Man is Hard to Find 1st draft

'I just pick his shit up with a plastic bag, right?'

Andromeda Van Zandt (Buren? Doren? Derbilt?) has kindly offered to take Midas (Phaedrus? Remus? Squeemus?) because there are no dogs allowed in the Bellclaire. She thinks he'll feel better if we both take him up to her apartment and settle him in. I go along with it, and say I'll come over and walk him every day, before and after work, until I can sort out a better arrangement. She says she could easily walk him some of the time, maybe bring him down to her bench with her, for protection.

'I can't talk in here. I'm scared of it.'

The elevator on her side of the building is dimmer and slower and older. She stands an inch from the door, her hand in a fist over her heart, Midas' leash hanging down from her grip like an umbilical cord. The door scraping each floor we pass. When we get to eleven she twists sideways and squeezes out the moment it opens wide enough. We're in a hall unlike Lara's and mine. It hasn't been fixed up, because renters live here. The wallpaper is peeling off, an ancient fleur-de-lis pattern with gold and green leaves. avz pushes open one of the two doors on her floor; on our side there are six. 'You don't even lock it?'

She shrugs.

The front hall, what she calls the *anti-way*, is tiled from floor to ceiling, though I might not have noticed if she hadn't pointed it out: it's filled with junk. Newspapers, puffy jackets, lambskin coats, cross-country skis, a cat carrier, a stroller, a shopping cart from The Red Apple that closed ten years ago. She moves a coat rack aside; she's already lit a cigarette. The cigarette moves in her mouth as she speaks, she's like a shifty antique dealer:

'Check this out.' Behind the coat rack is a mosaic. Bacchus with long red ringlets flowing down a flabby naked chest, a red blot of a tongue poking through his black circle mouth. His eyes are closed – he has curled black lashes – and he's holding a jug above his head, as if preparing to ... pour it on his head.

'A *fine* example of a *fin de siècle* High Hotel interior ...' She drops the shyster accent and reverts to herself. 'Doesn't it look like a bathroom? Or the subway station? They're the same fucking tiles.' She taps a square with a chewed purple finger, then shoves the coat rack back in front of him. The rack looks like it belongs to a drag queen: a pink boa, a fur coat, a ¾-size umbrella with an ivory handle.

We walk into the hall. I hear myself say, 'They built them at the same time, the Apthorp and the first subway. They built the subway closer to the surface than they had to, because they didn't want to scare people by putting it as far down as they could have.' My voice is too low.

She turns on the light. Ceiling-high bookcases line both walls. That's the one thing my place has in common with hers – fifteen-foot ceilings. But this hall is as wide as my bedroom. I can't see to the end of it. She sits down on a ¾-size round green velvet chair, beside a ¾-size round table – I guess people were smaller when they made these things – and kicks off her high-heeled flipflops.

'I hate these. I can't take a decent step in them. You know what my ma called them? Catch-me-fuck-me shoes.'

Her feet are dirty and red. We start the tour. Midas follows us like a bomb-dog, his nose to the ground. He's with the band. You know how dogs get.

Off the hall on the left are the 79th Street-side rooms, the ones I've never seen. Facing the courtyard on the right, the ones I know so well: her kitchen, her 'new' bedroom, the dining room, what's known as 'Granny's Disgusting Boudoir'. In the living room vacant candelabras shine. The Persian rug is threadbare but spotless. The pillows on three maroon couches are fluffed up like cakes. In the center of the coffee table – I think it's been fashioned from a ship's door, it has a porthole – there are some dying lilies in a big label-less jar. I'm pretty sure it's a mayonnaise jar.

'It definitely looks like the person who lived here has died.' That was me. Nice.

'It's just Granny's morbid guilt-induced cleaning. She's sleeping with my headmaster. She stops in a few mornings a week to clean up and comb out her fuck knot.' I try not to look too hard at her body as I follow her back into the hall.

'This is my new bedroom. I moved here because I had nightmares in the old one. Not that it worked. I have nightmares here too. Last night I slept in the closet.' The room is dark but I can see it's a wreck. She goes in.

I stay in the doorway. 'What are they about?'

'I need to find this quote. I read it a while ago and it explained *everything*, but now I can't remember it, or the book. Has that ever happened to you?'

'Yeah. What are your dreams about?'

'Oh, mostly that I have to throw myself out the window too. Walk-the-plank scenarios. Last night Lew – that's granny's boyfriend – was telling me my turn was next.' She's picking books up, opening and closing them, in the dark. 'He was going through the alphabet, a roll call. When he got to you, you had to jump out the window. Obviously my name is always at the very end. He poked you with a stick, like a teacher's pointer, and you had to walk along this thing like a diving board, then jump. It was in the Museum of Natural History, actually. The school was. The window was on the third floor, the one in the round corner, by the park, the south end, where the dinosaurs are now? I got away. I outsmarted him. But he chased me and caught me in some anti-way and broke some mirror and he sawed my wrist with a shard of it. I felt like I was being ... drained. I started singing *Que Sera Sera* to distract myself.' She sort of laughed, and started singing it.

'So someone's always making you?'

'What?'

'Jump.'

'I don't know. Yeah. Usually.'

Across the courtyard I can seen the drawn curtains of my old apartment. It's only been two weeks. For a moment I host an unexpected Scott Fitzgerald-y, 'them's the breaks' old-school fatalism. From within the blackness, a blue-red stain; it blooms and lights up the room. Lara's home. Fast walk. Andromeda has her hand on the light switch. I reach across and stop her. Lara can't see me over here. I have Andromeda's hand in mine and my arm over her. The red batik she's nailed to the corners of the window is knotted at the bottom to admit the light. It fucks up the mandala design. In Lara's light I can now make out the hardbacks splayed on the rug in this room, the clothes and underpants, the record player turning, with no record on it, an ironing board in the middle of the floor ... I tug her slightly, towards me.

I am saved by a scrap of paper on the floor, in the triangle of hall light, by the door. I read the words *Andromeda Taylor*. Over and over again.

I move her away. I make an involuntary snort. I think she's seen it too. She walks past me, out of the room, and starts talking even more. We won't go in her mother's bedroom, she doesn't think. She's read about boundaries in the self-help aisle.

She won't look at me. We stand in front of her darkened 'old' bedroom. She's yammering. 'They say you are everyone in your dreams, that everyone's just a side of you. That makes me feel better. When I was a kid I saw a lot of horror movies. My mom loved gore and she would always tell me to think of the guy in the sound booth, playing the saw or slamming a door or walking in a gravel tray. That makes me feels better too.'

She turns on the light in her old bedroom. A very different sort of room. Bunk beds and a poster of Rosie the Riveter. I go and look out at the window at St. Paul's: its uneven spires, red tiles, its crooked position on the corner because it was there before the road. It looks like a prop in a fish tank. Now she's behind me.

There's a smell of turpentine. Some cotton balls are on the windowsill, smeared with purple varnish. I think I might actually puke up Big Stav's fish burrito. I go and stick my head between the bunks of her old bed. I don't know what possesses me, why I want to look there. There's a little curtain around it, lavender checks, with bows at the top. I move it aside. There it is, taped to the underside of the top bunk: a picture of her father and his family. A wife and a small boy.

'I made my mother get them. I slept one night on top and the next on the bottom. I wanted a sister. OK, sometimes I pretended I *was* my sister.'

Trying to close the fucking ... bunk-valence or whatever I rip it down, then knock my head on the underside of the bed. It's a bit slapstick. We laugh, once. I decide I'll fast-forward the tour, and walk past her into the hall. The dining room, a narrow table – not unlike a plank – and chairs, that's it. On the wall, a John Singer Sargent of her grandmother as a girl. It looks like Andromeda, the same eyes. The mouth like the blade of an oar.

She stands in the middle of the room, holding handfuls of her weird dress in her hands, wringing it.

'What about a father, did you want one of those?' I cough it out.

'What about him? The Other Leonard Cohen? A session drummer. He toured with Aerosmith. He writes me letters

104

sometimes but I don't write back. I used to tell people my parents never even met. It was a joke, but everyone thought I was artificially inseminated. I mean … Oh, forget it.'. She sits on the table, puts her face in her hands, her elbows on her knees and looks at her lap. Dejection becomes her.

I leave the room. And go into the hall. And read the titles of books. *The Tenant of Wildfell Hall. Good Morning Midnight. To Bedlam and Part Way Back.* What section *is* this? I want to call 'let's finish the tour', in a jolly way. But I can't say anything.

'Sam?'

'I'm reading.' The poem 'Funnel' is upside down in my shaking hand. It's shaped like a funnel. An upside-down one, a dunce cap, at the moment.

'That's only the second time I've ever said your name.'

I go back in, saying, 'Listen … ' I'm going to tell it like it is. I'm going to nip this in the – I look at the way the dress cuts in at her waist, the pale cloth pooled around her on the table. I'm going to push her hair aside and kiss her on the mouth, lean her back on the table and reach up under the dress. You always forget what it feels like: you can't quite imagine it.

'What?'

'What what?'

'You said listen. I am listening.' She gets up, comes over and puts her hands on my face, smiling. Her touch has a kind of placidity that almost infuriates me. I take her hands off. I hold them a little too hard. Then she panics, tries to pull them away. I won't let them go.

'God … Let's just finish the stupid tour.'

I'm not drunk enough to not know what I'm doing. I do it anyway. I walk her to the table and sift through yards of the infinite skirt. The dress has a thousand tiny buttons that would take a year to undo. I'm putting my hand under it. I reach right up to her ribs. I feel the prehistoric material ripping. Andromeda reaches down my pants. My hands between her legs. On the warm curve between her hips, the high plane of her breastbone. I can't tell what her mouth tastes like. Like mine.

'Sam.'

People always say each other's name at these times. She's just saying it for the hell of it. I ignore her. Sex is my one goal-oriented activity. I am. I'm in a goal-oriented stupor.

I hear '*Sam?*' A bit odd. A bit *off*. I pull my head out from her skirt. Put my face in hers and touch her hair. Her face is sparkling. I wouldn't say sparkling unless I had to.

'Guess what?' She turns to the wall of windows over the courtyard.

'You're a hermaphrodite.' I watch her eyes. Hold on. What a ... what a stupid stupid fuck I am.

'Oh
my God. Oh
my GoD. Oh God.
I've gotta get out of here.
Sorry. This is. Not right. Sorry. '

I straighten her skirt and leave the room. I walk down the warm, dark hall with its serrated rows of books to the ceiling and into the bathroom. I turn on the tap and splash water on my face, like they do in the movies. I look in the mirror. Like they do in the movies. It's not working. I look in her tub. She has ancient ochre rubber flowers you used to be able to get from Woolworths, the ones that stop old ladies from dying alone in the shower. I get in. I turn on the cold, in my cheap, stiff new suit, with the fly still open. I stand there freezing, for as long as I can take it. Probably about two seconds.

But it works. I get out no longer Undrunk. I get out Sober. The pink sponge is still half-out the closed window. A dim yellow light from the courtyard shines through the thick corpuscular glass. The only things on the towelrails (marble, with generations of paint drips on them) are an orange lace underwire bra and a giant pink silk kimono. Midas has followed me into the bathroom. Now he's whimpering, getting underfoot, his long unclipped nails clicking and scraping on the tiles. I abandon my wilted suit in the tub and put on the giant pink kimono. I'm going to gravely make my apologies, and then get the hell back to the shithole Bellclaire where I belong.

She's shut off all the lights. I start to walk in one direction, then stop, turn around and walk in the other. Midas barks. He has two barks: one to throw him a stick, and this one. But there is no one here. I'm freezing.

'Andromeda!' I trip over the kimono and step on the dog. I find a doorknob and turn it.

The wide leather back of an office chair, a calm view of Broadway in front of it, and the sound of a calm view, single sounds that begin and end: the whoosh of a cab heading uptown, a car door closing. THE WORLD IS ALL THAT IS THE CASE is written in neon-green duct tape above the window. The chair creaks. Smoke poofs out above it. A little mushroom cloud.

'Anyone would have nightmares in this place. Right, Scooby.'

In reply, she takes a drag. Or a half-drag, half-sigh. She swivels the chair slightly and I see her profile; her knees are pulled up, and she's tied a strand of her long hair around her big toe like a noose. I half-sit on the desk, which seems a ... friendly way to sit, like a guidance counselor.

'I've been meaning to ask, are you a bad writer?'

'The worst. I ... can't help you, Andromeda.'

'You can.' The noose is tightening. Her toe is purple. 'Come back in the other room with me and help me get rid of this thing. This little *barrier* I have.'

'Jesus.' I jump up like someone threw water at me. The

kimono flies open but I catch it in time.

She stands up too. 'I mean, *what*? You want me to save it for *the one*? Can't you just think of it as a favour?'

The empty chair is between us. To stall for time and give me something to do something with my hands, I spin it. It's much lighter than you'd expect. It spins and spins, fast. On each turn it makes a high squeak. There's a photograph of Andromeda on the bookshelf, in a little fairy get-up, with a magic wand.

'The first time SQUEAK yeah I *do* just think it should be with someone who SQUEAK with someone you're uh SQUEAK...'

'Are you a Promise Keeper?'

SQUEAK

I stop the fucking chair. I look at her, again. She's staring me dead in the face. She looks like Catherine Deneuve. In *Repulsion*. She says 'Do you like Flannery O'Conner?'

'*What?*'

'Just answer the question. Do you like her? I mean, you think it's *symbolic*? You think it's fucking symbolic!' She's yelling.

'No. No, it's significant.' I speak quietly. I notice my kimono is covered with parasols, some opened, some closed, some half-opened.

'I would have thought you'd be beyond the symbol. It's *very* out of fashion.'

'Listen to yourself.' I'm whispering.

'Listen to yourself.'

I am.

'I fucking *hate* Flannery O'Conner, all right. I fucking failed a class because I fucking hate her so much, because she hates everyone so much, *all fucking right*?'

I storm out into the dark hall. The kimono, which I'm holding closed, billows majestically behind me. There is a dim grey splotch somewhere far away. I head into its weak light. It's coming from the archway to the living room, where a Swiss

Cheese Plant looms. Its huge leaves are cut-out, gouged-out, against the few lights left on in the apartments opposite and the perpetual lavender sky above the dark buildings.

Why is the view so clear? Why is it so sharp? Because all six windows are open to the night; the air outside is a continuation of the room. One step onto the radiator and I could walk out.

She walks towards the windows.

'This is the one she chose. Not the middle one, or one of the end ones. I know because she left her cigarettes here. I went into the other room, to get this Kafka paper I was writing, to show her, and when I came back she was just ... gone.' She laughs.

'Shit.'

She leans out. Her purple hair falls all the way to her waist. She stands on her tiptoes, her ankles rocking. I calculate how long it would take me to grab her if she tried to jump. Finally she sighs and turns back into the room. She sits down on the couch and tucks her feet up under her. Behind her on the wall is a large bad picture, in lurid pastels, of two naked women eating watermelon on a picnic blanket.

'Anyway, maybe you *are* the one.'

I kneel at her feet, reach under her ripped dress and pull out a foot. I hold it.

'Wanna sleep over?'

'Christ, *no*.'

'I mean on the couch. Maybe if you're here then I'll sleep.'

'If I do stay I'm not staying because this is part of the story where I demonstrate my heroic self-control and consideration. This isn't the story of anything.'

'Whatever you say.'

'When you wake up, remember I'm here, and go back to sleep. Don't wake me up. Just go back to sleep.'

'Yeah, OK.' So long as I stay.

'God, this should be in *The Guinness Book of Records*. It'll

be like the first thing I've ever done without an ulterior motive.'
I rub the rough edge of her foot, gently.

She says, 'I've only looked at it once, in elementary school, at PS 87...'

'That's where Escobar went.'

'Karlotta – as in Marx – Speilgelmann – she was in love with me, and used to follow me around telling me that I suffered from the lack of a father. This was in about fourth grade. I didn't like her but she was my only friend. Anyway, she had it – *The Guinness Book of Records*. There was this guy who had the world's longest fingernails, a guy in China – and they were twisted and long as willow leaves, and it said he couldn't do anything, even eat, he was so afraid of breaking them. God it really depressed me. I hated that picture.' She was radiant. I'd never seen her look so happy, or so young.

R.

Lit Crit

Novels presuppose
A conspiracy theory of life.

In reality, even
cabals of one, acting in the smallest
compass,

Are subject to
Dissension, misunderstanding, and accident.

At least
That's my story.

svz, 1977

* * *

Andromeda/Rembrandt

6/15

The last day of term and my teacher Rob follows me down into the subway then just stands there reading the Voice. Finally I'm so bored I go over and nudge him.

'Oh! Hi, Andromeda.' Fancy meeting you here etc. 'So ... how things going with you and Ed?'

'How do you know about it?'

'Everyone knows.'

'St. Mary's is supposed to be an independent school, not a codependent one.' I thought that line up a while back. It bombs.

But he's easy to crack: Apparently he's on a mission from Granny and Lew. Ed told Lew I was demanding his Ritalin, and plus they all thought my insistence on an planned non-romantic

111

deflowering was sociopathic. Lew is too busy wooing Granny, so he sent Rob to suss me out; he had a dentist appointment uptown anyway. We get on the 2/3.

Rob's wearing a white, big-collared nylon shirt, open at the neck. His chest is hairy and he's got a mother-of-pearl crucifix on a fake gold chain. He used to be a Jew from Great Neck but now he's a semiotician. The train roars, it's one of the last of the old ones, the kind with a real voice on it, with an accent. We take the screaming curve out of Wall Street. I get lost in the vortex of women bankers, their neat clothes, hemlines, briefcases, mules... How the hell could Sam marry her?

By 14th Street Rob and I are officially bickering. 'Ritalin is a PRESCRIPTION DRUG. If you're using it without a prescription you may as well be doing dope.'

I choose not to discuss my nascent drug addiction in front of all the coke-snorting bankers. 'Ed's the one with a Ritalin problem.'

'They're PRESCRIPTION.'

'He's not HYPERACTIVE. You know who prescribes them, don't you? HIS DAD. They bet at pool and his dad gives him more if he wins.'

'We're not here to talk about Ed Hanes.'

'No, we're here cause I'm going home and you're going to get your teeth whitened.'

'A happy coincidence.'

The crowd thins out at Times Square. Now we can see the advertisements. The whole car is covered in the same one: Kenneth Cole REACTION. I think it's the model from the Samsung ad. I hate the shoes. Fake croc.

'You should model, Andromeda. You're prettier than her.'

I'm kind of surprised to hear it from Rob, though someone must ask me like once a week on the street if I AM one. Gay guys and tourists mostly.

I mean, maybe I'll call the *Sassy* lady back and see what happens. A lucrative summer job. I've got nothing planned. Gorling The Reichian suggested I be a counselor at a day camp for kids with special needs. I told him I should probably enroll as a camper.

* * *

Sam / Mead

6/13

The Story of My First Day of Work When My Suit Was Wet
1st draft

First day at work, and I hit the laundrette because my suit is wet. The label says dry clean only, and I know it's gonna shrink, but I have no choice. My boxers are navy blue. I convince myself they can pass as running shorts, and I'm wearing an undershirt, what Andromeda calls a *wife beater*, what Janet calls a *vest*, what Lara calls a *tank top*. I decide to take up smoking. I stole one of Andromeda's cigarettes to get started. I go outside to light it up. And of course, standing on Amsterdam Avenue in my underwear and Dexters and smoking my first American Spirit, I run into Hillary.

'Good morning, Sam.'

'Fine morning.'

She decided to move on, to *keep walkin'*. A good idea too. But after a few steps she stopped, tapped her toe three times, and turned back, with a twinkle like a gold star sticker in her eye. Behind her trucks roared past with dirty doors. In the cement playground of the public school across Amsterdam, a graffiti mural loomed in shades of lime and pink. Rest in peace Tico, with a skull and crossbones, flowers, and a smoking gun.

Hill took a long glug out of her Starbucks reusable thermos.

'Beautiful morning.' I meant it.

113

This confidentially. 'You know I saw you last night, in La Caridad, with a very young and beautiful girl, and what's so funny is she's the *self-same* girl I saw in the street last week and left a note for, asking her to be in this real people thing we do. Is that not amazing? I left her a card because I just thought, Wow! She is the *Sassy* girl.'

'It *is* amazing. Sounds like synchronicity.'

'Just tell her to call, OK?'

'I don't think she wants to do it.'

'Why not?' It irked her deeply. 'God, why the hell not? She'll get paid a thousand bucks an hour' – the thought of which sent her into a mini-reverie. Her eyes fixed on the imperceptible progress of a washing machine behind the glass. She came to. 'What are you doing anyway?'

'Going to work at Barnes & Noble. Information Officer.'

'Bah ha ha ha ha ha ah ah aha ahha ha baughhh!'

But her mirth soon gave way to boredom. She can see her day ahead. Models, lattes, emails. She looked at her watch. 'You fuckin' her?'

I stepped on my American Spirit and went to get my suit.

Hill called after me, 'I thought you *believed* in honesty!' The laugh resumed and did not subside until I had walked all the way to the driers at the back.

The Barnes & Noble staff room is an airless, windowless shit-hole in the center of the building. Plastic-backed purple-carpeted chairs, the smell of B.O., coffee and newsprint. I'm the only white guy in there. All the others are in management, on the upper level, in a football field-sized room that used to be my first girlfriend Sasha's ballet school. Up there, management, they get high, openable windows and modular cubicles. I know this because they've already taken a shine to me. One of them, Todd, who I think may be an alien, leads me into the shit-hole

114

and waits with me for Geraldine, my supervisor.

'Don't be too scared of her. Her bark's worse that her bite.'

'So long as she doesn't hump my leg!'

He thinks I'm a laugh riot.

'I saw on your application that you were a writer; I was bored, so I pulled up one of your old stories online at the *New Yorker* archive.'

'Oh Jesus.'

He touches my shoulder. 'Great stuff, dude.'

And in walks Geraldine, a small chubby black lady holding a pink perspex clipboard. Her hair's in a dated Grace Jones fade, and she has gold stud earrings around the rims of both ears. She's eating a cinnamon raisin bagel. Todd gets beamed up.

'OK.' She finds my name on the clipboard, 'Samuel Taylor. I'm supposed to tell you that the customer is always right.' She turns a page. 'And I am supposed to tell you that you can consult your supervisor, that's me, with any questions or concerns you may have.' Licks her fingers, another page. Her nails are very long and … scrimshawed? 'We prosecute for sexual harassment.' Lick & flip. 'Don't steal books, and don't abuse the security code i.e. don't sneak in the store with your boyfriend.'

'Okey dokey.'

She hands me a copy of the rules. I sign them, then follow her into the store, with its cold processed air. We are not open yet. Outside, in the heat, ten hunched old people are waiting. Geraldine says they're regulars who come to buy one coffee then sit around all day. Probably can't afford air-conditioning at home. About once a week there's a sweep and they throw them out. On our side of the door, the security guard, a scary looking guy – tall, with red hair – is taunting them: fingering his bunch of keys that hang off the lock.

'You stand here' – Geraldine smacks the *People's Court*-style

115

lectern, wobbling the information computer – 'and tell people whether we have the book they want, then where they can find it. All you have to do is type in the title. That's. It.' Then the doors are flung wide and she starts work. I stand beside her for an hour, smelling her patchouli oil and listening to what people ask for. Diet and self-help books. Diet and self-help books. Diet and self-help books. Someone asks for *Nancy Reagan's Interiors*. Geraldine types in the wrong title and says we don't have it.

In a lull, after studying me for a while as I read some in-house propaganda on effective customer care, she says, 'Why you here?'

'They gave me a choice, this, cashier, or security.'

'No. I mean why are you here?'

'You really wanna know?'

'…maybe later.' She looks at the redhead. 'Take your break now. There's an OK pizza place on 78th Street.'

'I know.'

I stand outside in the ninety-degree heat, sweating my ass off in the shrunken suit, wishing I didn't have a break. The last real job I had was when I was a short-order cook in Martha's Vineyard when I was sixteen. Andromeda's age. I thought I was part of a clear horizon. I'm birdshit on the window of a clear horizon.

I watch the shop. Barnes & Noble isn't bustling in the slightest. But the way the aisles on the ground floor (I can't bring myself to call it 'the Grand Mezzanine') are arranged make it look more crowded. The bookshelves are low, so you can see everyone's head above them, and there's a mirrored dado at eye-level so everyone is repeated. I wait fifteen minutes, watching the milling and churning, the buying and returning, and go back in. My hangover creeps up. A white-wine-and-gin hangover starts *hey! I got off easy there!* then slowly morphs into a very clear understanding that *I am the cause of the suffering of the world*

… till finally: *I will soon die of cancer.*

The afternoon is a blur. Geraldine stands beside me, in case I have any questions. I don't. She eats a few Slim Jims. She herself, she admits, is on the Susan Summers diet, 'but it ain't working.' She also files her nails and reads a book of essays on the poet Audre Lorde. She's getting her Masters at The Graduate Center, in American Poetry. Who's my favorite poet?

I don't have one. 'Anne Sexton.' I produce *To Bedlam and Partway Back* from my pocket. I stole it from Andromeda's dead mother. *Ex Libris Sophie Mary Van Zandt.*

She's thrilled.

The hideous catwalk of bookseekers continues. I keep looking up at the ceiling, which is richly paneled in fake cherry wood. Grandmothers are after out-of-print children's books. Trim forty-five-year-old women are wondering where the spirituality section is. Why wasn't Sophie Mary Van Zandt like them? Once she embarrassed me in the elevator when I held the door open for her. She said, 'How *gentlemanly.*'

Geraldine pokes me in the ribs with her pen. Paul is in front of me, his arms folded.

'The Go-Fuck-Yourself section's right at the top of the escalator Sir. Next.'

'Lara's looking for you.' He stretches his arms out and cracks his knuckles in my face. True.

Geraldine put down Audre Lorde.

'Give her a call.'

'Sir, what can I help you with?' We've alarmed Geraldine.

'Just get in touch with her, dick.' He turns and *strides* out of the store. You could cut the tension with a knife!

I get back to work. 'Large Print, adjacent to the café. Adjacent? Next to the café.'

Geraldine looks at me askance. She's re-combobulating. If I'm not gay, what am I? She clicks the point of her pen in and out.

'Occult and Idiotic, top of the escalator, sir.' I'm losing it.

'You can't talk like that in here.' But she's amused. She clicks some more.

'Out of print. Try Gryphon across the street.'

'You're not supposed to refer them to other booksellers! ... What's the story with that guy?'

'No story.'

'Why does he want to kill you, then?'

'I'll kill him.'

'Please. You're the skinny wimp who gets sand kicked in his face.'

So I told her. He's in love with a girl I never loved. He hates me because she thought I was deeper than him. But now she realizes that not only am I not deep at all, but that even if I was, she wouldn't give a flying fuck. All she wants is 'a prewar classic six', some kids, and a man who isn't a total loser. Is that too much too ask? I, for one, think not. As for her 'needing to talk to me', I can't imagine it has to do with anything other than money, or the title deeds on the apartment, or maybe Midas, though I doubt it, because although she's responsible for his dumb name (I wanted to call him Flipper) I've always been his owner.

Geraldine has decided she likes me. She launches into the story of how she met her estranged husband. It was sort of similar. Like mine it was an economically motivated maneuver. She had to 'get out from under'. Anyway, now she's come out of the closet and she and April have just bought a place in Inwood. Have I ever been up there? It's up and coming. It's a good area. I shouldn't rent, renting is for losers, it's a waste of money. I agree wholeheartedly. I hear the sound Andromeda made when I put my fingers in her. A quick inhale, the length of my fingertips. If I have any money at all, I should put a down-payment on a place uptown or in Brooklyn. She kisses me goodbye on both cheeks and I smell her Patchouli oil and remember, suddenly, who it reminds me of: Sasha, my first girlfriend, who wore way too much of it.

* * *

Written on the back of a manila envelope left in the lobby of the Apthorp, addressed to 'Andromeda Van Zandt. By Hand'

A reflection on your failings as a muse.

* * *

Un-spellchecked Mellel document on cheap copier paper inside the manila envelope

6/15

Sam's Shoe Story

Maybe it's out of fashion, like symbolism, but I've always been one to believe in inspiration. At fourteen I looked in girls' faces for a muse, but just found zits and lipstick. At nineteen I began to wander, and this wandering confirmed certain things, only two of which turned out to be relevant. The first: unless you can forget yourself you can't know anything, and that includes yourself. The second: you'll need very comfortable shoes.

Sasha Lipinski. Was going out. With Tucker Frix. And he wore. Bass brown loafers. Lipinski was exceptional, if a bit zitty. Oh, she could make you feel so welcome on the cross-town bus! Like one invited to an exclusive party. I wasn't. I was wedged over in the corner with the old ladies whose furs smelled of mothballs and the kids with whole-head braces. But as the weeks of my fourteenth year passed and winter gave way to spring etc. I came to believe that I was owed more; that grander things could and would be made available to me, if I could convince my mother to buy me Tucker's loafers.

Now Janet – I never called her mom, mummy, or mama unless I was being sarcastic – had not spent a thin dime on my wardrobe since she left my dad in '81. The last thing I can remember her buying me was my spacesuit. A ski-suit, actually. Back then it hung in my closet like a glow-in-the-dark mobile. I kept the closet door open at night. It was my night light. Anyway. There's a photo of us in front of our apartment building on 100th and Riverside, her hands firmly on my puffy superhero shoulders. We are about to get in a livery cab to JFK, about to embark on an early attempted escape from the menace of my dad, by way of the Swiss Alps. Weirdly, even a year later, at eight, I couldn't remember what Janet was talking about when she boasted, 'Samuel skied down Mt. Blanc.' I can't remember the trip. I still have the suit, in a bag, on the floor of the closet, in the Apthorp.

I was a big liar as a kid. I'm not any more. I lie very little now. But you couldn't blame me too much. I'd learned it from my dad, who never told the truth about anything. He would go out to buy *The Post* and tell my mom he was going for a coffee, for no reason. That's a cliché. And the reason I try to avoid talking about him is simply that he *is so cliché*. He lowers the tone.

So: one particularly rough bus ride, I became determined to get the fucking things. I pinned all my hopes on shoes. Sasha was having a party, a real party, not on the bus, a slumber party, with boys, and it was pretty clear I was not invited. I read my book the whole way (*The Prince*, as assigned) and then, once I got home to our apartment building, I waited for the elevator man to descend, till I heard the scraping elevator door get several floors down. I took off my shoes, put my hands in them and rubbed the soles all over my school uniform. I stuck them in my backpack. Next, I half-unclipped my fraying, clip-on tie and spat in my hands, then pulled at, teased my hair. I turned to the dim hallway mirror and – to psych myself up – made some psychotic Alfred E. Newman faces. I opened my mouth so wide it hurt. I went, 'GLARARGHH.' Then buzzed.

Four times.

Janet opened the door, gave me a blank glance, sucked her Moore deeply, muttered, with mild surprise, 'You look like shit,' turned her back on me and walked down the hall to her bedroom slamming the door behind her. I'd calculated on our heading straight into the living room. She was usually in there smoking and reading a novel when I got home from school. But there was her book (she was going through an endless Zola phase) spread open on the couch. I stood there in my sham pathetic state and became truly pathetic. I'd wait in the living room; I figured she'd probably tie up her phone conversation and come out for a chat. But the conversation dragged on and on, interminably. An hour passed. Words floated out her open window and into mine: 'oil', 'rigging', 'macho', 'shit', 'the real thing', 'bore'. I knew she was talking to her second-best friend (I was her first) about her new boyfriend, Allan.

Allan. Janet didn't have a nice word to say about him and he was not a nice guy. (I'd met him once for drinks on his sailboat, the *Scorpio*. On that occasion I had taken a bite out of my ginger ale glass, but that's another story.) Nonetheless, boring macho oil-rigging shit that he was, Janet appeared to think of no one but Allan. She clearly didn't think about the house. Every piece of furniture in our living room – Janet's mother's couches, my dad's mother's armoire, her mother's white baby grand piano, his mother's antique lamps, my dad's mother's wide rocking chairs, the paisley beanbags they bought when they got together, even the dining room table that came with the apartment – was shoved up alongside the window that faced the river. It looked as if the whole room was tilting towards the water, like we lived on a sailboat. It had not always been this way. My father and mother had put on a good show early on, but after she threw him out and refused to let her other lovers into our apartment, she had less and less regard for the intended purpose of things. I sat on the dining room table and stared out the window.

Sasha. Sasha had been to my house before, for a Latin class Janet had set up for an unemployed boyfriend-of-short-duration to teach. Sasha and a few other girls were recruited from Brearly. My mother felt we should mix. Collegiate was all boys (I am ashamed, but there it is: I went to Collegiate). This was the first time I laid eyes on her. She was the second person to arrive, and the first girl. She sat opposite me. She took out a brand new pink plaid Claire Fontane notebook. I said, 'Nice hat,' because she was wearing this absurd Fedora over an asymmetrical haircut.

It was lust. But it was lust at first sight: young lust, which is love. Old lust is sleazy and has lost its ideals. Old love, though: old love is as pure as it gets. I'm old. I'm thirty-three. But – I reflected as I watched the river – it was good she had at least been to my house, caught sight of the things that made me, the fine river view, the marble tiled lobby, and not least my mother herself. If it had just been down to me alone she wouldn't have offered me the rare smile I got. And I did: she laughed at things I said. I thought there was a chance she liked me already. Really. The loafers were just the catalyst. An … enzyme.

I watched a heaped garbage barge make its slow way towards Staten Island. Next door my mother was getting sad. And loud. 'Well, what if I did? How much worse could it be? It'd shut him up if I said yes. But what I don't get … ' The seagulls hung over the boat like they were on sticks. The boat got smaller and smaller and disappeared in the haze. It was spring, and still light at seven. Cars sped down the West Side Highway, unfurling behind them the red of their tail-lights. Couples bicycled home in single file on the path next to the highway, then came together side by side where it widened. Puerto Rican families closed up elaborate, noisy barbecues. Sasha's mismatched earrings were so fucking great! Her clunky lace-up boots and short skirts were great. She dressed like a Go-Go, which in theory I disliked – but boy did she wear it well. I opened the Rolodex (this was the 80s) of what we might do once we were alone. Once she was my girlfriend and not Tucker's we'd be on a rowboat in Central Park and I'd kiss her. I'd only ever kissed one girl before, two years before at a party, for my two minutes in the closet. It had been disgusting. But I knew it would be so different with Sasha.

The red sun finally sank behind New Jersey. The little amber lanterns in the park were all on. Nana, on the cover of my mother's book, held her half-open fan beneath her eyes, and looked up at me.

It was eight-thirty. The picnics were history. Drunks were beginning to holler. I rolled off the table, my uniform still on. I always took it right off, but now I felt I had to leave it on. I walked slowly through the dark hall, past the never-used dining room and rarely-used library, to the kitchen. All was cool and quiet. I stood there and wondered about other people. Did the world open for them the way it did for me? Sometimes, when I looked at something – something small, like the little curvy blue glass vase that always sat, dusty and empty, on Janet's bedside table – the world seemed to breathe through it. Its insignificance was suddenly vital. Something hinged on it. On my appreciation or attention to it. Life: delicate, stupid, full of light. It was so clear then. If only I could have put the words to it.

I quietly opened the fire door that led to the back stairwell. The walls had a thick coat of shiny grey paint. The trash chute was the size of a bread box. It opened out easily on its well-oiled hinge. I took off my bag – I'd had it on the whole time – unzipped it, took the shoes out and dropped them down the chute. I listened to them bang against the aluminum walls as

123

they flew towards the giant garbage bag, twelve floors below, in the basement. I really expected her to be there in the kitchen when I got back in, with a look of wild worry on her face. It's always like that when I do something dramatic, actually: I spin around to see who's watching. But there's never anyone there watching when you think there is, Andromeda. You have to put them there.

I fixed myself a gin and juice, in the dark, and sat drinking it at the weird green and very 1979 plastic kitchen table.

When she hit the light, I saw my white knuckles on the half-full icy glass.

'You're not drinking again?'

'Just a weak one.'

'Have you done your homework?'

'No. Janet, we need to talk.'

She was in her long heavy silk gay-divorcee robe, and her hair was pinned up. She had no make-up on, and little lines around her eyes, but they were smart lines. (She does not have them anymore.) 'What – d'you get mugged again?'

'My shoes were taken.' I intoned. Gravely.

'Oh, baloney.' She threw her cigarette out the window and started opening and closing the cupboards. 'No one would want those shitty old Dexters. You can have tomato soup and peas or a grilled cheese.'

'I had pizza.'

She sat down, looked at my drink, then picked it up and finished it. 'I can't eat kid food by myself. What am I supposed to eat?'

'I'm not a kid.'

'Oh, right. My mistake.'

'Janet, I need Bass loafers. They cost forty dollars.'

'Forget it.' She thought it was hilarious.

'Mom, I'm trying to impress a girl.'

124

Now she really looked at me. I thought she was counting the zits on my face. But I was in a rush. It was hard to muster the words but I managed.

'It's tough being fourteen.'

Jackpot. The ocean of self-pity she tapped into was better than empathy: she had a really horrible time at fourteen, off at some finishing school, learning to enunciate and hand-wash panty-hose, sneaking out the window at night to neck with townies.

'It is important to feel good about yourself. That's true. I sometimes think that if I had had. The confidence. At your age. None of this,' she gestured vaguely in my direction, 'would have happened.' Then she poured herself a gigantic gin.

Next morning I was up at the crack with an erection. I waited till eight, made Janet her coffee with hot milk and brought it to her in bed. Then I watched her elaborate toilette, which was thankfully half its usual length as she was playing a mom-in-Adidas-on-a-Saturday-morning and not some oil tycoon's girl-friend. After she finished making up, she said 'There,' and gave herself the fake smile she reserved solely for herself in the mirror.

It's a good walk down to Harry's Florsheim Shoes. Janet passed the time teasing me about Sasha and my 'little moustache'. But I didn't care. I was happy. It was probably the last time I was happy. I loved every girl we passed. I loved the young leaves shimmering in the trees. At Eighty-sixth Street, passing the Normandy Apartments, I thought about the same thing I still think about whenever I see it: the scene in *The Thin Man* when Nick knocks Nora out with the butt of his gun. It's my favorite part. It's so she won't see him fight.

My mother wanted to talk to me about Allan. 'What do you think his intentions are?'

'You mean are they honorable?'

'No, wiseass, I just mean, what the hell does he want from

125

me? He's such a creep but he won't let me break up with him. You saw the flowers.'

'He probably just likes sleeping with you.'

She laughed. *Oh my urbane, virgin son.* I wished I hadn't said it. Boundaries, you know.

Harry's was mobbed. It was just before Easter and hundreds of little girls needed Mary Janes. Their anorexic mothers sat smoking on camel-colored vinyl couches, ashing into full trays like endtables. Ship's ashtrays, I think you called them. When we came in, they all stopped and stared at my mother. She cut quite a figure.

She shook a black Bass loafer at the sweaty irritable shoe salesman. 'Sammy needs these in an eleven.' Then started chatting with a woman sitting next to her.

He came back boxless. 'We're outta his size.'

I took over. 'I'll try the bigger ones.'

'Your size is the biggest.'

'Give me the next size down, then. Please.'

I walked around the store, admiring the rich brown gloss of the leather in the little floor mirrors. My feet were curled up in the toe. They looked great with my cut-offs and sweat socks.

'They're fine. They feel fine.'

Janet was gossiping to the woman next to her about a new restaurant, The Back Way, that had just opened down the block, and about how the owners made their real money selling coke. I wore the shoes out and we headed down there for brunch. Janet wanted Eggs Benedict and a Bloody Mary, but just as we were about to go in she decided she'd call up Allan. We turned back to the phone box on the corner. She folded the glass door shut behind her. A long argument ensued. She started crying. It was hot. I sat cross-legged on the sidewalk. My feet hurt too much to stand. She hung up. I watched her put on pink lipstick in the reflection of the coin box.

'Change of plans. We're going to Regine's to meet Allan and his daughter Scarlet.' She already had her hand in the air for a cab. 'Scarlet's dying to meet you.'

'I don't want to come.'

She was glad. In return she gave me ten bucks. Ten bucks in my pocket and a whole Saturday to myself! I walked downtown, through the park, looking at couples spread out for the day on bath towels. Airplanes trailed banners through the blue sky over the river. 'Get out of New York State Before It's Too Late.' As I walked, I daydreamed about the man I wanted to be when I grew up: A civil rights lawyer, a doctor, someone who would 'do good' in stylish shoes. I wasn't going to make my mother proud. I was going to set her a good example.

Every so often I stopped, and sat on one of the chipping sea-green benches, took off the loafers, and stretched my toes. Kids my age passed and giggled – they always did though, no matter what, because of the hair. I'd been very young when I realized that it had its advantages: I could do almost whatever I wanted because I'd get laughed at anyway. I could wear clip-on ties, too-short suits, Sex Pistols tee-shirts, my cut-offs to Phys Ed. My crippling mutation allowed me to inhabit myself more fully than the other kids. At around that time the hair was (it could be argued) even a very slight advantage. It was trendy to be kookie, Adam Ant, that sort of thing.

Sasha's attitude was gonna change. It wouldn't exactly be the shoes, but how the shoes made me feel about myself. I knew that even then. She'd pick up on it. Maybe I'd have to come right out and ask her to the movies, but that was the worst case scenario. What I hoped was that we'd be ... thrown together by circumstance, that we'd end up together, lost on a Latin trip, stuck in an elevator ...

I decided to go play video games with the beginning of the ten bucks. I was never very good at them, but I felt I could improve. I was crossing Broadway – I could see over people's heads even then – to check if the pizza place was crowded and if there was a long line for Donkey Kong Jr., when I noticed his trademark Kangol atop a glossy cascade of Jheri curls. I spun around to get back across the street, but the light was changing and a herd of taxis and delivery vans were coming my way. I was a few steps from the traffic island where he was waiting. The shoes clacked loudly as I ran. I stopped in front of him. I didn't want to hand over the ten bucks – it was much more than I usually had – but started to get it out of the tiny coin-pocket in my cut-offs.

Escobar seemed distracted. He was looking past me, down the hill towards the park.

'Hi, Sam.'

'What's up.'

'Nice shoes. They new?'

'Not very.'

He was acting different. More distracted. Maybe he wanted some conversation? I kind of did. I had the urge to tell him about Sasha, to ask his advice.

'Give me 'em.' He said it like someone was prompting him, like he had a receiver in his ear, like in *The Conversation*. He kept looking over his shoulder, looking all around. He wasn't usually so cautious. There were some old ladies and a drunk on the island with us. I looked to them, but they ignored us. They probably thought I was buying pot off him.

'Come, on, man.' The light changed. I considered running, but I was too chickenshit.

'Give me your fucking shoes.' He was really worked up. I though he was going to cry. I didn't bend down. I stepped on the heels and kicked the shoes toward him. He didn't pick them up or even look at them.

When the light changed I turned back toward the park, the

way I'd come, in the brand new white tube socks that Janet, in a blip of maternal concern, had bought me at Harry's. A doorman in the entrance of the Apthorp called out, 'You gonna let him get away with that?' And cackled.

I kept walking, past the poster in front of St. Paul's ('Christ died for you. What are you doing for him?'), past the trees that manage to grow in dirt squares cut out of the sidewalk, past girls and boys, on roller skates, in high-top sneakers, in loafers, in jazz shoes. And I didn't try again for years. I never tried to be anything I wasn't. Contrary to popular belief, this was not a good thing. To thy own self be true and all that crap. Nope, dear: it's healthy to believe in things, to hope, to delude oneself as necessary on the way. You have to. You have to think: I am a great this, I am a wonderful that. You have to think that from twelve at the very latest, because if you don't you'll have nothing in the bank when the truth starts to kick in. That's the only way it works.

But suppose you have a premature realization that that's what everyone else is doing too – telling themselves stories with themselves as the hero, shit they make up to store against the grand disillusionment – then you're fucked, fucked, fucked: because now you're locked out of the grand illusion too. And what about the fact that I lied and told Janet my shoes had been stolen before they were? Let's just say I became superstitious. It stopped me lying.

So: that story had no point, precisely because that was the day I threw the point away.

Oh, and I got her anyway.

* * *

St. Mary's Kafka and Film teacher Rob Hartman's diary, what he calls the 'Italic Diaries', an ongoing MS Word doc on an iBook

Operation Andromeda Van Zandt, in which I am to follow a hetero vixen student (who is pretty smart, but tends to the Marxist polemical) home from school to get the lowdown on what kind of trouble she's in. Orders from big father-figure, shithead Lew. Initially, I objected. It seemed above and beyond the call. But he laid on the sob story: first, her mom's dead; fine. And she's never had a father (big deal. Who did? But I remained 'concerned'). And then, what he called his *selfish motivation*. (See. Why didn't I just use quotes?) He's sleeping with – he actually said, 'You see Rob, I've been sleeping with –' and I held my breath: I thought, if it *is* (intensifier) Andromeda I *will* (50s-style, old-fashioned emphasis) call the authorities ... but he finished ' – her granny, Polly.' He was eager to elaborate, licked his thin, purple-blue lips. I promptly agreed to shut him up. The thought of two old people fucking makes me physically sick. Need to look into that ... Plus, truth be told, I'm considering using Andromeda as a heroine for an indie screenplay. But a high-budget job, where Natalie Portman could prove how deep she is. Told from different points of view. Maybe even her dead mother's? Maybe I've got unrealistically high hopes for this workshop I'm going to next month. For the transformative power of queer proprioceptive writing. Probably.

We sat in Riverside Park and *rapped* (re-appropriated term). She told me about some guy who lives in her building. He wrote her a story, and she's concerned it's a veiled *kiss-off* (such a cool retro expression I have to call attention to it). I was bored and regretting skipping my dentist appointment. I'm one blast away from a gleaming smile, the sixth and final session. Andromeda had put her bare feet up on the fence and started retouching her blue toenails. I mean, why buy *six* (emphasis; comic) teeth whitening sessions? Because the sixth was *free* (emphasis; comic) when you buy five. And here I was, in the Park with this *girl* (because it's a *girl* [because it's a *girl* {because it's a *girl*}]).

I took her Sartre out of her bag and read something she'd underlined. *To the extent that a pattern of conduct is defined as the conduct of a pederast and to the extent that I have adopted this conduct, I am a pederast. But to the extent that human reality can not be defined by patterns of conduct, I am not one.* (Uh … Strunk & White.) That put me in a better mood. I laughed my ass off.

'You know who you've gotta get into? Your mom.'

'Andromeda won't read mommy. Says she "wrote her". How pretentious is that?' – He has materialized out of the wine-dark river, reeking of Paco Rabanne, in a white plastic visor, cargo shorts, a yellow Cuba tee-shirt and flip-flops. It was *instant*. (I'm bored with this.) Another fucking Puerto Rican. A Puerto Rican Robert Downey Jnr.

'Where the hell have you been, Club Med?' Andromeda held the mini paintbrush over her toe, and spoke to the hot Latino number. I've never seen her look so upset, however. She usually makes this affected, aloof face. It turned pink and little white spots came out on her cheekbones.

He put his hand towards me, and looked at my crucifix. Andromeda said, 'Escobar, Rob. Rob, Federico Escobar.' She gestured from one to the other of us with her little brush, not looking up. He had a *firm handshake* (uhhhh) and he looked me in the eye.

'You know where I've been? I've been in rehab in fucking Washington Heights. They wouldn't let me out. Because I tried to kill myself. I jumped over the verandah but landed on a fucking mattress. Sprained my shoulder.' He pinched it through his tee-shirt and made a very pleasant hissing noise. He poked Andromeda. 'That was after *you* (emphatic) told me to fuck off.'

'Good idea. Blame me. Least you lost some weight.' She

131

started putting all her books back in her enormous bag. We watched in silence. And then, mercifully, *Miss Thing* (eponymous) hobbled off in her cheap high-heeled sandals with her toes splayed to protect her pedicure.

The rest is inevitable. I shouldn't indulge in writing this. I need to grade my film class's final papers. Not looking forward to that malarkey.

He stood up and walked a bit. I followed him. He climbed over a fence, and alighted on a little hill covered in cherry trees. I took the path around the fence, and only just saw him slip through an open iron door. It led into a railway tunnel, half a mile long with ceilings four storeys high. It was beautiful. Who knew that this is what the Promenade hides? Its *raison d'être* (foreign).

His voice echoed. 'This is where I live.' I couldn't see him at first. Then my pupils widened and I found him and I sucked his beautiful cock.

* * *

Handwritten by Rob, in neat, legible lines, on unruled paper

Escobar's Shoe Story: For Iowa Queer Proprioceptive Writing Workshop, August 10, 2001

The Allegory of Shoes

We sat in the dark of the Amtrak tunnel, under the Promenade: what he called 'the white verandah'. He told me a story. One day he just went off the deep end and tried to kill himself. His life was saved by landing on an abandoned sofa. His life was too literary for words, he said. He said it was an allegory. Why an allegory? Don't I know what an allegory is? Not wanting to condescend, and yet physically unable hold back the information that I have a Masters in Comp. Lit, I told him yes, I do know what an allegory is. And that this wasn't one.

Federico Escobar was a sickly child, but he liked it that way; this point must be stressed. From a very young age he understood and appreciated the extra attention his asthma afforded him. He would have preferred to be thin and sickly, but as bad luck would have it, he was a invalid of the fat and wheezy variety.

He grew up with his mother and abuelita on West 83rd Street, a few doors down from Brandeis High School. This was before and during the gentrification of the neighborhood. His earliest memory was of getting his finger stuck in a roach motel, and after that, most of what he remembers about the pre-verbal apartment revolves around sensations of stickiness: dirty linoleum, jars of face cream, coconut iceys from the man who came to the playground in summer.

At around the age of five he began to notice more. His mother, Carmen, had a series of abusive boyfriends for whom she spent – so it seemed to young Escobar – her entire life in front of a copper-tinted mirror. She was a great beauty. A large mole at the corner of her mouth, thick curls of black soft hair, the body of a girl in a beer advertisement. Abuelita used the phrase 'a great beauty' always with a forlorn and theatrical tilt of her curlered head, because she believed – and this is an opinion the grown-up Escobar has come to share – that her daughter's looks were a curse. The red phone would ring and ring and ring. There would be fights, black eyes, presents of bouquets and potted plants with little plastic signs stuck in them: #1 Mama, To the Woman I Love, etc. She had many, many boyfriends, but she was always faithful, to each in his turn.

After his grandmother retired from Woolworths his quality of life took a nose-dive. No more hanging around staring at the hamsters in the cages downstairs, no more free candy, grilled cheeses and Pepsis at the lunch counter. Abuelita got depressed, being home all day with nothing to do but watch soaps. *All My Children, Another World, As the World Turns, Santa Barbara* – these last two in schedule-conflict. This would mean a horrible anxiety, what with having to estimate the length and timing of two sets of commercial breaks, which storyline was at a more crucial stage, the risk of taking a pee. All she dreamt of was two televisions, one in the kitchen, one in the toilet.

Carmen didn't want to be in the house with her mother all day, but she wasn't about to get a job. He'd known her to only have one, waitressing, but she was fired after a month for getting too many calls. She really couldn't be blamed; her conception of herself as a great beauty kept her from being able to do anything else. She was not exactly one for self-reflection, but once she did say to him, during a lull between phone calls while smoking a joint on a lazy summer afternoon, 'It's like wearing sneakers and a dress, being like me and working at Big Stav's.' This with a high-heeled shoe hanging off her big toe, her Nair-smooth legs crossed under her on the orange pleather couch. This was her heyday, the early eighties, when Escobar was a fat teenaged fag.

Escobar didn't get to school much. Officially because of the asthma, though the real reason was that he hated it, and felt worse than a nobody. The other kids said he smelled and he probably did. He didn't bathe very often; no one bothered to remind him, and he recalls times when he was too lazy to even wipe his ass. Still, they were not unhappy days. He'd watch game shows and eat Co-Co Puffs while his beautiful mother took clothes off and put clothes on, sashayed through the apartment in high heels and lace panties, asking him what he thought looked best, discussing with him the likely ramifications that certain outfits would have for certain nights out. Escobar wished she would solicit his advice on her lovers as well as her clothes; but she didn't, and the few times he'd offered it

134

she'd rolled her eyes and told him that he did not, for some reason beyond her, understand the 'male species'. Her words stuck. Grown up and sad, the tragic outcome of 'allegorical' circumstances, he still feels that he cannot understand men, and yet he yearns to know them, to understand them, to move them.

But abuelita's presence in the house had put an end to the sad peace mother and son shared during the day. Los dos got at each other, the elder calling the younger a *puta*, the younger calling the elder – and this with good cause – a motherfucking hypocrite. It became unbearable, and as Escobar was fourteen, he decided it was high time he descended from the fourth floor walk-up to the street below.

But bear in mind that it is easy to see the past as simplified because we were more simple in it, and the now grown-up Escobar, as he relates this story, has to watch himself and not fall into the nostalgia trap. That said, he does feel that there was a different vibe in the early eighties, which he chalks up to mundane causes: there were fewer people on the Upper West Side; the drugs in common use were pot and rum, not Prozac and cocaine; the Latin culture still had a foothold, and for all their faults, they were better at enjoying life than the Jews who have since taken over.

Here Escobar takes pains to assure me that he knows the Jewish intellectual tradition is the greatest the world has known. The barbarity the Jews have suffered through the ages allows them special dispensation, and we can overlook their somewhat annoying stinginess. Still the facts stand: the Jews drove out the Hispanics. They intentionally put up walls between themselves and the Hispanics in order to break down then take over the neighborhood – when it could have been such a happy cohabitation, a flowering at the crossroads of cultures…

…back to the story. Explanations of his delinquency – psychological, cognitive, chemical – bore him; however, he knows

135

that for most people this sort of thing is very important. When he left the fold and headed out, a man, onto the streets, he had no role model. So, for the small-minded, for the unimaginative: no father-figure. His grandfather abandoned abuelita in '69, and ran off to Miami with his secretary. He'd been on the Board of Education, a real 1960s Puerto Rican Success Story. The mistress, Isabel Maria, had Cuban connections in Miami and when they got there he got an even better job in the local 'café con leche bureaucracy'. Escobar's father – always one in awe of his own father – had run off too, but in a way more befitting the times. He left lazy and hazy, could only make it halfway down the block, to an apartment in the same building as the liquor store he still runs to this day. Escobar didn't speak to him, ever, even though he passed him all the time. Escobar would see him in summer, sitting outside on a lawn chair drinking rum and cokes, or leering at mommies through the steamed-up plate glass in winter. He saw the young girls ignore his father. It still fascinates Escobar how a pretty girl can do that, why she would, when clearly she dresses to get the attention in the first place. Why is it that when she gets it she acts insulted?

Anyway, that was backstory. Here's where the actual story begins. It's the summer of 1981. Escobar is fourteen and he's been on the street since spring. He's started to look at girls, because he thinks he should, but he has no impulse to whistle, blow kisses, or grab his dick. He does wonder about them – what motivates them, in their halter tops and pink-tinted sunglasses, in their Fame sweatshirts and high-heeled boots – but it's a curiosity without desire. When a girl asks him for the time, he turns away without an answer. When she giggles and presses him, he is surprised to see himself turn around and tell her to go fuck herself. He is twice warned for loitering and twice for causing a nuisance. His mother is called into the 20th Precinct. All the cops have to pick their jaws off the floor when she shows up. A hundred fans couldn't cool the cramped room, and there are only two, in either corner. The cop who takes her to his desk has a sheen of sweat on his moustache. He positions her chair so she gets the best breeze. It blows up her hair, feathered and dyed red. Her son is headed for trouble, he tells her. He ought to be sent away to a special school where they'll straighten him out. She listens and nods. Plays it soft. Weeps. She will talk to the boy, tell him to smarten up. But at home that night, they share a six-pack of Miller and a joint and she tells him she laid it on thick, and had to think about her miniature poodle getting run over by a car to make herself cry.

As night falls, Escobar sits on the fire escape as she makes up, and abuelita fries cod. The sky goes from orange to blood-red over the rooftops spiked with clotheslines and TV antennas. It doesn't even occur to him that it might not be a bad idea to finish high school, learn a trade. Carmen comes and sits next to him. In a stoned daze, watching the evening wind down in other people's windows, he decides that he and his mother share an understanding of the world that separates them from everyone else. They're romantic pragmatists, lovelorn hustlers with no time for life's drudgery, and they know that to watch the sunset is the greatest joy of all.

His crimes start out small and stay small, the crimes of a fat kid. The first involves a stink-bomb that he throws into a local bodega when the owner calls his mom a slut in the course of asking for the fifty cents she owes. They are short on cash; his dad does a good business, but his mom has too much pride to ask for help. So Escobar mugs the boys from Collegiate. He perfects a menacing androgynous appearance with the help of Jheri curls and a Kangol. He opens up his shirt and wears big chains. In the past year he's grown thinner with drinking, and is almost handsome. He likes to stand behind the brownstone stairs and lunge out at the boys he mugs. He likes the smallest ones best, the way they step back, and twitter.

But he only robs as much as he needs too. He is ashamed of the little thrill he gets out of it, and prefers to sit on the traffic island or down on the Promenade, watching the people go by. He likes to have a snack, a Hostess cherry pie and a Dr. Pepper, and think. He reads too, constantly. His aunt Rita is a librarian and he stops into the St. Agnes branch once a week. Rita lives in a fantasy world in which Escobar is a straight 'A' student with a girlfriend who's going to be a lawyer.

That summer a new shop, Mueller's Cheeses, opens on Broadway, across from La Cardidad. This was one of the first shops the Jews opened. At first, he didn't go, and he kept to the bodegas; but the multicolored gallon jars of candy proved impossible to resist, and buoyed by having just read *Night* by Eli Weisel, he ventured in one afternoon. He was soon their best customer. He was often their only one. He bought Guava paste and queso blanco for his grandma, and gummi bears and Pop Rocks for himself. The owner, a mustached, yarmulked, dirty-collared, middle-aged man never returned Escobar's pleasantries. Perhaps he knew where he got his money; he took in about fifteen bucks a week from the Collegiate boys. But even if he did know, or even just suspected, it really should have made no difference. This is America, and every second dollar is stolen. Nonetheless, one day the ugly man out and told him to take his business elsewhere. Well, what he actually told him was that the paste and cheese were cheaper at Zabar's. But for a Jew to send business elsewhere? Anyway, the hitch was that young Escobar adored, relished, was addicted to the gummi bears the Jew sold. He did look, but there was nowhere in a twenty-block radius that sold that same kind. He started hanging around in front of the shop, insulting the customers under his breath at as they went in. His abuse was extremely catholic. To a rich old lady in furs: 'Fur is murder'. To Hasidic wives in wigs: 'It

138

works OK, fucking through sheets?' To a little boy: 'There's maggots in the marble halva.'

One spring the owner disappeared and one of his Israeli nephews materialized behind the register. Escobar had never seen anyone so beautiful. His features were even and cherubic, his eyes dark and piercing. He watched him for a few days, and when the boy noticed him, he went in and got paste, and bears, and cheese. They understood each other instantly. They became close, genuinely close, closer than Escobar had ever even dreamed of being to anyone. They could look into each other's eyes and know that the other thought the same things. Of course none of this was spoken. They stood divided by the counter and talked about books and history and what dreams meant. But never girls.

Escobar started to pay more attention to his own appearance, to trim – but not shave – his peach-fuzz moustache, to wear clean clothes. For the most part he managed. Abuelita was happy to iron and wash. It was just the shoes that posed the problem. He absolutely could not afford the right shoes, the shoes that would have completed the picture, that would make him the boy that would draw the Israeli out from behind the counter. At that time there was only one kind of shoe for a good-lookin' boy on the make. Bass brown loafers. But they cost fifty dollars, and even taking in ten rich white boys' lunch money a day, that would take a long, long time.

Escobar waited. He saved. He even stopped buying his ma her beer. But after three weeks he only had twelve bucks, and was getting desperate. He didn't have the chutzpah to ask the boy how long he was staying. It was a Saturday. Mueller's was closed, and he was hanging around on the traffic island in the middle of the Broadway Mall on 79th Street when fortune beckoned. ('This is the epiphany. Do you know what that is?' 'Of course.')

He stood in the blinding sun. It lit up the four corners of Broadway, the plastic back-to-school-display in the Woolworths window, the rainbow booze bottles in his father's storefront on 79th, the gray, grand limestone blocks that build the thick square of the Apthorp, and the sapphire-and-blood stained-glass windows of the Baptist Church. Sam Gordon Taylor, a boy he liked but nonetheless mugged habitually, stood before Escobar in Bass penny loafers that gleamed like the Chrysler building. And suddenly it seemed as if everyone on the sidewalk, crossing the street, in shops and cars even – visible through the windows of taxis – was a thin, pale-as-milk, red-headed white boy. Escobar had never noticed his face before, the symmetry of it, its wide delicacy, but he saw it now, everywhere, as Sam made his approach. He had a lovely face. Sam held his money out.

'Your shoes too.'

'How about the jacket?'

'If you don't take off your fucking shoes I'll follow you home and cut your throat.'

He watched him head back the way he came in mismatched socks. Both black, but mismatched. God, did he look pathetic. He had holes in the knees of his pants, and this was way before that was fashionable. Escobar felt a horrible wave of regret. Did the Israeli love him? Would the shoes elevate him in his eyes? He never even saw them. Escobar went home and stood on the table in front of the smoky copper mirror, twisting around to see the shoes from all different angles. They were two inches too long and looked ridiculous. He stuffed the shoes in the closet. When he went to Mueller's the next morning the ugly man was back and the boy was gone.

He asked me if I got the story and I said I certainly did. Then I kissed him, trying not to think about how he used to be really fat and hadn't always wiped his ass.

O.

Sobriety

You don't need
drugs and alcohol
to make you feel
miserable and lonely.
svz, 1986

* * *

Andromeda / Rembrandt

6/30

Granny's finally taken her hairbrush over to Lew's. Escobar's evaporated. Ed's on the Vineyard for two weeks. Sam moved out. The curtains over there are always drawn. I sit in her chair and smoke. I walk through the house picking books off shelves. *The History of Sexuality.* The more repressed you are … the less repressed you are? The Reichian thinks I should be on meds.

The swastika floating over his head. I wander into the Meaningful Closet, and try on the black and white dress she was wearing the day before she died, the one with the huge, silk-screened tulips on it. What were we doing that day? Talking about my Kafka paper, about the sex scene in *The Castle*, the one in 'little puddles of beer'. Then we went for a walk in the park. It was a cold bright winter day. It was so cold there were small icebergs in the river.

I look at myself in the smoky mirror and make the same surprised face she used to. I make the same face when I see myself as she did when she saw herself. I open the drawer under the tilted mirror. Half-looking for the Shoebox of Self-love. I'm coming around to the idea that I might just have to JUST DO IT myself.

There are two prescription bottles. She was on Prozac. My Bach starts ringing. I say Fuck because that is what I am thinking and because I assume it's Ed on the phone; he's the only person that's ever called it.

'Fuck you too.' It's Trish. 'I thought maybe we should have coffee later. Talk about the fact that you're FUCKING my boyfriend.' I hold the two orange bottles in my hand and sort of collapse on the closet floor.

'I only kiss him. I'll stop if you want. My mother was on Prozac. Is that possible?'

'What about "Beware the Corporate Pharmaceutical Complex"?'

That was a well-known piece of hers. I make it a point not to read anything she wrote but I think it's safe to assume she was anti-meds.

'Maybe she was going to write an article about the effect it had on her, or something? Anyway, I just found the bottles. I mean this is bizarre. She would have told me. She told me everything. It was a precept.' I was babbling.

'Are you seeing a shrink?'

'Some friend of Lew's. Some pervert Reichian.'

'Meet me?' She sounded concerned, actually.

I suggested that café, Edgar's, the one named after Edgar Allan Poe, on 84th, a hop skip and a jump from where he died in the gutter.

Now I can see my fucking hero out the window, in his tacky white shirt and stupid hair. He's crossing the street, right under the ledge where I've propped the twin bottles up, my diorama, my mini skyline. I called Midas and he came and looked down too (Sam hasn't been around to walk him. Me and José the Doorman are doing it). Right at the top of the subway stairs

Sam stopped, and looked up, with his hand above his eyes like the captain of a ship, then he went down to the train. He looked right at me. You can look someone in the eye from very far away. That night he stayed over I watched him sleeping till it got light. I sat on the floor next to him. I fell asleep with my head on the side of the couch. When I woke up he was sitting on the window ledge. He said, 'You'll give yourself a stiff neck.'

I'm gonna go meet Trish now. I think I'll just wear my pyjamas.

* * *

Sam / Mead

6/30

Dinner with Janet. I'm painstakingly sober. She ended up forcing her wedding rings on me, saying I should sell them, or give them to my sixteen-year-old, or shove them up my ass. The lady's got class. Stav's again. Except I was paying. It cost my whole first paycheck. Unc Sam's giving her a hard time about what he calls the *Mother and Child Reunion* – that he could abuse such a heartfelt Paul Simon song! I mean, *what the fuck* kind of threat am I? I don't want anything from her. I don't want to take her away from him. None of it makes sense to me. My boss Geraldine is a big twelve-stepper and she says I have the 'alcoholic profile'. I play along. You don't say? I pretend that she's convinced me to lay off the sauce. But it was that night with Andromeda that did me in. Not like I haven't quit drinking a zillion times before. Eventually the novelty of feeling like a stupid kid, constantly on the verge of fucking tears, wears off.

To get off the subject of Sam, who I was about to boringly deconstruct yet again, I brought up that Escobar is still in the vicinity. Janet remembered the whole saga. The shoe-stealing. The hair-dying. The Sasha-deflowering. (Sasha's hippie mom called up and tried to bond with Janet over it.)

'What rock did you find him under? Why were you looking?'

'I wasn't. This girl Andromeda told me.'

'First of all she's a *woman* – they're women now. Secondly, what the fuck kind of a name is Andromeda?'

I told her. Because I had to tell someone. I told her everything. I told her I almost slept with her. I told her I might love her. I told her she's a virgin. I told her she's called the Bellclaire twice and I can't bring myself to call back. I can't even get over there to walk Midas. 'Sixteen? That's it. That's classic. That's exactly what you need!' The alleged jubilation, however, prompted a switch from 'a light Greek white wine' to martinis.

Janet brought Stav in on it. He's got the hots for Janet and was hovering around drinking shot glasses of Ouzo and little cups of coffee that he rests on his gut. He kept whispering 'Little Andy? Little Andy?' He knows her, too. He said, 'Terrible about the mommy.'

'What?'

'Her mother killed herself a few months ago.'

'Whoa.' Janet finished her drink. 'Poor thing.'

'Shit happens.' I hated them both. Take my drink away, and I have no sense of us all being in it together. From there it got ugly. She switched to the free Ouzo. Who knew there were better years. Stav wisely retreated. I got going on Uncle Sam. Shouts were exchanged. Rings were proffered.

I'm looking at the rings now, on the white Formica surface of the Bellclaire desk. The red lights of Broadway bathe everything, every blessed corner of my garret, the powder-blue Artex walls that breathe plaster dust, the dirty empty TV screen, the little pus-colored tiles in the shower – but, inexplicably, not the desk I've been writing at, though it's next to the window. How can the white desk suck up all the light, and leave these jeweled rings looking like pull tabs on coke cans?

E-mail from Paul to Lara

7/3

------ Forwarded Message
From: Hill Schwinn <hills@sassy.com>
Date: 3 Jul 2001 11:32:57 -0700
To: Paul LeBrok <icarus123@aol.com>
Subject: re sam's supermodel

Dear Lara,

This just gets better and better. I'll pick you up at 7.

xxx Paul

Paul,

What's the emotionally intelligent way to deal with this?

Sam is seeing a teenager. Last weekend, Friday, I saw them together at that toxic Cuban Chinese place on his corner. I called and told Lara and she ran out and gave him the dog. Ha! Coincidentally, I had spotted the girl on the street last week and followed her home. She lives in the Apthorp. God, is he lazy. Anyway, I'd left a note in her lobby asking if she wanted to be in our 'Real NY Chick' thing. Nothing new, I stalk teenage girls all the time. But just now she comes into the office. She hadn't even made an appointment. She just stood at reception like the Queen of Somewhere on Something. Andromeda Van Zandt, sounds like the heroine of a bodice ripper, no? She dresses like one. I so know you don't care but she was wearing a bizarro floor-length Victorian that'd had the sleeves cut off and was held together with safety pins at the waist. And a detachable copy of *Being and Nothingness* and a pack of American Spirits.

I saw all this from my glass office with my pretzel croissant

145

hanging out of my mouth. I was thinking, you know, maybe I could do a column from her cool point of view, maybe work it up into a book – I mean if that crap you write can get published ;) – but it would be a joke, a dismantling of the cool girl and then I'd stick it to her in the end. But not until she'd blinged her way round the globe. When they showed her in, I failed to restrain myself. 'You know – I know someone you're seeing.' She's nonplussed, looks out the windows at the treetop view of Central Park. All the models do. They all say, 'Wow, what an awesome view!' I actually have a sign up that says, *Please do not mention the view.* She didn't. She asked how I knew Ed. I said I didn't know *Ed.* I knew Sam. She said who's Sam. She stared off into space. I think she may be on dope or something. What was she looking at? My Robert Doisneau poster? They love that too. My find-of-the-season fuzzy purple scarf that was flung over the filing cabinet?

Then she decided to cut the shit and laughed and said 'Ohhh. That was *you* who saw us. Oh Oh Oh. Ha ha ha. I'm not seeing him.'

I told her that was really good news. (I really couldn't control myself.) I told her she looked smart and that she could probably make it as a model. And that Sam Taylor is very bad news. He has Bad Faith. I asked her if she had gotten up to that part yet? That's all I remember from Intro to Recent European Philosophy – Bad Faith – but I wasn't just showing off. I mean. I was, but I also meant it.

She said she was past Bad Faith. I told her he was an alcoholic. She yawned then smiled at herself yawning. She has a great Colgate smile. Honestly, she reminded me of him. They sort of look alike.

Keith came in with the Polaroid. And here's the best part – I assumed she would continue to exude the same kind of bookish snottiness on camera, but she didn't. She transformed. She

146

became really lovely, placid. Queenly. It was kinda sickening. But I'm used to it.

When she'd left, Keith called her a *tall glass of water*. Which is, like, the biggest compliment he can give. Giselle isn't even a tall glass of water. He sat on my desk, called up Elite and got her an appointment for tomorrow. He says he's going to put her on the September cover, and suggests that we run a story about her. He loves the name. OK, gotta go look at shoes.

xx Hill

* * *

Sam / Mead

7/3

Feminine Sexuality 1st draft

I make Barnes & Noble back into Sasha's old ballet school. It's easily done. I can point them to the café and Self-Help and the toilet, and as I do a slow-motion tornado blows through, ripping out eyeballs, walls, fitted shelving, books, and then settles everything in the past, rearranged as it was 1981. Have you noticed that we are surrounded by celebrities these days? When I was growing up, normal people lived in this neighborhood; our life-size dramas didn't seem so shamefully small. Gwyneth Paltrow, who was in Sasha's ballet class, was then just called Gwyn, and one of us. What did distinguish her was that she had this awful fucking manner. She used to laugh at my punk tee-shirts and called me Dead Kennedy. I once heard her whispering to some of the other girls that I *lived* in the park. I gave her the finger. She wasn't even pretty. I'd sit on the bench with my back to the wall of mirrors, facing the barre. The old paned windows went all the way up to the thirty-foot-high ceiling. They kept them open. You hardly feel that anymore, that feeling of wide-open windows and the muggy street air. The very air is different now. Inside, outside.

There was a photographer who lived across 84th. His spot lights would shine into the room, and we'd see his umbrellas and light reflectors and all the other paraphernalia these guys use. In the mirrors the flashes would blind the girls. In winter it was already dark at four in the afternoon, and the girls were jumping in that stiff ballet way, smiling, because that was part of it; and when his lights came in, they screamed and ran and hid under the stairs like a herd of gazelles. They thought the photographer was a paedophile taking pictures of them with a telephoto lens. The old duck-footed teacher and I – he loved me, we laughed at them.

It was mostly when Sasha had a recital, or when we were just getting along very well, that I'd go and sit in. I'd read. (All that I read, I read because I thought the titles were cool. I had a book called *Feminine Sexuality*, by Lacan. I had *Naked Lunch*.) Or write. I wrote poetry then.

I wish my hands would fall off.

The class pianist, the accompanist ... what a noble calling. The tupperware-full-of-cabbage-soup-bringing, daydreaming polite wino moved her feet heavily from pedal to pedal, banging out ballet music, waltzes, mazurkas. She broke my heart. The first time I used the word *pathos* it was about her.

When they announced that the school was closing, Sasha took to the streets, mad. She looked nice very angry. She was always nearly bald, her hair like a boy's, and she had very large expressive dark eyes. She liked to yell about everything.

'I'll show them. Hell no, we won't go.' Her mother was a civil rights lawyer. I watched as Sasha made a pathetic giant sign to hold up, in protest at the school's impending transformation. First she had to spend twenty bucks on markers, poster board, glitter. We stood in the aisles of Menash the Overpriced

148

Stationers. When I was fed up looking in the tall glass cases at the gold fountain pens, with nibs like the Chrysler building, I got to bothering her about her doomed-to-failure stand. I followed her home and sat drinking her dad's Grolsch beers and bothered her some more. I told her I thought it was progress, a good idea; a big bookstore would be nice. Our old local, Shakespeare and Co. was, as I put it then, 'a den of elitism'.

We were in her parent's big living room, in a haunted building on 81th Street and Broadway. 219. Go in sometime, even just to the lobby. It's too cold. And if you make it into an apartment (over the years I've had three girlfriends who lived there) there are scratching noises inside the walls. Usually the bedroom walls.

I recall Sasha sitting with her legs out the window, wearing white boxer shorts and an undershirt. She lived on the second floor. I pretended I was going to push her out. 'Progress. Progress, dear.' Her parents were in the Hamptons for the weekend. It was this time of year. We were both virgins. We went into her parent's bed. Two fourteen-year-olds. Non-similar people. Investigations into non-similarity. I liked to watch her face in close-up, the art movie of her mutable feelings. She was walking through the apartment afterwards, crying, naked, into the brown kitchen, in search of one of her dad's beers. I felt like I owned her.

So.

Dear Andromeda. They blocked up the thirty-foot windows with six-inch leaded squares of glass, sealed them right into the walls. And they tore out the old wooden floorboards, softened by generations of little girls' feet. And they sold the industrial fans that stood in the corners of the high rooms. They ripped out the ceiling roses (what Janet calls 'ceiling tits'), and now you can buy them in antique shops for ten bucks a pop.

When the place was finally finished in 1984 I ran in, asking for a book I'd seen some *dude* in a motorcycle jacket reading on the 1 train. *Death on the Installment Plan*. The clerk typed the title into the putty-colored prototype of the Dell I use today. I thought it was only a question of him giving me directions. How could they not have every book ever written? It wasn't even in the 'system'.

And now I'm him. I disappoint everyone who can be disappointed by the lack of a book. I can tell who won't get what they want as they approach my station.

* * *

Granny, on a brown paper bag, left with Lew's doorman on Bleecker Street

7/6

Comrade,

You can too be too old for some things. Waiting in your lobby. Ashamed in front of the doorman. Counting the squares of gray marble on the floor: 46. And white: 38. Missing: 7. Dinner with Andromeda unmitigated disaster. She got drunk, like her mother used to. When she was little, at what Sophie called our 'summit lunches' at Florent, A. would be so polite and quiet, eating all her blood sausage. Sophie would drink champagne endlessly, rant, and be miserable. I'd put them in a cab on 12th Avenue. I felt sorry for her, but what could I do, call social services? I should have. I was back at the Apthorp, blanketing the duck in Cooper's marmalade. She asked me what I was doing there. I tried to explain how you and I decided we were being selfish, and that I ought to be spending more time with her. Her response: she unpinned a falling-apart dress of my grandmother's and sat on the kitchen table, in Sophie's orange bra, and drank red wine. She says she's trying to see how fast she can get through Sophie's reserves. When she was drunk,

150

which didn't take long, she got going on my charade. She said that ever since Sophie died, my attention to her is 'a charade.' I think I said something like I felt an obligation towards her. She screamed at me and began quoting Sophie's miserable aphorisms. Something about a supermarket with beds.

I left after she held a lit candle in my face, as if she wanted to burn my eyes out. I'm sitting here like a little girl who's run away from home. I have a little case and a basket. I'm going out for a bottle of wine for us. I will manifest you. On my return, standing in the doorway, in your red Che tee-shirt.

x P

P.S. – I still think your idea about writing a book about her, in which some great wire or whatever it was connects her à la Calder to the fate of the city, is not great. She isn't as important as her hormones are telling her she is. Right?

* * *

Rob's Italic Diaries

7/14

Escobar and I begin another day arguing about our *love* (important concept). Me saying – how can someone who has slept with hundreds of men, been raped countless times, seen his own mother's life destroyed by *Romance* (ditto-ish), persist in such abject stupidity? He asserts we're soulmates, because we can have this kind of conversation. I correct him. He calls me 'a stingy Virgo'. Finally I have to ask him to leave. I have to work. I'm applying to do a PhD at Santa Cruz, in the History of Consciousness – I've yet to break it to him. Plus I really want to get to this Jivamukdhi yoga class tonight.

He goes, but then about an hour later I happen to look out the window, down the Slope to the skyline and there he *still* (emph) is, on a sweaty stoop across the street. He looks up and waves. He's drinking from a Styrofoam cup of coffee. He's so *old school* (knowing) he won't even go to Starbucks. He calls them *fascistas* (Spanish). But I couldn't help admiring him out there. His buzzed scalp under the plastic visor, his big arms showing through the mesh tee. The skyline that rose behind him: it looked like the skyline twenty years ago, smoggier, more alive. Even the heat was nostalgic. Heat that asks for a fan, not an air conditioner; for a Rolling Rock, not a Volvic.

He was standing in front of a blue graffitied van and I was sitting there at my good boy's desk, trying to grade Trish's paper on the 'Hunger Artist' with a fucking hard-on. I went down. The whole thing was getting too goddamn cinematic: it was even starting to *rain* (stress). The door of the laundry van was not locked. We got in. Rolled around on hotel linens. I couldn't come. I was thinking about a pummeling from fucking Mr. Clean (Christ do I need to go back to therapy)... Everything was right, the hot van, the soiled sheets ... except me, of course, as usual. After the van, I kvetched about this. E. cajoled me onto the F train and I found myself on Coney Island, on the boardwalk amid the throng. We *contemplated* (self-conscious about the touchy-feely connotations) the Atlantic Sea. I told him I wasn't up to it.

'You *are* (emph) it.' He stands behind me and put his hands in my pits.

'I want a *clean* (joke to self. 1979. Brooklyn. My mother mops the no-wax floor. Mr Clean stares at me from the bottle; he's also on a commercial on TV. I love him because he takes care of my mother and he's magic and lives in a plastic bottle and he wears earrings. He's also strong and incredibly good-looking. No one can measure up to Mr Clean. No one should *dare try* [foreboding comic book voice]) house and a retirement fund.' I whine.

'Oh my God, me too!' He leans his head on my neck and

speaks to my ear, 'Anyway, are you happy? Estoy muy contento.' He kisses my neck and whispers, 'What you gotta learn, *mon ami* (his foreign language), is to just fuck it!' He dances down the boardwalk singing *Fuck it, Fuck it, Fuck it! Fuck it Fuck it, Fuck it!* (lyrics) A cha cha. Under the boardwalk I finally let him fuck me. I let myself think of Mr. Clean. My goddamn gypsy! It's been a little over a year, since Mel.

The future stretches before us: little more than baby talk and profanities. When I'm not with him I think it's all I'll *ever* (dead serious) want; but when we are together, and not making love I get dead bored.

* * *

Andromeda / Rembrandt; hard to read, due to interlocking red circles from the bottom of a glass of red wine

7/15

Having picture taken tomorrow. Am going to be in *Sassy* magazine. The 'Real People' story, i.e., not models. This Hillary keeps calling me up wanting to know if I'm 'psyched.' I think she would positively expire if I said no. Tomorrow someone from Elite is going to meet me there. Then there's something with some photographer I've never heard of but is famous ('don't I remember' those seventies-style overlit CK ads that were banned as child pornography? Can't say I do). The same team (this guy and Calvin) has learned its lesson and is looking for a new face to put in some new, more wholesome ad campaign. Trish said two things at Café Edgar Allan Poe. One: given that my mom had never tried to kill herself before and that she did it in such a 'wacky' way, it was almost certainly 'Prozac Induced Psychosis' (PIP for short), and two: I'd be the biggest fucking moron ever to walk the face of the planet if I didn't get in there and try to milk the modeling thing for all it's worth. She called

153

it a 'no-brainer.'

Pacing around the apartment wanting to talk to someone. Someone who would tell me whether I should do it or not. I broke down and called Sam (OK, for the third time) at the Bellclaire. A short depressing conversation. He said not to call him when I'm drunk. I said I wish I'd never met you. He said 'The feeling's mutual, dear,' and fucking hung up on me.

I went into my mom's bedroom and stood under that reproduction tapestry of the unicorn from the Cloisters and cut my hair, right to the level of my chin. It looks like it got caught in some machinery and cutting it was the only way to get it out.

Then I tried Ed on his mobile. I'm getting determined. I told Ed he had to do the job Sam wouldn't and Escobar said is long overdue. (No, I don't follow 'girl code'. No, I don't fucking care that he's Trish's boyfriend.) Ed mumbled into his mobile – I could hear the tinny engines and screaming women of GTA in the background. I saw him in his clean and organized Dr. Father's beach home, his bare tanned toes on rugs white as vanilla ice cream. He said I should be patient and enjoy the gifts I have or some shit. I think Deepak Chopra was at their house last week. I was looking at the triangle pattern on my Persian rug. Anti-representation. Islamic art is anti-representational. I was looking out the window at people with their forks going into their mouths. I was looking at my blue toenails and the lights like red streamers going up Broadway. What's all the fuss about fucking? I hung up on him.

Where's my old fucking conviction? I wouldn't have set foot in *Sassy* six months ago. Or have kept meeting Ed between classes to let him kiss my tit above the nipple under the fall-out shelter sign. Thank God it's the summer vacation. This is so much fun.

Now I'm crushing a Ritalin with the back of a monogrammed spoon. AVZ (Alice). It actually has a devil's face on the handle.

It does: it has horns. Someone bought a set of these? These were a wedding present? I'll put them in my trousseau. Now I'm all pepped up, feelin' chatty, nowhere to go.

P.I.P.

R.I.P.

PIPRIP

M.

Confessional

The Romantic
Equally the Platonist believe
Before the eye can focus
The heart must.

To believe otherwise
Is to transform life
Into a supermarket
With beds.
    svz, 1984

* * *

Sam / Mead

7/23

The Black Eye 1st draft

Last night after work (a week passes, you lie in your polyester sheets at the Bellclaire looking at a shrinking moon) I went out to La Caridad with Geraldine and her girlfriend April. Such *nice* people. They give self-help a good name. Say they've been *empowered*. Once were weak but now are strong. Have learned to love themselves *unconditionally*. Don't I believe in unconditional love? Sing along now. *The kind of love I deserve? The kind I want to return?* Fuck you, Musical Youth featuring Donna Summer.

Geraldine says what I need is a man. Huh? April says a woman. And that Geraldine is being heterophobic. Either way this man or woman will show me what's what. I'm not holding up my end of the repartee. In the bathroom I stick my head under the cold tap then spend five minutes staring in the mirror. I look like Howdy Doody. I look like Kenneth Fucking Branagh. When I get back to the table, my friend the waiter puts a Presidente in front of me and unscrews the cap. We all watch the little vapor-cloud in silence, like Papa Smurf might appear in it. Then I ask him to take it away. I tell him I'll pay for it anyway.

I left April and Geraldine and headed back to the SRO. I was planning on writing and not sleeping, which is what I've been doing for weeks, when I found Janet slumped in a mauve pleather recliner in the lobby. She had her Gucci sunglasses on. I said 'What do you want?' and walked past her. She stood up and followed me into the bright elevator. On the wall there are plastic pockets with postcard ads for cologne and Broadway shows, and Stav's to-go menus. Unwashed, backpacking, blonde dread-locked, body-pierced, Swedish or maybe Dutch teenage girls in push-up bras got on and off at every floor. Giving us, me, the eye. Me: gay, looking down, fingering postcards. With my mom.

When we got into my room, she took off her sunglasses and had this big black eye. First prize black eye. Blue-ribbon black eye. I think I made a noise like someone was pouring alcohol on a wound.

'Shit, mom.' That very rare, genuine usage.

I hit my father once, after he hit her. Very clear memory of her head smacked sideways, a right angle to her shoulder, her red hair sticking to her neck. I'd wanted to hit him for years but that day ... The sight of her eyes. The circuit breaker above her head. I threw all my weight – which could not have been more than 145 pounds – into his fucking face. He didn't spin around as I hoped, and land splat! on the wall with his arms splayed. Just tucked his chin down for a second, then looked up, with his best psychotic smile. I'd thought it was reserved for women. My mother said, 'No, Gordon. Don't.' He broke my nose with an open palm. And apologized endlessly. For years. I've always told myself that in an ass-backwards way I *did* save her, because she left him after that. In retaliation for his hitting me. Janet sat down at the Formica desk and picked up the page I was writing. 'The Story of my ...'

'Leave it.' I took it out of her hand and turned it over.

Over countless cigarettes and tooth glasses of Sterling Sapphire which she had in her Gucci handbag, I listened about Uncle Sam. It's my fault. She didn't tell him about the thousand dollars she lent me. And it wasn't about the Money, it was the Principle, I have to understand: he grew up with less than nothing, eating pebbles off the roadside in fucking New Hampshire ...

My father was awful to her and everyone in between has been too. And to see her, to hear her, her brashness – everyone thinks she's such a hard-ass. Takes no shit. What a joke.

I have no inclination to tell her to pull herself together. I have no curiosity over why she repeats her mistakes. I can hear rational Paul and rational Lara: they would blame her. She's not some welfare mother with no alternative. Thing is, if she isn't being hurt she doesn't feel alive. It's not an epiphany. I've thought this before. I'm less horrified at the thought than I once was.

After a while, Janet drinks enough to pass out, which was her stated aim. Her phone rings and I press all the buttons at once and say, 'Fuck you. I'll fucking kill you.' Then I shove it under the mattress because I don't know how to hang it up.

In the middle of the night I am writing, listening to her familiar, uneven breathing, when the house phone rings. I don't want to pick it up. I know who it is. I try to unplug it from the wall but the cord is attached. I can't get it to stop ringing. It's a very loud, old-fashioned ring. Janet moans, 'Hon, Pick it up!' then curls on her side in the dip in the bed, like a shrimp.

In my mind I'm still where I was in my story, watching a crowd of trees climb over that wall in Central Park. Giants dressed as trees.

I didn't answer the phone. I picked it up and held it to my ear. 'This is the manager of Duane Reade, on 60th Street.'

'Sixtieth and what?' I'm … suspicious? You can't be too careful. Jesus.

'Between Fifth and Lexington. I have a young lady here who says you would be willing to pay for a fragrance she tried to steal. I'm sorry to bother you.'

The whole time I'm waiting for a cab on deserted Broadway, then riding through the curvy, lamplit Park, I'm thinking about how I can extricate myself. The idea that I'm responsible for Andromeda is clearly the child of the idea that I'm responsible for Janet. But I still half-believe I can help them. I roll the window down and lean way out. I might have said no. But then they would have called the police.

The absurdly young driver is smoking a joint rolled in red paper, and after eyeing me for a while, he offers it to me through the grate.

'Why is it puce?'

'Cherry flavour, it's all they had.'

I never said I wasn't smoking pot.

Bit by bit, tree by blurred tree, the clanks of the cab, the lights of buildings rising on all sides of the park, the coughs from the benches, I get that old gargoyle feeling. I come to life. I'm on the way to rescue my Andromeda from the sea dragon of Duane Reade. And Janet in the room with her black eye.

The cashier knows what I'm there for, and points me toward the back with a look I interpret as spiritually advanced detachment. Aren't all retail employees more adept at sizing people up than even the best writer, with their stupid agendas?

It's clear what I'm here for. This must happen at least two or three times a week. I listen to my squeakers on the linoleum, the rows of ugly candy-colored crap spring out like a parade of faces in a convex mirror: baby wipes, toothpaste, eyelash curlers, hair gel, soap scum remover, rubbers. Endless, layers deep, probably the length of Central Park if you lined them all up. Of all the things she might steal, why toilet articles? I stop for a moment and make myself look. I'm superstitious: I close my eyes and think, whatever my eye lands on will tell me what the hell's in her. I open them and I'm face to face with a life-and-a-half-sized woman selling Revlon lipstick, her blood-colored mouth half open, her lips and eyelashes so full of goop a fly would get stuck in them.

Next to the children's cough suppressant section, there's a fireproof door with a red and white sign: EMPLOYEES ONLY. To my dismay, I give it my joke knock. Shave and haircut… The door floats open. An Indian woman looks at me over her *Enquirer*. A mountain range of tabloids, paper plates, pens, folders and a ten pack of Fritos snakes across the desk. Next to her there's an open window one foot from a brick wall so grimy it's growing hair. Andromeda's back is to me, and the door. All I can see are her long, tanned legs, which have cuts and bruises on them, her catch-me-fuck-me sandals, and her big yellow hat.

The manager says, 'She's gonna get herself into trouble. It's inevitable. Talk some sense into her.' She shows me the palms of her hands and smiles.

'Thank you. I will.' I pick up Andromeda's heavy book bag and then, without thinking about it, I pull the *stupid fucking hat* off her head.

'Wait.' The manageress throws a small, red and black shrink-wrapped box, about the size of a pack of cigarettes. It hits me in the chest. Paloma Picasso.

On the way out I stop in the shaving cream section. 'Hang

160

on.' I pick a can off the shelf and study it. 'Vanilla?' I put it back. Pick another up, look it over, return it to the shelf. She flips her sandal against the sole of her foot. Packs her cigarettes. 'No. Wait. What about this one – Edge Gel? You see, it's incredible, actually. It comes out gel, but it turns to foam! Ah ha! Barbasol? Classic, masculine ... cheap ...'

'Don't be mad at me.'

Andromeda: do you know your voice completely changes depending on what you're talking about?

'I'm not mad.' I'm not mad that I have to go to work in five hours and listen to my boss tell me I'm a fag. I'm not mad that Lara's boyfriend keeps showing up everywhere to tell me what an asshole I am. I'm not mad that my stepfather beats my mother. I'm not mad because I have not had a drink since last we met. I'm not mad that I lack the authority to write a decent fucking line. Not mad at all. All told, it's sixty-three bucks at the register. It's the middle of the night on 60th between Fifth and Madison. The air is wet. There is nothing, nothing, no one, no one. Beautiful emptiness. An empty yellow dumpster with nothing in it but a layer of concrete dust.

Andromeda's yammering. 'I'll pay you back for real this time. I'm expecting a windfall. My mom's most accessible book, *The Queen of Nothingness* – it's been added to like fifty freshmen English lists. We – I even have an accountant. The royalties will be massive.'

'Andromeda.'

'You always say my name when you're being condescending.'

'I'm concerned.'

She chants: 'Condescending ... concerned. Symbolic ... significant.'

'I've no idea what you're talking about.'

We walk a few blocks downtown on deserted Fifth Avenue and stop near the entrance to the Pierre Hotel, in front of that jewelry shop La Vieille Russe. In business hours there are Fabergé eggs and diamonds in the window. Lara and I went to brunch at the Plaza a few times and she liked to look in the windows afterwards. She actively pitied herself that I hadn't given her a diamond. Anyway, at night, they take them out but leave the spotlights on, shining on abandoned little velvet thrones, bare, neck-shaped necklace displays. Across the street, Ivana's gilded horse is frozen in the Plaza fountain. I raise my arm to hail an invisible cab.

'I'm gonna walk through the park. I need some air. I've been stuck behind Duane Reade all night. It took me a long time to get up the nerve to call you.' She passes by a semicircle of limestone with a bronze plaque sunk in it. It tells of – who knows – some dead guys: firemen burned to a crisp, soldiers in some squabble, long forgotten. The Franco-Prussian War or some such. History, life is always full of random things. They can be symbolic. They can be meaningless. Sometimes they can be symbolic and meaningless. What is *symbolic*? What is *meaning*? I haven't been stoned in ten years.

She enters the park and disappears from my vision for about five seconds. I run in after her. I follow her around the pond, beside a hill of schist. The pear trees and miniature willows are stooped and ashen in the lamplight. Andromeda's sandals make a clop clop. I am holding her hat. Her skirt swishes from side to side. Once, on a sunny day, I saw a businessman jerking off into his trench coat while he stared at two oblivious secretaries lunching on wraps. That was when I was twenty-five. I was on my way to meet someone at the *New Yorker*, to talk about the last story they didn't publish. My cynicism was settling in, like an auto-immune disease. It coincided with the invention of wraps. *Coincidence, or something more sinister?*

The plan was to walk twenty yards behind Andromeda and escort her the whole way but not say a word. I didn't know what the hell to say. She lights up under the glow of a park lantern, her half a head of hair that she'd obviously cut herself, glowing like a purple bulb. She lights up: her neck, her hair, her arms through the loose-knit shawl, then fades out. She flashes, slowly, a billboard of herself. Or a lighthouse. Sometimes when she goes over a little swell, through a tunnel, or around a corner, I lose sight of her and hold my breath until she reappears.

The tan dirt in the playing field near the GM building – of late, the Trump Hotel – is unnaturally light: dry, funny stuff that stains the white soles of your sneakers forever. It's dry, but it's slippery. Once, I sat here in the bleachers and wrote Lara a Self-Conscious Love Letter while watching her real estate team play a bunch of meatball hedge-fund managers in a corporate baseball game. When I married her, I thought I was the most honest man alive.

I keep thinking moving shapes and sounds in trees are men ready to jump out at my charge, but I'm ready. I have a coil in my foot. Everything is of great significance and concern. I start to laugh. Andromeda turns back and waves and smiles at me with a flutter. She has a very true and trusting smile. A big healthy smile. Someone whose mother really loved her.

The little white diamond lights are on in the dead trees outside Tavern on the Green. In the lit-up conservatory there's a bald man vacuuming. It's the wrong time to be vacuuming. It's the middle of the night. Andromeda's cold. She holds her shawl tightly around her. You'd think that in those silly shoes and slip, she'd strut or stumble, but part of what is remarkable about her, I muse, is her composure. Furthermore, back in the day, she would have been considered *exactly* the right age for me. What with my life-experience and vast accumulated wisdom.

Sheep Meadow is so lushly green it looks fake. Like a huge square of Astroturf in the middle of the dusty trees. The buildings of the East Side and downtown rise up in layers, purple under black, red under black, blue, rose. As she emerges from the pagoda on 72nd Street and I enter it, Harrison Ford and some dude walk in with a black standard poodle. They are both smoking cigars and turn around to watch Andromeda. When they turn back they see me, and HF gives me a look as if to ask if I'm a psycho, so I put my hand in the shape of a gun and say '*Top Gun*, right?'

At the bottom of the hill she goes into that little wood gazebo down from the ring-road. The one on the lake. I stand outside a minute, then go in. A bench on either wall. She sits.

'Can I see my perfume?'

I take it out, look at it, flip it around in my hand, then throw it as far as I can. It's a superhuman throw. We hear it falling through the leaves in the Ramble, on the other side of the lake.

'You remember those two teenagers who killed that homeless guy? That was here.' I can barely hear her.

I'm standing by the door, or the space that stands for one, with my back to her, looking across the lake. I say, 'Oh yeah. Very much your thing. Very symbolic. Elemental. She was sick with love. He was sick with hormones. The old drunk, well – that was pure karma, just the story talking – it takes its victims too. But so what, eh?'

Actually, I read a far-fetched article by her mom in *New York Magazine* about it. Something about 'bodies without boundaries'. She managed to tie in *the geology* of the Park. I wait for Andromeda to say something, but when she doesn't I turn around and look at her in the corner of the bench, her knees pulled to her chest, the shawl around them.

'You look cold.'

'What are you really thinking about?'

'Your mother.'

'What do you think she was like?'

'I don't know. I have no fucking idea. You tell me.'

The Hall of Human Evolution

Your mother, Sophie Van Zandt, was on the board of 'lots of places.' I imagine this to mean the Museum of Modern Art, the Metropolitan Museum, the Frick, and the New York Historical Society.

This story is about the time you went with her to a gala at the Museum of Natural History. She picked you up early at school, so you could help her get ready. You were very excited, sitting outside the principal's office, waiting for her. You felt like you were more important then the other kids on the bench: you were being taken out of school on official Feminist Business, not because you had diarrhea or head lice or something.

She came in wearing her long maroon coat. It had a tasseled fringe that swept the floor. It looked like the pelt of a mythical animal, a deep red unshorn sheep. She had on her little pink wire-rimmed Sean Lennon glasses and her hair was short and bleached. She patted you on the head, blew a kiss to the secretary, and you were free.

There is a mural in front of the school, a rainbow, and what the artist (who signed it, Melvin) imagined might be on the other side: an ice-cream cone, children of various shades, an open storybook, pea-green fields and purple mountains' majesty. 78th, between Amsterdam and Columbus. Across the street, the brownstones are expensive and sandblasted. They are all brown, except one, which is a sort of twilight blue. It's a nice street. That's the nicest house. You'd much rather have a house than an apartment. You'd like to live in that house.

First you go to the supermarket, to Red Apple, the one that isn't there anymore. Your mother stands over the steaks and calculates: she'll need about fifty. She is uncharacteristically nervous. She fills the cart. You stand back watching. Some delivery boys snicker behind you. Then she says 'For Christ's

165

sake Andromeda, give me a fucking hand,' and you join her, grabbing steaks two at a time and throwing them in the cart. They tell you one of the boys will deliver them in half an hour.

At home, you wait at the kitchen table. It's nearly summer and the window is open. Turquoise wool and knitting needles are laid out, all ready. You take a container of Breakstone's cottage cheese with pineapple out of the fridge and sit down and start to eat it. She circles around the table, smoking. She leans out the window and ashes her cigarette down into the courtyard. After several disapproving, over-the-shoulder looks at your dinner she says,

'You know what kind of life that cow had?' (You were a still little confused about what was OK to eat. The two of you had only been vegan four days.)

'It might not be dead.' You glanced at the expiration date.

'Please, *it*. That's a thousand different cows you're eating. All in lightless prisons. Force-fed hormones to make them produce more milk, and when they aren't making enough – Hello Big Mac.'

You pushed it away. She put it in the garbage and handed you a jar of Skippy and a carrot.

'That's a girl.'

It was better anyway.

'This is taking for-fucking-ever.'

Across the way Mrs. Kasbaum's husband Werner, who wasn't dead yet, was screaming at Mrs. Kasbaum that she was a useless bitch, as usual. He drank a lot of beer. Pabst. Your mother called out the window, 'Say one more word to her and I'll call the fucking police, you fucking Nazi.' She slammed it shut.

Actually, they both survived a concentration camp. But he was a bastard.

It got dark. Waiting is hard. Your mother quoted herself.

166

'Don't think of it as delayed gratification / think of it as immediate suffering.' She took two shots of gin in a row. Cork Dry. She ordered it special from Escobar's sleazy father's liquor store. It was her favorite.

You were really excited about the gala. It was for the opening of the new Hall of Human Evolution. You were desperate to see it. You were sort of a nerd at that time, and had read about the debate over whether we are descended from Neanderthals or just *homo sapien sapiens*. When this happened, six years ago, they were saying Neanderthals had died out. You doubted this very much and always thought they had interbred. If animals can, they will, you figure. The funny part is your mother stole your idea, went to the library one afternoon and wrote something for the Tuesday science section in *The Times*. And lo and behold: six months later it turns out they think you were probably right. The incident established Sophie as one of our foremost thinkers in evolutionary theory.

Anyway, the galleries were to be transformed, and you were dying to see – would they have thrown the see-through plastic woman into the trash, the one with the bright internal organs, the veins like spiders, and fat the color of daffodils? Or would she be stuck in a corner, or still there, shoved somewhere in the new exhibit? You had a dress all picked out too, but your ma said – better wait till you'd made hers to put yours on.

By the time the delivery boy arrived, steering the cart right into the kitchen, your mom had had about ten mini-martinis. She was so excited she gripped his forearm as he put the bags on chairs and helped get everything on the table. She gave him a ten-dollar tip. He was so weirded out he forgot the Red Apple cart in the kitchen.

The steaks were three deep, and each pack had two in it: a mountain, a volcano, of toxic white Styrofoam, glistening plastic wrap and red-and-light-grey meat. You poked your

167

fingers through the shrink-wrap and pulled the steaks out, then hammered them on the table with the tenderizer so they were flattened and wider.

Right after you'd got going she said 'Wait,' and ran into the living room. When she came back, Laurie Anderson was singing 'Sharkey's Day'.

Do I know that song?

Yes.

But when you tried sewing the steaks it didn't work. They kept ripping. The big knitting needles went right through. She said, 'All those wholesome years of knitting at Steiner! What a total waste.' (Polly had sent your mother to the Steiner school.) 'The poor things have no muscle tone. They don't get to walk around. Imagine if we didn't get to walk around. Imagine if we had to stay in here all the time.'

At that moment you felt like you *did*. You remember thinking, 'That's weird. I know I leave every day. But I can't remember it. I'm always here.'

It wasn't a bad feeling, but it was the first time you looked at what you thought, knew it was not *technically* true, but felt it as if it were anyway. If I know what you mean. You think that may have something to do with representation in art, but you digress...

Her face? Her cigarette hung out of her lipsticked mouth, she had on a pink tee-shirt with a picture of Malcolm X on it, and she was laughing. 'Go in my office and get the goddamn stapler, sweetheart. Not the little ladies' one, the one – the big mama – the staple gun!'

It worked. You stood up on the table. She held clumps of the dress in her hands and you sort of lowered the rest over her head. She had this thing about it not being 'age-inappropriately short'. When you were done, she insisted you add another hem of steaks. 'Only just above the knee. I'm not fucking twenty.'

She put her long velvet coat over it, and you left.

It was a beautiful night. You were happy in your blue silk dress.

'You do know about the lives of silkworms, Andromeda.'

You knew she was going to give a speech, and were happy about that, too. You liked the way people sat rapt when she spoke. You liked that they knew she was your ma. You held hands on the way, and walked up by the Planetarium (the old one) because she didn't want to be right on time. Have I ever been to one of these things? Apparently everyone is pleased out of their minds with themselves, and all dressed up. They think that if it were not for them, sponsors and purveyors of Science and Reason, we would all go to hell in a hand-basket.

Since most of the men there were ancient, your mom didn't get the kind of attention she usually did. Instead it was more civilized: 'Ah, so this is your delightful daughter' stuff. They were in tuxedos, the fat old ladies were in their glittery gowns, and there was a big spread of food. You specifically remember a spectacular platter of Nova in the shape of a fish. Obviously it was off-limits. You had a ginger ale and your mother drank about a bottle of champagne.

Then they let you through to the new exhibit.

It was no longer dark and mysterious.

The old recorded voice from the distant dark ceiling was gone. The thin beam of light on the plastic woman was gone. The woman was gone, and in her place they had dramatized The Stages in the Evolution of Man. Put him in these really dumb poses. His arm around the waist of the gal, like they were at a fucking drive-in or something, the both of them covered in hair, with dog snouts.

Your mother patted your head and said 'Poor thing, they took your plastic lady.' She walked to the stage. There wasn't a stage, just a little black platform. No one sat. She cleared her throat and waited for silence. You have to confess: the instant she revealed it you felt sort of proud. You made it, after all. It had not occurred to you that it might be offensive. She often 'exemplified' her points in similar ways, with masks, with props. That was her style. She was a performer. You imagined you would be congratulated roundly afterwards on your handiwork.

You could hear shoes shuffle on the brand new shiny purple- and black-flecked floor. A reproduction of Lucy's skeleton – her jaw wide open – was just behind your mother. You can't remember what she said or how it played out. You're sorry. You're not a good storyteller. You can't remember if she spoke a bit and then took her coat off, or if she took it off first. You do have the apology she wrote to *The Times* in the Meaningful Closet somewhere. In it she refers to the 'facile equation of Us with Them as a means of retrospectively justifying our own brutality towards other species.' You can't understand it. When she was wrong, defensive, or didn't know what she thought, she got really lazy. She set things up so they could have a thousand meanings, like an infinity mirror. Then when she was accused of being unclear she called her accuser reactionary, because everything can mean everything. Not that you ever discussed this.

Your mother called 'Andromeda' from the stage, and you walked out, through the crowd, which parted all right.

Outside, on the corner above the entrance to the A train, she tried to take the dress off in front of a garbage can. It got caught on her head. She had no bra on. She never wore a bra. Her tits were much smaller than yours; you have Granny's. So there the two of you were, the tower of meat stuck on her head, her chest bare. The long black velvet coat on the sidewalk.

Do I know what's the funniest thing about it? All you could think about was *your* dress. How if you had worn a different one, then somehow everything would gone differently, because you think that a tiny change in an insignificant detail can alter everything. When you got home she made a pot of instant miso soup and cried into it, then you slept together. You usually did anyway. You slept hugging.

E.

from Sayings of the Fathers

Better to cut off a
male child's foreskin
than to inspire obedience
by guilt.
But in combination –
unbeatable.
    svz, 1992

Andromeda/Rembrandt

7/24

'The membrane has been usurped by its absence.' As svz would
have said.

I got caught stealing, and called gallant Sam who came and
bought me some perfume. But he was a little touchy about
it. We went to the park. We sat in the gazebo. He wanted to
hear something about my mom. So I told him something. I've
practically never told anyone practically anything. We kept
seeing guys alone and in pairs, cruising in the Ramble. At one
point he said, 'Why do they get to fuck in public places and we
don't?' When I finished the story, which he kept interrupting
with FACILE EJACULATIONS like, 'O poor you!' and 'Jesus Christ!'
It was almost light. Soon there would be lots of rollerbladers
and people chasing themselves.

    He kissed me on top of my head and said 'Let's go,' in this
comforting but paternalistic way. He put his arm around me
and tried to pull me up. But I wouldn't move. I climbed on his
lap. He SORT-OF tried to get me off. He wasn't wearing the scary

yuppie suit. He was in those Bruce Lee pyjama things he usually wears. From what my mom said about dicks, I thought they'd be horrible to touch. She was always saying how ugly they are. But I like his. It's amusing.

I had to silence some coy protestations.

No we shouldn't get married first.

No I didn't want to wait for Ed.

I pulled up my skirt, a long camouflage-pattern one, and covered our laps with it.

He wasn't going to do it. I sat up and did it myself, felt myself widening, little by little. Then I found what I was looking for – I half-expected not to have one, but there it was, my STOPPAGE ETALON. I pushed down hard without a second thought. Sam made a sound like he got punched in the stomach.

It did hurt, a little. The tear. We stayed like that for a minute. I rested my head on his shoulder and looked at the sky over the museum; it was definitely pink. Then I started moving, because I felt like it, and he did too.

You can feel yourself opening, like a camera lens. And you can feel the inside of your vagina spaz out. I made hiccupy noises, realized they were mine, tried to stop them, forgot what I was trying to do, heard them again. I couldn't remember what I was thinking from one moment to the next. When I looked at him, he was looking at me, sometimes. Others he was turned away with his eyes shut tight.

He stopped moving suddenly, and lifted me off. He leaned over by the edge of the gazebo, did his pants up and stayed still. His hands were shaking. I waited a long time before I stood up and pulled down the long curtain of my skirt. A runner swung around the curve of the ring road that separated us from the hill.

The silence was killing me. 'Aren't you supposed to come?'

He came to where I stood at the non-door of the gazebo. He looked at me, took my hands, put them together, then put his around them. He rocked our hands, all four of them. 'I didn't want to.'

I'm actually writing all this at the cattle call for this perfume ad. I feel like I've been sitting here forever. I've determined from the INANE chatter of my fellow aspirants that they are looking for a model who 'doesn't exist yet'. That's me, fresh-faced Andy. Oh, Andromeda – the name Andy is taken. It belongs to Andy McDowell.

Actually, there are some blown-up *Vogue* covers on the wall, and one of them is her. She has sand all over her face. They ADHERED that sand to her face with Vaseline. Someone stood there, endlessly futzing with it, until…Oh My God That's Perfect!

Giovanni The Famous Photographer is on the other side of this gym-sized room. He's perched on a high stool looking at pictures on a light box, receiving grinning ninnies. He keeps looking over this way. Today is grey and rainy and I'm not wearing enough clothing because Alexis, my booker at Elite, told me to 'stop covering up with that tragic shawl'. He also gave me this sage advice: 'Just totally be yourself, Andromeda, only don't say anything negative.' Oh, OK!

I went back to the Bellclaire with Sam. His mom was in the bed. Sam took a shower. Janet sat there in her wraparound Gucci sunglasses, staring at me. I heard Sam's deep cough. I felt it in my chest. Like a helicopter stuck in one spot in the sky. Hovering over a traffic accident on the highway or something. Whatever that means. God, how poetic!

I am very good at small talk. She asked me where we had been and I told her. 'I got caught shop-lifting and Sam was the only person I could think of to call.'

She said, 'Don't waste your time making problems for yourself. You already have enough. It's impossible to be so pretty.'

I loved that. I thought that was a really cool thing to say. It's almost like being pretty is taboo: you aren't allowed to discuss it; you're just meant to be thankful and shut up. Ed got offended once when he complimented me on my shirt.

I said, 'It's not the shirt, honey.'

'Oh, you're not that good-looking,' he said, and kind of stormed off. (It was another Assignation Under the Fallout Shelter Sign.) But obviously he thinks I am. Can't we just get it out in the open and move onto something else? Because not talking about it makes it more, not less, important.

Janet and I decided to leave and let Sam get to work. She said he hadn't had a job in 'dogs' years.' My mom used to say dogs' years too.

Outside, she asked me if I needed money. It was a hazy muggy morning. Everyone rushing here and there. For some reason I noticed the stunted skinny trees in the sidewalk, and on the Broadway Malls. The leaves had turned yellow, and looked tired already, after the heat. And it was so crowded, more crowded than it was even a year ago. Last night didn't happen; no one knows about it, no one would care. But I feel different. A notch in my skinny belt. Anyway, I had no money and the thought of a bacon, egg, and American cheese from the Galaxy had an unearthly appeal.

I told her about the modeling and the windfall, but that yes, at that moment I could use some money as Granny was so flustered after I told her I hated her that she forgot to leave me my stipend.

'Allowance.'

Janet gave me a hundred-dollar bill and told me not to drink too much. Then she took a half bottle of Sterling Sapphire out of her bag, handed it to me, and got in a cab. While I was waiting for the light, she drove past. She'd taken off her shades and I saw she had this huge motherfucker of a black eye, like she'd walked into a doorknob.

175

On four ripped-out pages of the Rembrandt, left in the lobby of the Bellclaire in a manila envelope marked 'By Hand, For Sam Taylor'

7/30

The Pamphleteer
by avz

Once upon a time there was a girl who lived with her mother in a huge mansion on Riverside Drive, where Schwab House is today, except this story takes place in the future, which looks like a Tim Burton movie. Old and new.

They lived quite happily and undisturbed. The mother was a local politician and the daughter was her canvasser. She could often be seen with a large bag over her shoulder, heavy with pamphlets. She handed them to old ladies with fake droopy flowers on their hats. She handed them to young men with matted hair who, though they were carrying unwieldy guitar cases, turned around to look at her after they passed.

Was she pretty? Technically, yes: skin like glass, hair like onyx (or something black that shines). She had an openness about her, an air of expectation. She knew this and it bothered her, because you know what? It was completely inaccurate, Sam; misleading, even.

Her mother, always eager to exploit the smallest, dearest, most defenseless things, tried to tell her (she was called Magpie) to 'work it'. She bought her frilly dresses and lipstick. Magpie stood in front of the mirror looking at her face, and could not tell what all the fuss was about. She couldn't see her own face.

Her single solitary friend liked to throw up. They sat in an attic room eating Entemann's Chocolate Chip Cookies, looking across the river to the Palisades Fairground that was always lit up at night. The carousel spun silently (it was miles away), the little seats on the Ferris wheel bobbed. Her friend Ezra (she was a girl named after Ezra Pound) stuffed and then excused herself. Magpie stood in her window looking out. It was a big round window that could be seen from the fair. She knew this because last summer she had gone there on a Greyhound, across the George Washington Bridge, just to find out. All she could make out for sure was the little grape-fruity light fixture in her window. A human figure you would have mistaken for a curtain or houseplant.

Like her mom, Ezra also though she should be an actress or a model, something remunerative. She said, 'Why not exploit yourself instead of letting the world do it for you.' This rang true enough.

Still, Magpie couldn't bring herself to. She really couldn't. She liked to stand all day in the snow, or in the sun; New York's extremes of temperature were even worse in this future, and there were no seasons. One day she wore Ugg boots and seal coats, the next nothing but a bikini (and her bag, of course); besides, she liked her job. While she handed out the endless pamphlets ('Know your Garbage!') and tracts ('Why You Should Get Paid to Do Your Own Dishes') she thought about ... nothing. That was her secret. She never thought about what she was saying, what she was doing, where she was. There wasn't even a song in her head, which was heavy and wordless as a church bell.

She wanted to take a boat across the river. ·

So I guess she did have a tiny imagination.

Anyway, at the happy end, she becomes a common fraudster named Ms. Rosa, a palmist. She covers her mansion in Christmas lights and has fake moles implanted by irreversible surgical procedure.

* * *

From Escobar to Rob, sociopathically written across both sides of a Hallmark card with a picture of two Labrador puppies on the front. 'A friend is forever' is printed inside

8/6

BROOKYLN
YOUR HOUSE

ROB,

I'VE COME ACROSS YOUR TYPE BEFORE; BUT NOT IN
YOUR PARTICULAR CONFIGURATION; GUESS THAT
IS ALL THE DIFFERENCE THERE IS BETWEEN PEOPLE.
YOU HATE ME. YOU HATE ME AND I WONDER ABOUT
MYSLEF THAT I KEEP COMING BACK. I KNOW YOU SAY
YOU LOVE ME BUT YOU MEAN HATE. THIS HAPPANS
ALL THE TIME THIS IS THE FEELINGS ALWAYS MUTUAL
MAXIM. YOU CAN CALL IT LOVE; I CAN CALL IT HATE.
BUT THE FEELING THAT EXISTS BEFORE THE WORD;
ITS THE SAME; IT'S SOMETHING SHARED. IT IS IN
THE ROOM WHEN WE ARE THEIR. ALSO ALL LOVE
IS SEXUAL LOVE; THE ONLY KIND OF LOVE THERE
REALLY IS; EVEN BETWEEN PARENTS AND CHILDREN;
THOUGH REPRESSED. EVERY OTHER KIND OF LOVE
BEING LIP-SERVICE, AN EXCHANGE, PREMEDITED AND
OUTCOME ORIENTED.

BUT WE CAN BE HAPPY. YOU CAN GAIN TEN
POUNDS AND I CAN STOP WALLOWING IN THIS MIAMI
SWIMMING POOL OF NARCISITIC DESPAIR. PEOPLE
LEARN TO COOK; PEOPLE GROW HERB GARDENS ON
FIRE ESCAPES. PEOPLE DRINK LESS AND SMOKE MORE
POT. THIS IS DOMESTICITY AND PERFECT FOR US.

I'M LEAVING THIS UNDER YOUR DOOR. I KNOW
YOU SAID YOU DID NOT WANT TO SEE ME WHEN YOU
GET BACK FROM THE WORKSHOP BUT I ALSO KNOW
THAT YOU REALLY DO. ITS NOT FINISHED.

THESE WOMEN. THIS WOMAN LET ME IN TO
YOU'RE PLACE WHEN I PRETENDED FUMBLED FOR

MY KEYS. DOESNT SHE KNOW IT ISN'T SAFE. I MIGHT
HAVE KILLED HER.
     YOURS INFERNALLY,
     RICO ESCOBAR

* * *

Andromeda / Rembrandt

8/6

Trish and me and Escobar and Ed are down at the new café
above the boat basin, The Rotunda. I'm paying. First big paycheck. I'm going to be a supermodel. I'm even bringing Trish
to England with me tomorrow to do this shoot for the cover of
some very cool magazine I've never heard of. I said I wouldn't
fly without Trish. I said she was my lucky hat, like the babysitter
in *Goodfellas*. Alexis, my booker, didn't get it. He sits at this
big table all day with the other bookers, making calls about
how great I am. He calls me The Philosopher.

Trish has gone to try and sneak into the marina. She said
she was surprised I have such a fear of authority, such lack of
bravura, that I would rather stay here and listen to Ed and
Escobar argue about *Dog Day Afternoon*. Escobar calls it
homophobic. Ed says it's 'of its time'.

An hour ago I was at home with Trish, trying to choose
what to bring on the trip, when Ed called. 'Hello, hot stuff…'
And then Escobar buzzed from the lobby saying, 'Hello, baby.'
HOT STUFF? BABY? We told them to meet us here. Trish says it's
like Venice.

Up until a few years ago it was not. My mom wouldn't let
me walk the quick way down to the river, because a woman
got raped and killed in the public bathroom in '86. We had to
take a circuitous route – onto the Promenade, down the paved
hill, past the Amtrak tunnel. Now Adolf Guiliani has got all the

179

trains running on time, and everyone dressed up and drinking Margaritas. When's the coup? Here we are, pretending to be in the courtyard of a Palazzo, taking in the view of those pocked high rises in New Jersey, beside the crappy cement fountain, which at least still stinks like it used to.

It was kind of a bad scene, me and Trish, at home. First I tried to talk to her about Sam but she was totally uninterested; she thinks it's gross. So does the Reichian, who only wants to talk about Sophie. All Trish could think of was my image. Not ironically. She hauled all my clothes off the floor, off the chairs in the kitchen, out of the bathroom (the house is really getting out of hand since Granny left) and threw them on my mom's bed. Then she said my signifiers were all wrong.

'Look – I can see the humor in it this dressing-to-deconstruct thing, but going into Calvin Klein tomorrow dressed like an old lady who rides the bus is NOT ON.'

(Giovanni the Photog liked me, so now I've got to meet Calvin tomorrow. It's his perfume.)

'Sam's really smart. I think he might even be a GOOD writer.'
'Please!'

She flipped through the Polaroids I've accumulated. I don't even have a portfolio yet. I'm riding a wave of hot air. I'll laugh all the way to the bank.

'These suck.' She threw them on the bed.
'I think I'm in love.'

She unconsciously braided little braids in her bangs and consciously chain-smoked her weird herbal cigarettes. She looked at the clothes-mountain. 'One thing that's VINTAGE is OK. But this. This ... this is all too ... eugh.' Words failed her. She sat weakly down. She always looks hungry.

I reassured her. I told her I had a lot more stuff, and took her by the hand, into the Meaningful Closet. I haven't been in there in days. Her eyes glassed over. Then she took the bull by the horns and told me I had to get a META-NARRATIVE. Where do I want to be in five years? I dunno. A model? No. Grad school? Nope. Under this same pile of old blankets? Perhaps. We sat down on the closet floor and I opened THE LAST bottle of wine. Trish didn't drink much. Says she hates to feel out of control. I say I never feel in control, except maybe when I read, and that's only because I know what everything means.

'You don't know what anything means.'

I twiddled my toes and giggled. Looking into her sunken eyes, her blue-red mouth, that perfect nose, the jarring collarbones.

'You look kind of like Louise Brooks.'

OK, I sort of made a pass at her. I think I stroked her cheek. She thought it was pathetic.

'I'm as straight as they come.'

'How straight is that?'

I swear I only did it out of boredom! Trish tires me. She makes me want to drink until I drown. She's a lot like Ed, actually. They've both got this close-down thing. This list of things they think are gross, a waste of time and money, not worth thinking about. I told her about the Deflowering at Doorless Cabin. I said that ever since then, I had wanted to fuck everything that moves. Which isn't without some truth.

'He didn't make you come?'

'I … no, I guess not.'

'You didn't make HIM come?'

As in: what the fuck is wrong with us.

This was once we were down here, at The Rotunda. Midas was with us.

Escobar was similarly disgusted. 'No wonder he hasn't called you, baby.'

Ed said, 'Still, he's an asshole to abandon his dog.'

I'd been kind of thinking he did it to be nice. That he knew that Midas would make me feel better, since I'm all alone in the house. And he does. I adore him.

Ed was drunk. 'I'm sure he has a pattern of this kind of…
contretemps.'

'I don't think that's what you mean, sweetie,' said Trish.

'Dumping dogs, seducing sixteen-year-old virgins…'

'Not making them come…' Ha ha ha, Trish. People at other tables were listening in. The whole ROTUNDA was in on the joke.

Suddenly Midas started yelping and wagging his ass and head like crazy, then ran off, his leash jangling behind him, towards Sam, who was coming down the steps. In his suit. Looking like a low-budg NY1 anchorman. I had to tell them it was him.

'OK … he is kinda cute,' said Trish, sheepishly.

Ed muttered. 'Sorry-ass-cheap-ass-Mo-Black-Fowad-suit.'

I met him halfway across the dry fountain, which he'd climbed into, after Midas. He didn't kiss me hello or anything. He actually backed away. I haven't heard from him in, God … it's a week now. I have been not a virgin for a week.

'You hate *The Pamphleteer.* I shouldn't have left it. God, it was only a joke.'

We stood there looking at his shoes. Finally he said, 'I love it,' then looked at me for a second and didn't smile. Then walked away, towards the boat basin.

I told my *posse* (retro) that he said he had to get back to the newsroom. Sam Taylor reporting live from the Rotunda in Riverside Park.

Trish went back to my house to sleep in Granny's Disgusting Boudoir. She has no tolerance. She drank two glasses of wine and a tenth of a margarita from Escobar's pitcher. It's ten. Escobar and Rob are going to buy coke somewhere downtown, and bringing Midas, 'for protection'. It's dark and I'm the only one left at the café.

I think I'll go get something. A yoga video or something. I'm going to get into shape. Trish said I should. She said even though I'm skinny my body lacks DEFINITION.

* * *

Sam / Mead

8/6

I took Geraldine's shift tonight. It was her anniversary. They went to Tavern on the Green. You assume that because someone is gay they won't be into such clichéd shit. Not sure why you assume that. I guess you think if you can reject certain social pressures, like being straight, you can reject others too, like tackiness. Whatever makes them happy. They are so fucking happy and nice and well-adjusted. And that's because they have worked for it, and they deserve it. This is true.

I was there from four till midnight. It's different at night. The café is closed, and there is a calm, an almost human feel to the place. Frau Kasbaum was in again. She misses me. When she first started hanging round my podium I was afraid I'd get in trouble with Geraldine, but she doesn't care. So now we meet there, and Kasbaum talks at me and I sit, which I'm not supposed to do. I'm supposed to stand, in the middle of the football field-sized room, a pillar of information.

Kasbaum's got it in her head that Lara and I should reconcile. When we were together she made no secret of the fact that she hated her.

'Samuel, you have to think of the solemn promise you made. Till death do you part.'

'I already told you.' I'm actually a little worried she's losing it. 'We're *divorcing*.' Paul served me with the papers the other day.

183

While she held forth, I went back to re-reading the story Andromeda left for me. I had it next to the computer, where Kasbaum couldn't see it. I like her handwriting. It slants the wrong way, towards the margin. I even like the shape the whole thing makes on the page. It's like an open fan.

Kasbaum and Werner had their problems, but always got through. She'd had a daughter with another man, and she never ever saw her, because Wern didn't want anything to do with it, and this was a sacrifice for Kasbaum, but she was willing to make it, because she had vowed herself to Werner. Or something.

I had managed to switch the topic from myself to the more general decline in morals when Andromeda came in, walked right past me and got on the escalator. I turned around to watch her. She had on her Ronald MacDonald hat and the mourning shawl.

'She's too young for you.'

Josh, my psycho-doppelganger, came off his post at the door and followed behind her.

'Can you just wait here a moment? If anybody asks, Self Help's at the top of the escalator.'

I got on behind them. But when Josh got off he turned left and went to bother this pretty Chinese girl Regine, who works in Spirituality.

I hid behind a display of the *Larousse Encyclopedia of Wine*.

Andromeda picked up the *Moosewood Cookbook* then put it back. She picked up *Sushi for Dummies*, then put it back. Finally she took something enormous, a *tome*, from the bottom shelf, and got on the escalator going back down.

I followed five steps behind. I cleared my throat. She didn't turn around. Once off the escalator she wrapped her hat half around the book, walked over the silent taupe carpet and pushed her shoulder against the glass door to open it.

I was walking backwards towards my podium, I think with my hand over my mouth, when Josh came barrelling down the stairs like fucking Rambo. He followed her out of the door, grabbed her elbow and the book. Andromeda's face when she looked up ... I told Kasbaum to wait another sec.

There were mobs of boys on the street. Some action movie had just let out at the Old Loews.

'Can I handle this, Josh?'

She stunk of booze.

'What? She's tryin' to steal this.' He held it much closer to my face than he had to: *Healing with Whole Foods*.

'You don't, actually. It's the first time. I've read the in-house pamphlets. They say, the first time, they say, it's down to your discretion. She's – '

'Well, *my discretion* – ' he gave her a horrible once-over. Suddenly we were in a sea of well-heeled juvenile delinquents. Some little shit tugged on the edge of her shawl.

'Fuck off!' I really yelled. The short crowd scattered. 'Look, Josh – she's my cousin, OK? She's just lost her mom. My aunt. She was a famous marine biologist.'

Josh gave up. He turned to Andromeda. 'Come in here again and I'll fuck up your face.' He threw the glass door open so hard it bounced back again.

No thank you. No thank you, Sam, for saving my ass. She just disappeared around the corner. Sobriety is not good for anger management: must point this out to Geraldine. I caught her fast. I almost hit her. Instead I kind of chucked her down on a stoop around the corner.

'What the fuck was that? You wanna end up in the back room with that fucking lunatic? Oh God. Maybe you do.'

As if in reply, a pencil-thin stream of blood trickled out of her left nostril.

I wiped it on my thumb, 'And you've got a nosebleed.'

'It's just an abrasion. From snorting Ritalin.'

'I don't think *Healing with Whole Foods* is gonna cover it.' I sat down. I had to. There were red bars on her bare arm in the shape of my fingers. I covered my eyes. I thought 'You want *me* to *rescue* you?' And then I said 'You *want* me to rescue you?' She looked at me like a codfish. I started again. 'That first time I talked to you by the Planetarium ... I thought that if I took my fingers off the rubbers in my pocket I'd fly off into space. Like the guy in *2001*, the one Hal disconnects?'

'What the fuck are you talking about?'

'What you want this to be versus what it actually is.'

'What *I* want it to be?'

She lit the filter end of her cigarette and smoked it. I pulled it out of her mouth and threw it in the gutter. She lit one the right way.

'You think you are in this story, Andromeda. This story of Sammy and Andy, who come up against obstacles – things stand in their way but they fight for their ... whatever, and then, in the happy ending... Fuck! Fuck, I can *buy* you that book if you want it. I get a discount.' I decided, ' I'll bring it over after work.'

'I'm gunna look uh Escobar.' She stood up. The sole of her flip-flop folded under itself and she fell. I caught her by her elbow and didn't let it go.

'Let go.'

'Go home.'

'No.'

'Letgoame.'

'Go home. I'll be there in an hour. '

I maneuvered her up to Broadway, then gave her a shove in the direction of the Apthorp.

Inside, in the universe of processed air, out of the mug of the summer night, my double was reading *Loaded* at the fake cherrywood magazine racks. Kasbaum leaned on the podium giving me the hairy eyeball. Apparently no one had wanted any information. Like I fucking care.

After a minute I ran out again into the road. Her yellow hat was crumpled in her fist. The big triangle of her shawl pointed down at the sidewalk. She went into the gate of the Apthorp. I'd meet her.

When I got back to my lectern, Kasbaum said 'You know I get my blood pressure pills from Genie, at Plimpton's?'

'*So?*'

'*So*, she says Lara's bought three pregnancy tests in the past week.'

Carnival Flight to Miami. TOMORROW. 99 bucks. One way.

* * *

Andromeda / Rembrandt

8/7

I was supposed to see Calvin Klein at 10, but they called me up at fucking 7. Hungover. Nosebleed. Failed lesbian.

Could I be in at seven-thirty?

I wasn't AT ALL sure I could. What were the sums involved?

Nine hundred for two hours if I get the job, but for him to even want to see me … What the fuck is wrong with me? Alexis wants to know. ad naus.

On the train at dawn, distracting myself with thoughts of free will. Segued into that from the humiliation of Sam not showing up at *my place* (retro) last night, after being such a patronizing bastard, and how (this is horrible) it made him MORE appealing. Anyway, somehow I ended up all lofty, trying to figure out if modeling was a 'means to an end'. I tried on one of my mother's old favorites, when she accused herself of being a hypocrite for her high salary at NYU. She claimed she was infiltrating from within. Yeah right. She was as knee-deep in all the petty shit as the rest of them. She'd been known to INTERCEPT MEMOS. She was an academic overachiever masquerading as a fuck-up. Me, I'm the genuine article.

I don't see myself infiltrating. What am I gonna do? Overthrow the palaces of fashion with snottiness? The best I could come up with, and the truest, is that the whole thing is a testament to my morbid curiosity. I want to see everything. I'd look inside a dead body. I was the only one in the subway car. Me and the Reaction model, heading downtown.

The offices are on 31st Street and 7th – I mean 'Fashion Avenue'. The security guard didn't look up from the funny pages. I took the stairs up to the 8th floor because I didn't like the look of the elevator. This brought me to knock upon the back door, which threw them. Some guy smiled and kissed me. 'I didn't even know this thing was here! You must be Andromeda! You made it! Now this is for an in-house show. Angela was supposed to do it but she missed the Concorde. It's for Japanese buyers so Calvin wants it really natural. No catwalk stuff.'

I have to admit I was thrilled. I thought – maybe it is better at the top. Less inane, and it's just what filters down to popular culture that sucks.

Into a room lit like a morgue with shiny white floors and instead of windows, racks and racks of dark clothes.

I stripped in front of him and he helped me on with a suit. I looked like a stewardess.

'Oh my God – they're not too long on you! They keep sending us all these midgets!'

I felt proud ... to be tall? The assistant was tall too – that's what he's like, like one of K's assistants in *The Castle*. He kept touching my hair, which was kind of frizzy from the humidity, and sighing. I saw myself in the mirror. I had two red spots on my cheeks like a clown.

Calvin's face is dented like the moon but he has a nice, I guess what you'd call an affable, smile. His office is very eighties, gunmetal gray, as is his tee-shirt. And his hair. And the early morning out the window. There's no one in the offices across Fashion Avenue. It's still very early. Some matronly Italian woman in pantyhose and a skirt suit appears and offers me an espresso and I sit across the desk from them. Calvin, flanked now by two identical Kafkaesque assistants. I'm not making this up.

'Big break for you, huh?' smiles Calvin. He seems GENUINELY happy for me. 'Don't be nervous.'

'I'm not.'

'Angela is gonna regret she missed that plane,' says the one on the left.

The other adds 'She's always MISSING THE PLANE,' as if to imply something deeper.

Calvin says, 'OK, let's just have a spin around the room.'

'Go slow so we can see the clothes,' says the one on his right.

I walk to the corner, and then it starts: I CAN'T STOP SMILING. It seems so so silly. Fucking hilarious. What was it? The put-on. It's the put-on that's funny. I run my hands over my face, 'Sorry, sorry.' But the only thing that works is to bite the inside of my cheek. Hard. It hurts. Then I forget where I am, in a way. I disappear.

I walk naturally, all right. I tour the room, around and around. I stop and look out the window at the slight variation in the greys of the slats of the closed venetian blinds across the street. I forget the three of them are there. I pick up my cold espresso, tip my head back, down it like a shot. At Calvin's desk I pick a couple of things up, executive toys, and study them: a distressed metal yo-yo, a crystal cube. I actually toss the cube up in the air a few times. After a while I sit back opposite them and cross my legs. I can crack my ankle endlessly, and I start to do it, spinning it around and around in its socket. Until I notice the looks on their faces. They have not blunk. Is that a word?

'Thank you,' said Calvin. As in, don't call us, we'll call you. Or maybe just don't call us.

But anyway I've gotta go to London. Now. Trish is already at the airport. I'm in the Town Car. I've never been on a plane. My mother was scared of them.

A FEW DAYS AFTER I WROTE THAT, OR A WEEK, I THINK –

(8/14)

Today we did a shoot in Brighton for ID. I had to kick my bare feet in the cold sea. That was the best part. The rest was that kind of carny / trashy thing fashion people think is so cool. I don't get it. It's depressing to BE trashy therefore it is depressing to ACT trashy... No? Yes? Right? Am I wrong? I was so annoyed I pretended I was in PETA and against wearing furs. Then someone pointed out that I'd had a bacon roll for breakfast. Whoops.

All the other girls, and the stylists, and the photographer, were on their cell phones making dates. I wished I could call Sam but I think he's had it. I'm such a fuck-up. I'm never going to steal or drink again. Trish thinks this is a good idea. She says I'm an alcoholic. Right now she's at the Saatchi Gallery looking at an exhibition called The Body/Fragments.

The other models redo their make-up when the make-up artist leaves the RV, or refuse to wear things they think unbecoming. I don't even look in the mirror. I totally don't care. I mean, they can make me look however they want. That's what they pay me for. So far I've clocked 1950 dollars – which isn't great: I owe them 2500 for all the messengering, printing my new cards, and Trish's tickets. But they keep telling me to wait. They'll be more and more. I'm alone in the RV. I'm not in this shot because I refused to go on the roller-coaster. It's going to be some complicated thing – they have a poodle trussed up in bondage gear and the other girl, Cheryl, is holding a little mini-whip. I'm gonna be waiting here forever. I'll write part two of my story, which is based on actual events.

The Pamphleteer
Part II

So after years of pamphleteering Magpie gave up one day. It occurred to her that she did not know if she agreed with her mother's way of doing business. She'd seen her attend too many charity balls of late, and come back through their door laden with freebies – plates, pens, towels, sleeping bags. All labeled. All sponsored. By drug companies, tire companies, lightbulb and gun companies.

She was almost seventeen and she decided to run away, though she wasn't sure where to go. She was brave, but not that brave. And she traveled heavy: lots of shoes, lots of books. So she couldn't hike. She decided to visit her father, whom she had never met.

She'd been modeling, at everyone's insistence, and it made her richer but it also made her not trust anyone. All the friends – even the politicized anorexic ones, even the dear neighbor ones WOULDN'T FUCKING CALL HER BACK (rewrite) – said, 'Oh, just do it. You'll make a killing then retire.' Retire.

She and Ezra went standby for a first class ticket. Magpie had never been up in the air before, and though she knew it wasn't going to flap its wings, she was surprised at how noisy it was. She was also surprised at how easy and civilized it seemed to run away from her mother and the old Schwab mansion, and leave the lights of NY twinkling in her wake like Christmas.

When the plane lowered itself over gold-and-pea-green TV dinner-shaped fields, she felt more relaxed than she ever had. England was limiting: the food was bad, there was less energy. And people didn't look at each other. No give, no take, just surreptitious sizing up.

191

She and Ez stayed in a hotel for several days. Then one night, while Ez was at dinner at a friend's, Magpie (after drinking three wonderful Pimms at the hotel Bar; the hotel was called The Gore) asked the concierge to look up a number for her in the yellow pages. The good dignified moniker: Alfred Pupkin.

He answered on the first ring.

She heard a child in the background. A television.

'Who's that?'

'Um. Hi.'

'Who's that?'

'It's your daughter, Sophie's daughter. Magpie.'

'God. Well. God. You havin' me on?'

'Yes. I mean no. I'm in London. I ran away from home to come and see you.'

'How's your mother?'

'Dead.'

They met in The Gore for a sweet the next day. She'd noticed that the English often ate sweets instead of food.

When Al saw his daughter he had to steady himself against the maitre-d's podium. She was at a table in the back in a tight brown dress that shimmered like Coca Cola. Her long hair fell down her bare back. She was tall and thin and had her mother's face. Alfred was a failed rock star. He'd gotten into it for the girls, the pretty girls. Andromeda's mother was a pretty one, all right. But not ALL RIGHT. She'd taught him a lot, but mostly she'd disabused him of a notion: that pretty girls are fun and flattering and good to be around. Sophie, she'd been 'a right fucking pain in the arse'.

He bent to kiss her and it was awkward. She stood up and was taller than he was. He looked so inconsequential. The word *homunculus* sprang to mind. The homunculus in the mosaic in the antiway in Schwab sprang to mind like in a pop-up book. This little blob of flesh had caused so much trouble? She instantly wanted to leave but was polite and ate all the icing off her cake. Afterwards she walked him home to the door of his walk-up where he lived with his third wife and their son. 'She's not much older than you,' he said, before they said goodbye. He was staring up, chin lifted high, at what she surmised was his own window.

When she went home her mother was not dead. Or maybe she was.

When I got back to the Gore

Holy Shit Alexis just called to say Calvin LIKED the weirdness and wanted to use me for the LOVE perfume campaign and could I go straight to Miami. 'In the ballpark of 250,000 dollars.'

ANTOINETTE! MAKE ME A PIMMS! PEEL ME A GRAPE!

I'm just gonna sit here and wait and see what Trish says.

* * *

Sam / Mead

8/14

How Can Such a Man Exist?
1st Draft

People age. That's the scary thing. The whole idea that life is made up of moments that don't amount to a linear truth, or self, or hill of beans – I stand by that still; but people do change: they decay and fall apart. I have not seen him in ten years. The last time was at my graduation from the MFA. God, did the teachers there hate me, but that's another story. Or non-story. He hugged me at the airport. Smelled of Paco and Dentyne. He had a tear in his eye. 'Son.' The obligatory slap on the back.

'Gord.'

In his embarrassing SUV, passing low, lumpy hillocks beside jutting metal shapes that make up the disused post-industrial landscape that leads away from the airport, Gord says:

'I've been to a few Promise Keepers meetings with the boys

from the club, and they all say what a tragedy it is we don't get on.'

'What club?'

'Gun.'

'You're a … a … *Promise Keeper*?' Tears welled up in *my* eyes.

'Nah. Not a joiner.'

We passed lawns flat as plates. Then we got to his gated community. Pretty as patterned toilet paper. Hedges in box shapes. Pebbles on top of garbage bags to keep weeds from growing in driveways. Keeps the oxygen out, he explains. That sound: slow, spinning tires on rocks in driveways. His low white house.

On the wall in the guest room there is an inexplicable watercolor of a deflated football. A wash of blue behind it. It is a little boy's room, which might make sense if Gordon hadn't bought the place five years ago. In the shower I try to convince myself that it is unlikely that Lar is with child. Unlikely because in all my years of the tried-and-true withdrawal method, I've never fucked up. Except with Sasha. Sasha tricked me. I knew I was being tricked. Why? We both wanted the adventure. The drama and the tears, the closeness. We were teenagers. We ended up hating each other.

It got dark and Gordon and I sat in the twilit 'conservatory'. He drank martinis and I – declined. We didn't look at each other but out at the lights on the lawn, a pattern of flat glowing disks dug into the ground. Soon we saw ourselves reflected in the windows. We talked, not to each other, not even our doubles, but to the white glow of the reflection of his white leather couches. For a moment I snuck a glance at the similar shapes of our faces, our twin heads like two pissed-off pythons. One of the light-disks from outside was lodged at the level of his chin.

We'd been discussing current events. My dad's a Republican.

He felt the election had been fair. *Hanging chads his ass.*

I changed the subject. I said, 'It's so quiet and dark here.'

'Why not move down, away from the hubbub? Get outta NY. *O-ver-run.*'

'What the fuck are you talking about?'

'I just mean you can ...' – he patted his groin, warmly, and opened his legs wider – 'really spread out down here ... and don't you cuss.'

'Fuck. *Dad.*'

'Nor patronize me.'

'OK. Right.' I got up and clapped once. 'Let's go out somewhere.'

'You wanting to see my neck of the woods? You're on the wagon? Hmmm. Let's go to Maggie's.'

He'd driven about fifty feet down the road when he pulled over and asked me to take the wheel. He'd been drinking all day, he was embarrassed to say; but he'd been 'so mixed up' about seeing me.

I *almost* felt sorry for the bastard as I got out and walked through the headlights around to his seat. The stars were up. I haven't seen stars in the country in years. In NY you see one bright star, never a gorgeous swarm. And crickets. I haven't heard crickets. I drove us carefully down the skinny, dark, boggy roads. I pressed one button and all the windows went down and the wind ripped around us. It smelled of something, wet flowers, closed sleeping flowers. I thought about Andromeda. No, I didn't think about her. I never think *about* her. I thought *on* her.

He broke the silence with a yell above the wind. 'I know you hold it all against me! But she can hold her own, believe you me! You don't know what she's like! You've always had this idealized vision!'

'I'm not an idealist!' I was speeding up. I haven't driven in years. The road was attached to my body. It's fun. There was Rand McNally on the dash, flapping like crazy. There were very few cars on the road and those there were, were very polite. They let me have my fun. They probably all knew Gordon from the Gun Club.

'Course you are! You always were! Your mother – you know I was remembering this tee-shirt she had – *A Woman without a Man is like a Fish Without a Bicycle!* She wore this while we were married! Without a brassiere!'

Speed up some more. Change the subject. 'I've got a job! Lara left me! Threw me out, and I've got a job! Barnes! And Noble! '

He said, 'No! No! No! No! Niggers and spics work there! You went to college! What the fuck are you doing?!'

I floored the accelerator. Sobriety – another note to Geraldine – is simply a particularly volatile form of Undrunkenness. I was suicidal. I was patricidal. The twilight sky like the circuit breaker over Janet's head.

'Jesus fuck son! Slow down! I take it back! They're all wonderful! It's a big happy fucking family! We are the world!' He laughed.

I laughed. I started to laugh like Jack Nicholson. It doesn't seem funny at all now.

Of course Maggie's was a strip joint.

'Now, honest-to-god son, I did not know that. I thought the waitresses were just very secure in themselves.'

Under a tall neon sign of a woman in a cowboy hat with tassels on her nipples (like on penny loafers, but gold) spinning a lasso, several men in similar hats were talking on their cell phones. The bouncer said 'Howdy, Gordon.'

'I'm not going in there.'

'Are you homosexual?'

'Yes.'

'Whagheugneuh?'

'Dad – Lara caught me in bed with this guy Paul. But thanks for taking the weight off. Thanks. I feel … free. Finally.'

I got in and drove. Gordon kept saying, 'Christ,' and running his hands down the thighs of his pressed and creased Dockers. He muttered 'That's what you get. That's your comeuppance, Gordon…'

'I'm kidding.'

'Whannaheugh.'

It took him a full minute to pull himself together. 'You had me there. Hell, I knew you weren't. I knew you used to go crazy for that, what was her name, the dark one?'

'Sasha? She wasn't dark. '

'She wasn't a blonde. I have no idea what you get up to down there. I worry about you.'

'Well, I write and I drink. But right now I don't even drink. I just write and go into work with niggers and spics and fags.' I felt like whistling so I did. *Que Sera Sera.*

'You writing anything good?'

'A love story. A nice story. It's not good. Oh, and I have a girlfriend. She's sixteen and she's a model. Very pale, blonde as corn silk.'

'No shit. All right!' *YEE HAW!* 'This is an OK place. Here. Here!' I overshot it and had to bang a uey. 'It's a cajun joint.'

Sitting at the shellacked wood table in front of a free basket of chicken wings, he drank. I had soda and soda and soda and soda and soda. He got it in his head to convince me to go into his new bag, real estate.

'Writers are liars, and all you need to do to sell anyone anything is lie.' He accentuated his points by jabbing celery sticks in the blue cheese dressing that came with the wings. 'And what's a piece of property but another lie? Piece of a dream, of

197

someone's dream. Same thing.' Jab, crunch, eyes on the tits of the waitress. Me. Not him.

On the way home he started in on Janet again, how he'd never loved another woman. How she'd ruined his life. He fell in and out of sleep. The same Ambervision sunglasses he's always worn slid way down his John Voight nose. I turned on the radio and there was a Pink Floyd-athon. Perfect. I drove us slowly home.

I managed four days. Gordon wouldn't open the fucking windows. *Couldn't* fucking open the windows. His windows *don't open*. I wouldn't play golf. I floated around on a purple floaty thing in the pool and read *The Beautiful and Damned*. Thrice. *They* never gave in. You didn't see Antony Patch down at Barnes & Noble.

I checked and re-checked my messages at the Bellclaire.

Lara. Lara needs to talk to me. *Sweetie*. Geraldine thinks they are about to promote me over her and it's racist bullshit and she's gonna sue but she know's it's not my fault. Now, she's not 'litigious' but she really wants to talk to me about this. *Sweetie*. At least there's my pretext for leaving early. Something urgent at 'work'. Oh and Lynne, no *sweetie*, whatever that's about. I probably owe her money.

At our farewell dinner, under the patio umbrella, near the embedded lights, he spiked my ginger ale with gin. 'You need a drink. If anyone's ever needed one. You do.' I dumped the whole thing into this very expensive orchid in the middle of the table.

'I'm gonna give you some money. You want me to give you some money? I'm gonna give you the Jeep so you can drive down to the airport, stop off in Miami, whatever. You need to have some fun, son.'

His pen hovered over the check. I've seen this movement before, like a bee buzzing a flower. It makes me want to grab the Waterman and jam it in his eye.

'I'll pick it up in a week. I've got a meeting down there. We're starting up this internet business, selling time-shares. I thought you might want a piece of it.'

I needed at least a thousand.

'Sam?'

'?'

'I love you.'

Anything that comes into contact with his life turns into a bad movie. (I've left out the part about his maid Consuela, who came onto me, and who he's fucking, because it was too much. I mean it was truly *not to be believed*.) But he gave me 5000 bucks. I didn't consider refusing for a fucking second. I drove here, to Miami, and checked into a very expensive room. My ticket is not for five days. (For twenty bucks more I could get a return. You gotta love Carnival.) The bed's vast, the sheets are cool. The sea out the window turquoise, convex. I open the curtains and unfold the windows and stare at the sea. It glitters back at me like those tar and diamond-chip sidewalks in Midtown.

Also the place is swarming with models, looking at me, in this new linen suit I bought. No idea who the hell I am.

* * *

Andromeda, on Gore stationery, stapled into the Rembrandt

8/24

Nameless in the panopticon. It was three days ago. I'd been here twelve hours and it was going fine. The elevators float up into the light of the atrium. Rising, you see the interior terraces, the plants with leaves like elongated green hearts spilling out of pale wood window boxes. You see everything that's going on outside peoples' rooms. People down below, at the square mirrored bar. People in the other elevators. If you took film of it, and gave each door a note and then sped it up, you'd have a pretty interesting movie, and hopefully a tune, after a while.

I got in and stood with my back to the glass door, something I wouldn't usually do. My claustrophobia was turned inside out. As the door was closing someone stuck their foot in. It snapped back open. We looked at each other. He was in a different suit. New shoes.

'What the fuck?'

'WHAT THE FUCK?'

We both said it at the same time, twice.

I put my arms around his neck. He held my head on his chest, by the collar of his shirt. He held it like he was afraid it would roll off onto the floor and break.

When he got out I followed him down the exposed hall to his room. He was looking at the terraces on the other side of the building, and up at the dark hexagonal skylight. 'Isn't it a waste of the space? Couldn't they have trapeze artists flying around in here or something?'

He had the key card in his hand and put his forehead on the fake wood door.

I leaned over the balustrade or verandah or whatever it is and waved to Giovanni, who I'd left at the bar, who I knew would be watching. I was supposed to change my dress and come back down to do some set-up or something. Sam leaned over and waved at him too.

'Who he?'

I took the key and swiped it myself.

I went straight to the window and heard his jacket land on the bed behind me. It fell too slowly. Maybe it was very very light. Then he came and stood next to me, 'This is too weird. I mean the likelihood of this is – unlikely.'

There were some kids yelling Marco, Polo in the lit-up pool below. There was a party boat done up like a Christmas tree at the foot of the Atlantic. It was getting dark.

'What are the fucking chances? Think about it. It's really out there. It's like... '

I said, 'It's not fate, Sam. It's a coincidence.' The look on his face made me want to tease him. 'You think this is some story – Sammy and Andy, who overcome all obstacles...'

'It's worse than fate.' Then he touched the ends of my hair. 'Why is your hair blonde?'

'Girl-next-door.'

My dress was awful. It had these little flesh-colored tabs hanging off, like skin-colored seaweed. He pulled at one.

'I look like an ice skater.'

'Which one, the girl next door or the ice skater?'

We stood there for a while. Looking at each other. Then we fucked.

'Sometimes it's good. Sometimes it's bad. Sometimes it's ugly.' That's what he says when I ask what it's like with people who're not us. We are in this huge bed. We've spent two days there. I can't get halfway across the carpet without being pulled back by the ankle. I called Giovanni about this flu I have. Sam says to tell him it's 'coming out both ends', so I do. Sam says it shuts anyone up in any circumstances. It is a bit like the flu. Something you can't remember how it feels when it's not happening. So you do it over and over again. Very different from the first time. Nothing like it.

O.

Sorry, ma. Let's make that: AHA.

On the second night we realize we are starving and sneak out the staff door so no one will see me. We get Cuban omelets and eat them out of tinfoil containers as we walk to the beach.

The sea is noisy in front of us. He holds my hand over his heart and starts to tell me something: 'Andromeda – '

'I like the sound of my name in your mouth. It lacks the drone. You give it a drum.'

There are very few people around. It's happy hour and we have a bath sheet. We do it quickly and I watch the strange, the fascinating, contortion of his face as he comes in the sand.

After the beach, or maybe it's the next day, I can't remember, we walk through grubby pastel streets with low houses and salsa music coming through slatted storm windows. Multicolored lights. The air is different. It's changed. Blue, wet air. He's not letting me drink, and keeps saying we're the soberest honeymoon there ever was. I don't feel sober. He's singing '"Nothing on the top but a bucket and a mop and an illustrated book about birds." You don't know that one? What about – this one's topical – "Here comes success. It's plain bizarre. Here comes my Chinese rug…"' He kicks an old tennis ball down the street. He looks beautiful. Then he starts again. '"I kissed my girl by the factory wall. Dreamed a dream by the old canal."'

'I don't know any of them.'

'Which one do you like?'

'The last one.' I'm wearing his mom's rings. When you move your hand carefully you really see the light shine out. I don't want to give them back. He sees me looking at them.

'Gimme those.'

'No.'

'Fine, keep 'em. It's just I like to hold them in my pocket. They're my worry beads.'

'What do you worry about?'

'How I can get Gordon's Jeep back without actually seeing or speaking to him.'

'That's not what I mean.'

202

He stops.

'I can take it.'

'You sure? … You.'

I don't believe him. 'I wish we could live here. I'd like that house across the street.' It had a little roof deck out the back and the owner or whoever had lots of little sculptures, a Venus de Milo, colored bits of broken mirrors on string, a bush of fuchsias, potted plants, Buddhas. It was cramped and looked out at nothing but the tight little getting-dark street with air like chocolate.

At some point later that night I go to take my Ritalin.

'Do you have any refills? Let me see 'em? I want to see the bottles, I think they like changed them from when I was prescribed them. I'm feeling nostalgic.'

I give him all three. He pops the tops off, walks in to the bathroom and flushes them down the FUCKING TOILET. When he comes in the room I throw an empty Volvic bottle at him. It bounces off his head with a THWAP.

'You can do better than that.'

'You're a condescending fuck.'

'You're a fucking retard.'

I push past him, get the bottles (pointlessly) grab some clothes off the floor, throw them into the plastic bag they give you for your dirty laundry. When I get the door open he comes up behind me and holds it shut with one hand. I push him off. We kind of wrestle. He's laughing. I knee him in the stomach. Then he stops laughing and pushes me to the floor and takes my wrists and holds me down. He lifts them up and slams them down, twice, then rolls onto his back and presses his fingers into his eyes.

I say ' Have you ever heard of Prozac-Induced Psychosis?' As I say it I start to cry. 'Trish said it makes some people suicidal

203

and I could sue. My mom really was not the type.' (I was now hyperventilating) 'She was *kidding*! I know you wouldn't think so from her books, but in person she was usually … imitating herself.' I was yelling and crying and laughing. I was hysterical. The fight had kind of done me in. I AM a retard.

He holds my head under his arm, in a sort of headlock. 'It's OK. It's gonna be OK. You'll get older.'

'You're older.' I wipe my snotty face on his dumb shirt.

'Yeah. Honey.'

Day four. I think I've been in FL a week now. I hurt a bit. I thought they would have cancelled the shoot or sprung Angela out of rehab where they keep her. Anyway I decide to go downstairs and face them. I'm widely reviled. Forty people have been waiting. I find out when I get there that it's a commercial. I thought because Giovanni was a photographer – I don't know what I thought. The stage is all set. It's outside on the beach. I'm going to wear a bikini top and cut-offs, MUY short, all of which is fine by me. Except I don't want to act.

I put my mother's bag over my shoulder.

'I don't act.'

'Modeling IS acting,' says Giovanni, lighting a cigarette and continuing his conversation with the make-up artist. They are worried my dye job looks cheap. They wonder about this big hickey on my shoulder. They both think it would be 'fierce' to leave it. Some takes with, some without. I tell them obviously Calvin will hate it, obviously – it's supposed to be an innocent American girl, one who's saving it for THE ONE. They ignore me. I'm the model.

There I am, there Andromeda is, between two sheets of white fabric that are being blown by big fans, a PA behind each fan, a crowd of team-players behind the PAs: make-up, photographers, more PAs, props, craft services. I pretend to be someone else. A girl from Texas. I have a vision of her collection of sun-bleached stuffed animals on a shelf. Her room, her cherry-patterned curtains, her notebooks. Her tidy brain. CHRIST. FAMILY. LOVE. I pretend to smile. I pretend to laugh. I smile. I laugh. Finally, I deliver my line in a Southern accent, 'It's who Ah ahyem today…'

I'm afraid Gio hates it; he comes at me with a contorted face, his head tilted. 'You're – amazing.' Then everyone says so. It's the consensus. 'You're so different! Like a different person. A NICER person!'

I'm sitting here at Miami International in the first class lounge with Madonna, who's reading *Yoga Journal* out loud to three sycophants. 'The perfect downward dog…' She found time to give me a dirty look. Kabbala my ass.

Sam drove me here, too fast, in Gordon's car. He didn't say a word the whole ride. You go over this overpass that shines like a road into heaven.

When we pulled up at the terminal in that space they only let you stay for forty-five seconds, he said, 'It bit me on the ass, honey.' None too clear on what bit him on the ass. A man in an orange vest, a parking warden or whatever, stood outside my window.

I looked at his hand on the steering wheel and then I kissed it. 'Well, bye!'

I opened my door. Sam reached across and shut it. He kept his arm across me. I looked out at the low white roofs of the Miami airport.

'OK: what bit you on the ass?'

'Nevermind.'

'There are palm trees at the AIRPORT. I love that.'

The man in the orange vest knocked on my window.

'Do you remember that day you threw the ashtray into the

courtyard?' He said this to the steering wheel and through his teeth.

'It slipped.'

'Come on, you threw it.'

'No. I didn't. '

'You THREW IT.'   .

'It JUMPED.'

'DAMMIT! FUCK THIS! DAMMIT! ANDROMEDA! ADMIT YOU FUCKING THREW IT!' He slammed the steering wheel. The horn went. The warden looked worried.

I had only just landed on the pavement with my plastic bag full of free perfume and dirty clothes when Sam tore off like Lady Di's chauffeur.

I'm going to read this script Ed faxed me at the hotel. It's called *Meadow's Mom*. It's about me. I'm crying. I wish Madonna would stop fucking staring at me. My character's name keeps changing. He can't decide! Anyway I'm gonna ask Ed if it's OK if I do some kind of accent.

DUH

Faith in Things Unseen

*A damn sight more reasonable than faith
in things seen.*

* * *

8/29

Sam / Mead

Has it become, or has it always been, a big black scab? I
approach from Newark. The skyline is hideous. Spokes, prongs.
Pitchforks, dirt. And I have to remind myself in the Town Car
that there is land under us as there is a sky above. One day
it will all be gone again. I think about the invisibly fast and
strong glaciers, and how they cut out the Hudson, and left the
big rocks in the park.

I forgot that I lived in the Bellclaire and told the cabbie to
take me to the Apthorp. I remembered that I lived at Bellclaire
when we pulled up at the Apthorp, and I saw Lara and Paul
leaving it. So I told him to drive to the corner so I could get
out in front of Plimpton's, but there's no avoiding them. They
take up the whole street. And Genie's out front sweeping the
sidewalk. It's fucking *Mr. Roger's Neighborhood*. The sun is
so bright I have to hold my hand up to shield my eyes. Lara's
poised and sweatless and white as a doll. I say to her, 'Kasbaum
thinks you're pregnant.'

Paul makes a low whistle. 'You're not subtle.'

'That's right. I'm not subtle.'

'If anyone cares, I'm thrilled,' says Lara.

'Is it even mine?' I ask her. 'Can't she do some kind of test?'
I ask *Genie*, but she turns around and goes back in the store.

207

Lara's wearing tennis shoes.

I've never seen her in reasonable shoes.

I'm suddenly very weak. I put my hands out and hold myself up on a hot parking meter. I want to make love to it. Its heaviness seems so old-fashioned.

Paul asks, 'How's the little one?'

'Good. Great. She's gonna be a movie star.'

Lara says 'I saw her in *Hamptons Magazine*. Hill thought the make-up was all wrong. Too dramatic. Too vamp.'

I knelt down and hugged the meter's leg. 'Have you stopped your neighborly intervention?'

'You're fucked up, Sam.' Lara laughed. She did look happy, and well. She looked really really well. 'You are *so* fucked up. For the record, I'd undo what I did with Social Services, though my conscience *was* my guide. It really was. You don't fucking believe me, you fuck? You fucking Humbert Humbert fuck –' She crouched down next to me, and started to hit me lightly on the head, laughing and hitting me.

Paul rubbed her shoulder and pulled her up at the same time. 'Don't waste the energy.'

There was a new doorman watching us.

'Where's José? You managed to get him fired too? What'd he do, put his cap on backwards?'

I rose up. They both stepped back. 'He won the lottery! No shit. I thought you read *The Post*! He was on the cover!' She flashed her palms above her head on each word – *Yes Way Jo-sé*!'

I half-heard her, watching her nose, her perfect bow lips. I almost saw her compartmentalized, sane brain. What will a cross between me and Lara be? Or Lara and Paul? I picked up my bag, and went determinedly into the Apthorp, then remembered again that I didn't live there, and walked determinedly out again.

All along José believed in this grand thing: that he was gonna be the hero of his own life, his ship was gonna come in. And … *it fucking did*? How could something so daft be true?

And the punch line is … I call Lynne just now, and it turns out Janet *stole* my new thing off my desk and gave it to Uncle Sam because for the next month he'll do whatever he's told. And someone listened to *him*. People do. Then the someone called Lynne, who's now in the process of drafting out a contract. She used the phrase *water under the bridge* and I told her maybe she should use it to put the fire out *on* the bridge and then I apologized because it was so badly phrased she didn't understand what I was talking about and neither did I.

Look across the street. Look. At all. Those windows in the Ben Franklin Hotel. Another girl in a different window. She's just a girl. Telling me she loves me when she's coming. And I taught her. It was hard work, but it was worth it.

* * *

Andromeda / Rembrandt

9/9

The Pamphleteer (cont)

Magpie tried to quit modeling. She came home from Miami where she was much hailed as an ACTRIX. Elite had already arranged auditions for several cereal commercials and a soap opera. Andromeda wondered whether this was a respectable thing to do. So quit, and then what? Carry on the family business? Van Zandt and Daughter. Get paid to write nasty convoluted things about good movies, and other things that feel good. Get paid to dissect one's own pleasure. (She wasn't indoctrinated for nothing.) The phone would not stop ringing. She was sitting on the floor of her new bedroom arranging her clothes into piles. No more dressing to DECONSTRUCT. She was going into a tailor to have some things made. All the same thing. Several slight variations, but all a Mao Suit, of sorts. Light blue with black trim. She could afford it. She could afford anything. She had forty-five thousand dollars in the bank, the first chunk for the LOVE ad. She could afford to buy her apartment if she wanted it. She didn't want it. She wanted to get the hell out of here.

Alexis said that to quit modeling was fine; he said she could just do acting. He called it shrewd, in fact. There was just this one last show that they had booked in before. She did not want to do it. He'd arrange free clothes. She *really* did not want to do it. Had it not occurred to her that it made THEM look bad to have shot their mouths off on her behalf? OK OK OK, she'd do it. That was yesterday.

She was sober anyway, except for the Ritalin, which she had mes-merized weak-willed Genie into giving her without the prescription. ('You don't need to see my triplicate drug of abuse 'scrip'. Staring deep in her rat-like eyes, the bitch who sold her mother the Prozac said, 'I guess I know you since you're a little girl. Now you're a big famous model.') She was giving up Gorling, hence the lack of scrips. He just sat there, his legs wide the whole time, looking like it was all he could do to keep from jumping up and trying to screw her. Reichian. Yeah Rightian. He should pay her.

She spent the morning of the show (yesterday) really speeded up on three Ritalin, writing the personal statement for her early admission application for Yale Drama; it milked the suicide thing, and then was going to end up on something like … 'only when we pretend to be someone else, or no one, can we really be ourselves.' She wrote it easily. That kind of bullshit was in her blood.

The show was behind the New York Public Library main branch, in Bryant Park; backstage everyone was going insane. She was right on time, as usual, but was literally thrown to the floor in the mad rush. A bikini and a pale pink translucent plastic raincoat à la *Blade Runner* were slapped on her. Other girls crowded around. Why did SHE get that raincoat? They wanted it.

Then hair and make-up. Two cones off either side of her head, very *Muppets*. They wanted those too. Up on the wall, a list of the order. She was second, which is the biggest deal. No one was drinking. No one was doing drugs. Just the sheer adrenaline rush of total idiocy. Cell phones blaring. Several rockers and their girlfriends waiting over by the beer, not one soul bold enough to be the first to grab one.

Some awful disco music. Everyone so hyped up Andromeda wants to crawl under the table. Her cheeks have been painted pink, pink circles. She looks like 'a futuristic trapeze artist'. She says that, thinking of her dickhead neighbor who is not going to call, and the glass atrium in Miami. The make-up guy SCREAMS. 'YES! A FUTURISTIC TRAPEZE ARTIST! THAT'S THE LOOK!'

The girls line up and Andromeda follows ten seconds after Angela, who is actually pretty nice and doesn't seem as bothered as the others.

Have you ever been to a baseball game at Yankee Stadium? There are as many people at a runway show, or it seems like it. It's like those dreams where you realize you have no clothes on in public. But 'This is no dream, this is really happening!' (*Rosemary's Baby*). On either side of the long white plank of a runway, heads like strange, ugly, flowers in giant garden borders. Eyes. Lenses. Everyone silent and worshipful, and the fake clicking of digital shutters. And she's naked. Nearly naked. She has her cigarettes and a lighter in her hand.

Then, in front of her, Angela is walking funny; like a mechanical toy. Why? She was walking OK backstage. Andromeda stops still halfway down the runway and lights a cigarette. Two girls pass her. Jaws drop. She steps out of her Minnie Mouse round-toe spectator heels (they were too big anyway) walks to the end of the runway, sits down, then slides off and walks through the crowd. Which parts, all right. She feels her mother with her, walking out with her. Holding her hand and chucking her on the shoulder, 'That's a girl.'

At home, in the Meaningful Closet, she eats a huge meal. Osso Buco, delivered from Stav's. She dribbles meat fat on a first edition of a book of her mother's, her first, *Write of the First Night*.

211

She took it back from Escobar, who was her gay friend, once a drunk, now bright as a new penny. Says he's Seen the Light. But 'for real' this time. It was on a banner trailing a Cessna, through the sunset, over New Jersey. THE WISDOM TO KNOW THE DIFFERENCE. He goes to as many AA meetings a day as he can. I saw that banner too. But it said 'Magpie, my dear, it all comes clear – the only thing to do is DISAPPEAR.'

So at home she opens the book. She is very pleased to see it starts with a quote, one she has been trying to remember for some time. She must have opened the book before and not remembered. It's from that Ibsen play, *A Doll's House*. It was a quote of a quote she was looking for. Of course. "I could tear myself to shreds."

She thinks: that wouldn't be a bad part. She fetches from the drama section of her dead mother's library. The US first edition. And immediately starts to learn her lines. She'll bring it to her accountant appointment first thing Tuesday morning. She has Sophie's accountant now, at the end of the 1/9 line, in the World Trade Center. She'll buy a townhouse. (Prada's been calling, for a commercial, which is acting.)

Nora: *If that were to happen, I don't suppose I should care whether I owed money or not.*

* * *

Sam /Mead

9/11

Lara calls first thing. I call her back. Andromeda doesn't call. I don't call her back. I am a grown man. Grown men have sex with young girls who throw themselves at them, and I have not been unkind. I have been good. I've taught her things. (This like a loop in my head.)

'God. You're supposed to read *The Post*. What happens – we

212

break up and all of a sudden you're *civilized*? You didn't see the headline yesterday?' Lara and I are now standing in our emptied old living room. I'm looking across the courtyard at the scrunched mandala Andromeda uses as a curtain. '*Runway Runaway*? She walked off and *hailed a cab*? I think she's mentally ill.'

I forgot to stop looking at the mandala. I wondered if she was behind it. I sort of knew she wasn't.

'Are you sure you know what you're doing?' asked Lara.

'I'm not doing anything anymore.'

She gives me the old, warm, don't-bullshit-a-bullshitter look.

'Really. It was an untenable situation.'

'I don't care whose kid it is, you know that? I'll be happy either way. In fact, I almost like the element of surprise.' She's looking very well. Some lines have been erased from her face. She's grown hopeful.

'Let me to take you out to brunch, to that fancy fish restaurant.'

'It's Tuesday. They're not doing brunch on earth.'

'OK: breakfast. You know the fish place I mean?'

'It's called Fish.'

'Yeah, let me to take you out to Fish, wife. Fish-ex-wife.' I tousle her hair. Next thing I do, in the elevator, is tell Lar about the advance for *A Futuristic Trapeze Artist*. Her whole face changes. My stock is through the roof. It's what Heidegger might call a phenomenological transformation. On the way out the new doorman stops us to say a plane's just hit the Twin Towers; we shrug.

We're the only ones in the wide expensive restaurant. I order a bottle of champagne. Lara reminds me she won't touch the stuff. It's been almost five weeks of sobriety and WHERE THE HELL HAS IT GOTTEN ME? It's feathery turpentine going down. I want to be a father. I want to have someone look up to me, replicate

213

me. I'm eating a dozen oysters. Lara's eating wild, endangered salmon. The waiter is useless; he's glued to the TV over the bar.

'Two planes, what are the chances of that happening?' Lar muses.

When I tell her I want the baby she cries and smiles and makes no noises. She smiles the way she used to. She knows me again. And she says, 'It's yours. You know.'

I do know. I know exactly when, too. And I know who to thank.

After her crème caramel and decaf latte: 'Well, I've gotta go. Remember the Old Sloans? Sloan croaked. I've gotta show it at eleven.'

I stand up. 'I'll walk you. '

It's a beautiful day. I have not finished the champagne and I get Lara to put the rest of the bottle in her Kelly bag, then I keep drinking it out on the street. I feel fanfuckingtastic. My wife. My kid. My town. When we get to the Old Sloans, Lara puts her hand on my face and kisses me goodbye.

'Call me,' says Lara.

'Bank on it.'

It's my day off and I'm gonna quit tomorrow. I head into Central Park, into the Bramble. A whole day ahead of me and forty-five thousand dollars in my pocket. I sit on that rock that pokes out into the lake, contemplating the hut where my dick served its one selfless purpose. I'm going to tell Lara about that, some night while our baby is sleeping in our brownstone in the Slope. I take off my jacket and tie. There are three helicopters, stuck, like full stops in the sky. Couples are rowing by in rotting green boats. I think I'll hire one. I stand up, then sit down again. I decide to go home. Then slowly unlace and take off my shoes. I crouch there, on the rock, until it's dark.

svz
2006

214

All the aphorisms credited to svz are by Joseph Holland Chassler, 1944-2001. They were originally published as part of the collection Work Hard/ Play Dead *and later as* Addict's Damn.

Two Ravens Press is the most northerly literary publisher in the UK, operating from a six-acre working croft on a sea-loch in the north-west Highlands of Scotland. Two Ravens Press is run by two writers with a passion for language and for books that are non-formulaic and that take risks. We publish cutting-edge and innovative contemporary fiction, non-fiction and poetry.

Visit our website for comprehensive information on all of our books and authors – and for much more:

- browse all Two Ravens Press books (print books and e-books) by category or by author, and purchase them online at a discount on retail price, post & packing-free (in the UK, and for a small fee overseas)

- there is a separate page for each book, including summaries, extracts and reviews, and author interviews, biographies and photographs

- read our regular blog about life as a small literary publisher in the middle of nowhere – or the centre of the universe, depending on your perspective – with a few anecdotes about life down on the croft thrown in. Includes regular and irregular columns by guest writers – Two Ravens Press authors and others

- sign up for our monthly e-newsletter, filled with information on our new releases and our authors, with special discounts, prizes and other offers.

www.tworavenspress.com